NO MAN'S LAND

Also by G. M. Ford, available in Pan Books

THE FRANK CORSO SERIES

FURY

BLACK RIVER

A BLIND EYE

RED TIDE

THE LEO WATERMAN SERIES

WHO IN HELL IS WANDA FUCA?

CAST IN STONE

G. M.
FORD

NO MAN'S LAND

MACMILLAN

First published in the United States of America 2005 by William Morrow
an imprint of HarperCollins Inc., New York, USA

First published in the United Kingdom 2007 by Macmillan
an imprint of Pan Macmillan Ltd
Pan Macmillan, 20 New Wharf Road, London N1 9RR
Basingstoke and Oxford
Associated companies throughout the world
www.panmacmillan.com

ISBN 978-1-4050-5540-6 (HB)
ISBN 978-0-2300-1689-7 (TPB)

Visit www.panmacmillan.com to read more about all our books
and to buy them. You will also find features, author interviews and
news of any author events, and you can sign up for e-newsletters
so that you're always first to hear about our new releases.

Better to sink in boundless deeps,
than float on vulgar shoals.

—HERMAN MELVILLE,
Mardi and a Voyage Thither

NO MAN'S LAND

1

"As of this moment, we are holding one hundred sixty-three hostages. Starting at eighteen hundred tonight, I'm going to shoot one of them every six hours until Frank Corso is delivered to me." The handheld camera shimmied, but the voice never lost its tone of command and the hooded black eyes never wavered.

The picture rolled once, then the screen went blank. Governor James Blaine looked back over his shoulder at Warden Elias Romero. An unasked question hung in the air like artillery smoke.

"His name is Timothy Driver," Romero said. "He's a transfer from the State of Washington. Doing life without . . . for double aggravated murder."

A glimmer of recognition slid across the governor's pouchy face. "The navy guy? The captain?"

"Yes sir," said Romero. "Driver used to be a Trident submarine captain." Romero cleared his throat. "Came home a little early from a cruise. Found his wife flying united with some local guy. Lost it. Got himself a gun and offed them both, right there in his own bed. Blinded another inmate and stabbed a guard during his first week in a Washington prison. The con was a big player in the Aryan Brotherhood. The guard was an old hand . . . popular with the staff. Washington figured it wasn't safe to keep Driver around their system anymore . . . so they shipped him to us."

The governor jammed his hands into his suit pants pockets. "How the hell could something like this happen?" he demanded. "Meza Azul is supposed to be—" He stopped himself. "As I recall, the design was supposed to prevent something like this from ever taking place."

"Yes sir . . . it was." Romero pointed to the bank of surveillance monitors nearly covering the south wall of the security office. The screens were blank and black. Romero cleared his throat. "We've got the last minute and forty-five seconds of tape before Driver turned the security system off. It's quite—"

"Let me see it," the governor interrupted.

Romero crossed the room, jabbed at several buttons and stood aside, allowing the governor to belly up to the monitor. White static filled the large central screen.

"It's quite graphic," Romero warned.

"I'm a big boy," the governor assured him.

The picture appeared. Shot from above. Somebody in a guard's uniform putting an electronic key into what appeared to be an elevator door. The figure pocketed the key and bounced his eyes around all four walls before removing something from his inside jacket pocket and turning his back on the camera for a full thirty seconds.

"It's Driver in a guard's uniform," Romero said. On-screen, Driver had straightened up and was poking his index finger at the keyboard on the wall as Romero narrated. "He just used a security key in the elevator to the control module, then . . ." He raised his hands in despair. "And then somehow or other he disabled the fingerprint recognition technology."

"Say again."

Romero reached around the governor and pushed the STOP button.

"On any given day, only five men have access to the central elevator. The pod operator, who you're about to see in a minute, and the four senior duty officers." He dropped his hands to his sides. "Driver found some way around it." He moved quickly to the console. The figure started to move again "Look. He's punching in the security code."

On-screen, the door slid open. Driver stepped inside and momentarily disappeared.

Blaine's face was red now. "How in God's name did a prisoner get hold of any of that?" the governor sputtered. "A uniform"—he waved a large liver-spotted hand—"the security code. How could . . ."

Romero merely shook his head, refusing to speculate. He stuck to the facts.

The picture cut to the interior of the elevator, where the man in blue stood calmly in the center of the car, hands folded in front of him, bored expression on his face.

"Driver had an appointment for a medical checkup. We're guessing he somehow overpowered the team we sent for him." Romero shrugged and swallowed hard. "Somehow or other, he must have . . ." Romero searched for a word. ". . . he must have *induced* the guard sergeant to part with the security code."

"And the fingerprint identification?"

"No idea."

The two men passed nervous glances as the picture cut to the interior of the control module, where an African-American man in a starched white shirt swiveled his chair, turning to face the elevator door just in time for the man in blue to step inside and point to the bank of security monitors. "Check sixty-three," he said in a command voice.

Without a word, the man in white turned his back on the closing elevator door and began running his fingers over his keyboard. Whatever was supposed to appear on monitor sixty-three would remain forever a mystery as Driver looped what appeared to be a length of thin wire around the other man's neck, made a sudden twist at the nape and began to pull with sufficient force to lift the man in white from the chair. His fingers clawed at his throat and his eyes tried to burst from their sockets, as rivulets of blood began to pour down over the white Randall Corporation shirt and he began to convulse, his legs beating time on the hard stone floor, his open mouth spewing . . .

James Blaine turned his face away. While the governor was busy retaining his lunch, Romero reached around him and pushed the STOP button. Silence filled the room like dirty water.

"This wasn't supposed to be possible," James Blaine choked out.

Elias Romero kept his face as hard as stone. "Yes sir," was all he dared to say.

The governor was right. From day one, Meza Azul, Arizona, had been designed to hold the worst collection of criminals in the United States. Worse yet, the prison was the centerpiece of an entire community whose very existence owed itself to the twin notions that Meza Azul was one hundred percent escape-proof and that incarceration could be a highly profitable enterprise.

Unlike many of its predecessors, MA, as the residents liked to call it, had not started life as one of those quaint little mining communities, wedged high among the jagged sandstone-and-granite spires of the nearby San Cristobel Mountains or as one of those dust-covered stage stops masquerading as ghost towns down on the valley floor.

No . . . the privatization of the Arizona Department of Corrections had led to a complete rethinking regarding the placement and staffing of new prisons. While the state had preferred to use the opportunity to revitalize one of these long-dead towns, private enterprise had quickly recognized the folly of this approach.

First and foremost, to take on an existing town was to take on its residents, many of whom, it was sad to say, were ill suited to the rigors of employment in a modern maximum security prison. While the initial report to the state attorney general had used such terms as *trainability* and *technological recidivism* to describe the problem with the locals, it was generally understood that what they meant was that the kind of folks who chose to shrink from progress, the kind of iconoclasts who stayed behind when the circus moved on were generally either too smart, too stupid or too lazy to be of any use to a dynamic new enterprise such as the Randall Corporation had in mind.

Of course they couldn't come right out and say something like that, so they couched their recommendations in more positive terms such as *family friendly* and *self-containment*, and thus Meza Azul, Arizona, had been created.

Truckers along I-506 swore the facility had been born overnight, cut from a single piece of cloth and dropped whole onto the desert floor, prison, houses, school, post office, golf course, movie theater, swimming pool, palm trees and all. Bada bing. Gone today. Here tomorrow. Welcome to the twenty-first century.

For the past seven and a half years, the State of Arizona's cut from the Meza Azul Correctional Facility had been the difference between profit and loss, between surplus and deficit, and was regularly mentioned by the governor as being emblematic of the imaginative fiscal policy with which he had brought the state back from the precipice of financial ruin.

James Blaine had no doubts. Spin doctors be damned. No way he could distance himself from Meza Azul. This was his baby, and the longer it went on, the worse it was going to be for his chances of reelection.

"What now?" the governor demanded.

"We've got FBI negotiators on the way." Romero checked his watch. "They should be here by six tonight." His big brown eyes rolled over the governor. Waiting. Not wanting to be the one who asked the question. Ten seconds passed before the question asked itself.

"You think we can handle this on our own?" Blaine asked.

Romero shrugged. "Probably not."

"We've got over eighty State Patrol officers on the scene right now."

"Driver's opened two hundred forty of the cells. Mostly in Cellblock D. The Bikers. Maybe some of the Mexican Mafia too. We had to put some of the Hispanic overflow in with the Bikers."

The Bikers owned the south half of D Building. The African-American Congress had the north half. The Mexican Mafia and the skinhead Nazis shared B Building. The Bikers would have preferred to live with the Mexicans, but there was no way you could put the Nazis and the Africans in together. The Mexicans hated the Nazis, thought they were the biggest scum-sucking maggots on the planet. They'd have rather lived with either the Africans or the Bikers, but there was no way you could put the Nazis in with the Bikers. In addition to seeing the Nazis as mutants and as a disgrace to the white race, the Bikers also hated them for horning in on the methamphetamine business, both inside and outside the walls, and, most of all, they hated the skinheads for besmirching their much beloved Nazi insignia.

The governor winced and ran a hand over his face. Before he could speak, Romero went on. "They've got hold of the armory," he said.

"Which means what?"

Romero had to force the words out of his mouth. "Which means they've got access to every kind of automatic weapon available on the planet." He hesitated. Took a deep breath. "And about three million rounds of ammunition."

James Blaine ran a hand through his hair and turned away. He could feel how thin his hair had become in recent years. He'd once had *presidential hair*. That's what they'd called it, *presidential hair*.

A knock sounded on the door. Neither man spoke. The door opened a crack. Romero's executive assistant, Iris Cruz, looked from the warden to the governor and back. She was thirty, twelve years Romero's junior, her once hourglass figure turning into something more like a time clock. They'd been sleeping together for the past nineteen months. Ever since Iris's husband, Esteban, had tired of his life in America and returned to Mexico. Esteban's shadow was still in the yard when Romero made his intentions clear. He'd wanted to for a long time, but had resisted. Iris had known from the beginning. Women knew these kind of things. Just like they knew when a man was never going to leave his skinny wife like he'd been claiming he was going to do all these months. Sometimes a woman would block it out for a while, but she knew. She always knew.

"I got that book you wanted," she said, without making eye contact.

Romero crossed the room in four quick strides, plucked the book from Cruz's manicured fingers and closed the door. He stood for a moment looking down at the book's cover, then flipped it over and glanced at the picture on the back before opening the back cover and reading the flap copy.

"What have we got?" the governor wanted to know.

"It's a book by Frank Corso." He held up the cover so Blaine could see. *Red as a Rose: A Story of Passion.* "It's the book he wrote about Driver."

The governor started his way. "Says this Corso guy lives on a boat somewhere in the Seattle area," Romero said.

"Call Seattle," Blaine said. "Get this Corso guy on the way." He blew out a huge breath. "I'm calling out the National Guard."

2

With an ease often mistaken for arrogance, Melanie Harris allowed her eyes to follow the focus light along the overhead camera track until her gaze came to rest on number four an instant before the light turned green and the camera began to roll. *"This is Melanie Harris for* American Manhunt. *Join us again next week when* American Manhunt *once again turns up the heat on the criminal plague permeating our nation."* She picked up a sheet of folded paper from the desk in front of her. While it would have been more efficient to have included the copy on the electronic prompter, Melanie preferred to use the closing notes as a prop, lending, she thought, an air of spontaneity to a segment of the show that could, without careful tending, become a parody of itself. She handled the page with only the tips of her fingers, as if it were hot off the wire. She then tilted the page outward, as if to show the viewers at home. *"As of this week,* American Manhunt *and our millions of viewers at home are responsible for the arrest and successful prosecution of nine hundred and seventy-nine dangerous criminals."* She offered a twisted smile. *"Nine hundred seventy-nine felons . . . murderess, rapists, carjackers and thieves who no longer walk the streets preying on innocent citizens . . .*

thanks to the efforts of people like you." She pointed at the camera. "*Until next week,*" she intoned.

The red light went out. She got to her feet. A trio of technicians stepped forward with the speed and precision of a NASCAR team, flipping switches, sliding slides, turning knobs, disconnecting her from the collection of electronics she wore during a taping.

"Clear," somebody said.

She cast a quick glance at the control booth, where Tommy Allenby, her longtime director, stood with a fake grin plastered on his face, making the victory sign with his fingers. She smiled back and stepped away from the desk. The affirmation from Tommy was little more than force of habit. In the seven years the show had been on national television, Melanie had steadily taken over what would normally have been the duties of the director, leaving Tommy in the role of little more than a cheerleader. A well-paid cheerleader, as she'd been forced to remind him earlier in the year when he'd threatened to quit. Since then, their relationship had become cool and strictly professional. It had come to her ears that he'd been shopping his services to other programs. After considering confronting him on the matter, she'd decided to let him test the waters. Might be better that way. Better for both of them.

As she moved across the set, Leslie Hall, her executive assistant, began jabbering in her ear. "We've got another taping at nine-fifteen tomorrow."

"What have we got?"

Leslie ran down the list of crimes and criminals scheduled for next week's show. A pair of Midwest bank robbers, who, after nine bank robberies, were still at large. A missing father of four, whose slaughtered family had been discovered in the basement of their home and a recap of the year to date. Each half hour episode of *American Manhunt* consisted of three segments. The inclusion of a recap meant they were short on current material and were using the compilation as filler.

"It's not much," Melanie sneered. "We just did a recap. You tell Martin we need better content." They all knew. After seven successful years, the show was beginning to fizzle. The mob was fickle. The onslaught of reality programs was eating away at their ratings. Melanie jabbed a long, manicured finger at the floor. "Producers who don't produce find something else to do for a living."

Leslie assured her the message would get through to Martin Wells, the show's executive producer. She began to say that Martin was surely doing the best he could, but Melanie cut her off by throwing up what only Leslie could translate as a disgusted hand and kept walking. "Tommy wants to have an all-staff meeting on—" Leslie tried.

"We don't need an all-staff," Melanie countered quickly, her heels clicking harder on the floor. "Anything that needs covering we can go over on Friday."

Leslie jotted notes on her pad. "The Berens people would like to have a word with you about the—"

Another wave of her hand. This time negative. "Have them talk to Trudy."

They were off the set now, walking quickly down the hall toward Melanie's dressing room. Third door on the left. "This afternoon—" Leslie began.

"This afternoon. I'm going to the beach with Brian. Period. End of story." Another hand gesture. This one like the cutting of a knife. "I stood him up twice last week and it's not going to happen again today."

Melanie pulled open the dressing room door, stepped into the cool quiet and closed the door. She crossed the room to the lighted makeup table and began to work at removing the layer of makeup the technicians plastered and painted over her face prior to each taping.

Other than cosmetics, the only thing on the table was the framed photograph of Melanie and Brian's first and only child, Samantha, a smiling four-year-old whose guileless grin could warm the coldest of hearts. Samantha's headless and armless torso had been found behind a Chevron station in Grand Rapids, Michigan, ten years ago next month. Plucked from beneath the gaze of a nineteen-year-old babysitter whose anguished cries for help had gone unheeded, Samantha had been missing for four days before her mangled body had been found. Neither the missing pieces of her body nor her murderer had ever been found.

Once the funeral was over, once the pain and the initial shock had subsided and the endless stream of phone calls had begun to taper off, the experience of losing their only child had affected Brian and Melanie in completely different manners. Brian retreated into a shell of self-loathing, blaming himself for not being there when his daughter needed him most, neglecting his successful criminal law practice, alienating his longtime friends and his family in favor of a three-year drinking binge from which he very nearly failed to emerge. Only in the past year or so had his former relationships begun to take on the kind of genuine warmth that had been the hallmark of his earlier life. For all intents and purposes, he'd put the matter behind him. As long as you didn't look into his eyes too deeply. Nobody except Melanie did, so it wasn't a problem.

Melanie, on the other hand, had gone fey. Lapsed into a controlled rage, determined that no other child should suffer like hers had, the Michigan housewife began a campaign for the protection of children, demanding that local law enforcement agencies initiate school awareness programs, demanding that state lawmakers enact legislation designed to protect children from the kind of interagency jurisdictional finger-pointing that had allowed her daughter to be kidnapped in broad daylight from a public park, had allowed some scum to hold her daughter for four days before dumping her torso behind a gas station like so much garbage . . . a tragedy abetted in some measure because local law enforcement powers were unaccustomed to cooperating with one another.

By the time her rage began to subside, nearly three years later, Melanie had testified repeatedly before the U.S. Congress, had appeared on every talk show from Larry King to Leno, had been primarily or partly responsible for eleven separate pieces of legislation designed to protect children, including the Amber Alert System, and had, by virtue of her sheer ubiquity, been offered her own reality TV program, *American Manhunt,* which for the past seven years she had used as a personal medium for the expiation of her guilt and anger.

After seven successful years, all in the top twenty-five, ratings had recently begun to slide. It was no surprise. As any number of astute critics had pointed out, *American Manhunt* was the seminal program of the new "reality television" craze sweeping the airways. Everything from the *FBI Files* to *Survivor* owed its existence to the groundbreaking work done by *American Manhunt.* Not only had the show spawned its own competition, but, as some wit had once pointed out, no one had ever gone broke underestimating the attention span of the American public. Thus far, Melanie had managed to keep the matter in perspective. Not only was seven years a darn good run, but she was presently engaged in negotiations with a major production company for her own daytime talk show.

"Oprah with an edge," they said.

Having removed the last of the TV makeup, Melanie applied SPF forty-five sunscreen to her face, followed by a careful layer of translucent powder. She puckered up for a final application of Beach Coral lip gloss and was good to go. All she needed to do was change into her beach clothes and sandals.

Melanie rose to her feet She was halfway across the room when her dressing room door popped open. Assistant Producer

Patricia Goodman walked into the room. Patricia was fat and fifty; she was also Marty Wells's niece or cousin or something, which, as far as Melanie was concerned, explained why someone with a job description so nebulous was still on the set.

Patricia closed the door behind herself and looked up at Melanie. "The girls are ready whenever you are," she said in a bored voice.

Melanie stopped in her tracks, a small glimmer of memory picking at her consciousness. "What girls?"

"The twenty-five job shadow girls." When Melanie did nothing but frown, Patricia went on. "The high school girls. You're going to spend the afternoon showing them around the production lot. Showing them the ins and outs of the business. You're their hero. Remember?"

It came to her then. There'd been a contest. In all the local high schools. Selling magazine subscriptions or something. Winners got to come down and follow Melanie around for an afternoon.

Melanie walked quickly to the mahogany gateleg table she used for a desk. She pushed paperwork aside until she could read the cluttered calendar below. There it was. One to five, with a dinner in the cafeteria to follow. Right there in black and white. She banged the table with the flat of her hand. "Son of a bitch," she said.

Patricia took a step back to stand with the door against the back of her dress.

"Problem?"

"Of course there's a problem. I was going to—" She stopped herself, not wanting to lay out the dirty laundry of her life in front of Patricia. Unwilling to mention the growing distance between Brian and herself. The recriminations or worse yet, the silences. She waved a dismissive hand. "I'll be along in five," she said instead.

She waited until Patricia had let herself out, then jabbed a button on her phone. Leslie picked up. "Call Brian for me. Tell him something's come up. Tell him—" Again she stopped herself. "Tell him I'm sorry, but something's come up."

She returned the receiver to the cradle, took a deep breath and headed for the door.

3

Cutter Kehoe was a genetic rarity. A third generation Biker, directly descended from that aberrant strain of humanity for whom the term white trash had so astutely been coined. These were the recycled slag of an older civilization, the misfits, wastrels and whiners who became the dejected camp followers of the new nation's hardy pioneers. Always a day late and a dollar short, arriving after the good stuff had long been spoken for, they were without roots, so they kept moving west, toward the unclaimed land, until moving became a way of life rather than simply a habit, and the notion of honest toil became a last resort rather than a calling.

Some fell into cracks along the way, choosing life as Kentucky hillbillies, West Virginia coal miners, as Okies and Texas dirt farmers. Their inbred descendants are still there, still lolling about porches, eking out marginal lives on hardscrabble land, still hostile to outsiders and prone to unpredictable acts of violence.

Kehoe's grandfather Jimmy made it all the way to sunny California before the blood took over, propelling him on a suicide ride atop the new Indian Superchief he'd bought with his separation bonus. Armed and drunk, he was still looking back under his arm at the Highway Patrol car when the motorcycle hit the three-cable guardrail at just over a hundred. His pregnant common-law wife, Patricia Bostitch, identified the initials inside his engineer boots.

Kehoe was the only man outside the Special Containment Wing who lived alone in a two-man cell. They couldn't prove he'd killed the skinhead, so they couldn't officially adjust his sentence and stick him in Extreme Punishment. By the time the yard bulls had forced the crowd apart, the little guy with the red SS bars tattooed on the back of each hand had spilled his purple contents out onto the concrete, his pinched face quizzical, as if amazed at how his organs had slid through his slick fingers, rolling out onto the rough stone, where they gleamed and quivered like sea life.

Reviews of the yard videotapes were inconclusive, so Kehoe got ninety days in his own little cell in A Building, as far away from his Biker buddies as the heat could put him. A Building was where they kept the droolers and the chesters, the habitual baby rapers and those fuckers who were so out of it you couldn't even let them loose in a maximum security prison. The thinking was that a few months with the gomers and goners might give Kehoe a little humility. After a week, even the wet brains stayed on the far side of the yard. After two weeks, Kehoe had the yard to himself.

Kehoe was the first man Driver liberated. He came out of his cell with a swagger usually reserved for Saturday night bar fights, head swinging, silent, moving on the balls of his feet, checking both directions of the empty walkway.

"Kehoe," the voice rang from the overhead speaker. His eyes found the speaker and the little black camera. "Yeah . . . who's runnin' his mouth there?" he asked.

"Driver."

Kehoe scowled and thought it over. "That really you, Captain-man?"

"Sure as Kurtz is watching cartoons on the inside of his skull."

Kehoe broke into a grin. "They surely ain't gonna like you taking over the intercom, Captainman. Gonna get you down in the SCW for sure."

"No time soon," came the reply.

"Where you at, Captainman?"

"The control pod."

Kehoe stopped moving . . . looked at the camera again. "You shittin' me."

"Why don't you come on up and join me?" Driver said.

Before Kehoe could respond, the security gate at the far end of the concourse began to slide aside. Kehoe took a step back. The voice sounded again.

"No death penalty in Arizona, Cutter. What are they gonna do? Give you another life sentence?"

Kehoe grinned again and pointed at the camera. He moved with a loose-jointed quality that belied his long, ropy arms and enormous hands. "You got a point there, Doc. Other than ninety at a time in the SCW . . . really ain't much the blues can do to a pair of no-parole lifers like us, now is there?"

"Not a damn thing," rang from the ceiling.

"What you got in mind, Captainman?"

"I got hell to pay in mind, Cutter. Hell on wheels."

The notion seemed to satisfy Kehoe. He hooked his thumbs in his pants pockets and started down the walkway toward the elevator, knocking on windows as he ambled down the cellblock.

Driver flipped a half a dozen switches, then sat back in the chair. Watching Kehoe walk brought it all back to him. That first week in Walla Walla. How he could tell there was somebody else in the block other than him. How the trustees would make chitchat when they brought him meals, but would pass nary a word with whoever else was down there at the end of the row.

Just scrubbed the floor and hurried back to feed Driver, looking thankful to have returned at all.

Fifth night he was there. After the physical exams and the orientations. After the shrinks and the social workers. Just about the time they were about to assign him a cell in the general population. It was late. After lights out, when the voice broke the perpetual daybreak of the block. "Hey," someone called with an adenoidal twang. "You there?"

Driver slid from the bunk and padded to the front of the cell. "What?"

"The Mexicans sold your ass to them Nazi skinheads," the voice whispered, then paused in the darkness for the words to have the desired effect.

"What?"

"The Mexicans don't buttfuck," the voice whispered. "It goes against their macho thing. So, when it's their turn, they always sell the fish for cigarettes. Usually to the niggers, for like, two, three cartons. Somethin' like that." A dirty laugh rolled down the concrete like a steel wave. "I hear they got thirty cartons for you. You worth that much?

"No," Driver had answered.

A chuckle. "No is right."

The chuckle turned into a full, braying laugh. "Sheeeeet. You may be hot shit on a submarine, but around here you ain't nothing but food, baby. That's all . . . just food. That Kurtz ain't but a biscuit away from four hundred pounds. He's a lard bucket, but . . . I'm tellin' you, boy, I seen you come in. You in deep sewage."

Driver said, "No" again. This time in his full voice.

The sound of liquid moving through pipes suddenly filled the air. Somewhere in the distance, footsteps could be heard. And then a shout.

"Gonna send you somethin' first thing in the mornin'," the voice said.

And then the conversation was over. Later, sometime in the night, Driver closed his eyes and slept.

As promised, a surprise arrived before breakfast. Guy mopping the floor passed it to Driver through the bars, rolled up in a paper napkin. It was an old toothbrush. The sharpened plastic shaft had a small hole drilled through the blunt end. A thin wooden dowel had been slipped through the hole, forming a T grip. Driver pulled the dowel from the hole, laying it gently in his palm next to the toothbrush.

The voice whispered. "You put that in your shoe, Mr. Captainman. On the inside of your foot, business end forward. You can go the through the metal detectors all day long with that motherfucker in your shoe and nobody'll know. Time comes to use it, make damn sure it's together tight."

Driver had tried to stammer a thanks, but his throat had been too dry.

"Remember, the Mexicans won't help him none. They hate those Nazis damn near as much as I do. They're just there to make sure Kurtz gets a fair shot at what he paid for. You start messing him up, they'll be gone in a heartbeat."

The corridor lights snapped on and began to hiss. Kehoe talked more quickly now. "You best go for the face," he said. "Anyplace else ain't gonna stop that big piece of shit." The words poked Driver hard in the chest like a thick a finger.

And then the doors slid back and Cutter Kehoe came walking by with that same loose-jointed shamble Driver was watching now.

He paused at the door of Driver's cell. "You comin'?"

Driver shook his head. Kehoe curled his lip again.

"Nowhere to run, nowhere to hide, Mr. Captainman. Might as well have breakfast. The juice is in on this thing. Not eatin' ain't gonna make no difference." He smiled, then headed off down the corridor.

Driver stood at the front of his cell and watched Kehoe step through the security gate and join the other prisoners on their way to breakfast, watched as the torrent of prisoners instantly split in two, as every man sought to put as much distance between himself and Kehoe as possible.

4

The house was shrouded in shadows as she unlocked the front door and stepped into the foyer. Melanie Harris could hear the sound of the television floating from the den. The long, tiled hall was illuminated only by the sudden surges of electronic light as they bounced off the walls and ceiling. She took off her shoes and started toward the back of the house. The cold tiles massaged her feet as she walked.

Brian was spread out over the oversized Morris chair with a bowl of microwave popcorn resting in his lap. She stood beside the chair for a moment, hoping he'd acknowledge her presence or, better yet, scoot over a bit so they could sit crammed together, hip to hip like they used to. Instead, he kept his eyes glued to the TV.

"Hey," she said.

"Hey," he answered, without taking his eyes from the screen.

"Sorry about today."

"Yeah," was all he said.

She waited another moment, then crossed in front of him and sat down on the couch at the far side of the room. "How'd your day go?" she asked.

"Same shit, different day."

The tension in the air was as palpable as a breeze. She hesitated before she spoke, not wanting to start the argument they'd so carefully been avoiding these past few months.

"Maybe we could make the beach next week."

"I don't care about the beach. I can go to the beach anytime I want."

"I said I was sorry. What else do you want?"

His sudden burst of laughter was without a trace of humor. "Since when does any of this have to do with what I want?"

"Something came up. I was busy. What can I say?"

"Don't worry about it. You don't have to say anything."

She sighed. "Not tonight, huh? I've had a long day."

"You've always had a long day."

Her voice rose. "What's that supposed to mean?"

"Just what I said." He sat up. Lobbed the bowl of popcorn onto the coffee table, where it bounced once before coming to rest. He threw his stiff arms out over the sides of the chair like a baseball umpire calling the runner safe. "That's it," he announced. "I've had enough."

"Enough of what?"

"Of all of it. Of L.A. Of the sponsor cocktail parties. Of the network parties. Of the whole damn thing. I'm sick to death of all of it."

Her voice caught in her throat. "Of me?"

"I didn't say that. Don't put words in my mouth."

She was on her feet now. "A lot of people would love to be where we are." She clamped her jaw shut before she could blurt out something about being grateful for the two-million-dollar house in the Hollywood Hills, the matching BMWs, the maids, the gardener.

"Yeah . . . well I guess I'm just not one of them," he said.

Melanie took several deep breaths to calm herself and sat back down.

"I'd like to think I've done a bit of good. You know . . . that maybe what happened to Samantha . . ." The sound of the name stopped her for a moment. She couldn't recall the last time she's said the word out loud.

Brian waved her off, as if he knew what was coming and couldn't bear to hear it again. "That what you tell yourself? That it's about Samantha? What a joke."

"Oh really?"

"Yeah, really. Who are we kidding here? This isn't about Samantha anymore. It's about you."

"How can you say that?"

"Because it's true. Whatever you could do for children you already did. These days it's about ratings. It's about sweeps week. It's about what night and what time slot." He waved a disgusted hand. "It's about everything in the world except what we came out here for in the first place."

To Melanie, their past lives in Michigan were little more than a blur. It was as if her life had begun in that awful moment when the phone rang and the cold clear voice informed her that her daughter's body had been found. In that minute of time, the previous twenty-seven years of her life had disappeared, leaving her only with the here and now.

To Brian, living in Hollywood was a B-movie. Low production values and bad dialogue. A place where everything was big but nothing was real. He'd reestablished his law practice and was doing quite well, but he'd never taken to Los Angeles. Not from the first day, when they'd moved into that rental house in West Hollywood. Not for the past seven years, as the show grew in popularity and Melanie became a household name. None of it mattered to him. All of it just left him feeling empty and unsatisfied.

And then there was the matter of children. Brian wanted to have some more. Melanie wasn't ready. Wasn't ever going to be ready. They both knew it, but neither of them had said it out loud, like so many things left unsaid these past few years.

And then . . . like an alley cat thrashing his way out of a bag, the great unspoken phrase burst out into the air.

"I've had it with this place. I want to go home," Brian said.

"Home?"

"Michigan."

"You can't be serious. This is our home."

He got to his feet. "I spoke with my dad tonight. He's finally gonna retire. I can take over his practice. We'll be fine. Better than fine. We can—"

"I can't leave here. There's nothing back in Michigan for me."

His eyes held hers now. "Then we've got a problem."

"I'm in the middle of negotiations for a new show. I'm—" She stopped herself and began to massage her temples. "Not now, Brian . . . please, not now . . ."

"There's never going to be a better time," he said.

Melanie began to sputter out a denial but stopped herself.

"I can't believe I'm hearing this," she said finally. "There's no way I can possibly . . ."

The phone rang. It was as if a stranger had entered the room. It rang again, and then a third time before Melanie reached down and picked up the receiver. "Yes."

"You wanted fresh content well . . . I've got it for you, baby," her producer, Martin Wells, blurted into the phone.

"It's late, Martin," she said with a sigh. "And it's really not a good time."

He ignored her. "I've got the first unit on the way to Arizona as we speak. They'll be set up and good to go by morning."

"What's in Arizona?"

"Just the biggest prison riot in U.S. history. Prisoners have taken over the supposedly escape-proof prison. They're armed with automatic weapons. The governor's called out the National Guard. There's a hell of a fight brewing."

"Are you talking about that place where they send the worst of the worst. Meza somethingorother?"

"Meza Azul. Yep, that's the one."

"Are they holding hostages?"

"Something like a hundred and fifty of them."

She started to speak, but Martin Wells cut her off. "Here's the good part. You know who's leading this riot? Who's turned out to be in charge?" He didn't give her time to answer. "Guy named Timothy Driver. Name ring a bell?"

"The navy captain. Guy who shot his wife and her lover."

"Know what he wants? What he says he's going to shoot one hostage every six hours over until he gets?"

"What's that?"

"He wants Frank Corso delivered to him at the prison."

"The writer?"

"That's the one."

"How long before the first deadline?"

"Just under two hours."

5

"Can you zoom in? Can you get his badge number?" Elias Romero reminded himself to relax and not breathe into the microphone.

"He's too deep in the shadows," the CNN cameraman yelled over his shoulder. "I can't get anything from here."

"I don't believe it," somebody whispered from the back of the van. "You think he's really gonna do it?"

"Let's pray he doesn't," the state police captain said.

"Here he comes," the cameraman shouted.

All eyes turned to the screen, where a sandy-haired man in a guard's uniform was being pushed through the central arch of the administration building, out of the shadows into the harsh over-head lights. His gait was a stiff-legged stagger; his face was white with fear. His hands were manacled to a wide leather belt encir-cling his middle. The camera caught the clenching and unclenching of his fingers as he walked out into the stark artificial light, then zoomed in closer and closer until only the portion of his blue shirt holding his badge filled the grainy screen inside the van. The de-gree of magnification combined with a slight jiggle of the camera made the numbers on the badge dance before their straining eyes.

"One seven three four five," somebody finally read out loud.

Elias Romero repeated the numbers into his cell phone and waited for Iris Cruz, who was back at the command center, to look up the number.

They were parked on the grass, hard along the left side of the main gate, just as Driver had ordered. One remote truck providing the video feed for the multitude of media outlets now lining Boundary Road, the access road to the prison, a quarter mile to the east. Only the cameraman was outside, shooting the man standing in the prison's front courtyard from a distance of seventy yards. He had his camera pressed hard against the chain-link fence. Above his head, massive coils of razor wire garnished the fences for as far as the eye could see. The air smelled of dust and steel.

The manacled guard stood motionless. Movement could be detected within the deep shadows of the arch. He seemed to turn his head to listen. Seemed to nod in agreement before dropping to his knees. His face knew.

"Cartwright, Wally A." Iris Cruz's voice pulled Elias Romero's attention from the wavering picture of the kneeling guard. "Single white male. Only been on duty for a month and a half. Still on probation."

His given name was Waldo Arens Cartwright. He'd been named after his only reputable uncle, a steely-eyed beet farmer with a jaw like a bass, who, having had the great misfortune to have stepped on a land mine on only his second day in Vietnam, had thus earned a place of honor in the sparsely populated Cartwright family wall of fame, where he now rested in perpetuity on the north wall of Aunt Betty's dining room.

As the name Waldo seemed to attract derision in much the same manner in which a spring flower attracts the bee, the war hero's namesake had, early on, made certain that he was always known as Wally. The way Wally figured it, life was hard enough without asking for trouble, so he'd used Wally on his job application.

Ten minutes ago, Wally had been sitting on the bench in front
of his locker scraping the last of the chicken gravy from the plastic plate with a crust of bread. Some of the guys hadn't eaten at all.
Nerves, Wally guessed. Being held hostage affected some guys
that way. As for Wally, way he saw it, a meal was a meal.

The locker room had been crowded. The takeover had happened right at shift change, when there weren't more than two
dozen officers walking the cellblocks. Everybody else was either
coming or going. The guys on duty had been rounded up and
stuck in the locker room with both shifts. The duty sergeant had
run the roster for both shifts and, lo and behold, nobody was
missing. The announcement sent a shiver of hope through the
hundred or so corrections officers. Maybe they were all going to
come through this. Maybe the inmates were going to go through
the standard list of demands, then it would be over and they could
all get back to their lives. Maybe.

When the door was flung open and a half dozen inmates
armed with everything from Mac 10s to a machete strode into the
room silence settled like a mantle. Spoons stopped in midair,
mouths hung open as a pair of Bikers grabbed Wally by the elbows and lifted him from the bench. Had Wally the slightest notion that he was about to join his namesake on Aunt Betty's
dining room wall, he surely would not have gone so quietly.

"Thanks, Iris," Romero said. He snapped the cell phone shut.
Keeping one eye glued to the screen, he had begun to repeat the
information for the benefit of the others crammed into the interior of the CNN van when the chatter of automatic weapon fire
suddenly filled the air. He watched in horror as a withering salvo
of fire drove the kneeling figure face-first onto the ground.
Watched the body twitch for a few seconds as the river of fire continued, and watched still as the firing stopped and the body grew
still.

"Son of a bitch," somebody said.

Silence filled the air around them like molten metal. Seemed like there was nothing to say. A moment later, a pair of inmates came loping out of the shadows, grabbed the fallen guard by the ankles and dragged him back inside. The powerful microphone picked up the *click click click* as the victim's teeth chattered across the asphalt even after he disappeared from view. Still no one spoke.

At the back end of the arch, Driver looked down at the guard's carcass. At Kehoe holding the rifle in his arms as if it were a baby. "Put him with the others," Driver said.

So far, they had nineteen dead. Guys who'd finally had the chance to settle old scores. Guys like Harry Ferris, who'd spent the past eleven years as the wife of a con known only as the Butcher. Ferris repaid the Butcher for his sexual favors by emptying a whole clip into him, wounding two other cons in the process. Things like that were going on all over the joint.

Driver could relate. He remembered his sixth day in Walla Walla. Almost seven years ago. Remembered Kehoe's warning and how he'd stayed in his bunk that day. Literally hid under the covers like a woman, until the voice came.

"Let's go."

A pair of guards stood in the corridor. They took him by the elbows and marched him down two flights of stairs, through two checkpoints and two metal detectors, before depositing him in the custodial staff locker room.

Driver had tried to stammer out a question. "What's . . . I don't . . ."

"Orientation," the fat guy said.

"Yeah . . . orientation," the other guy chuckled. "You're gonna get your horizons expanded." The door snapped shut. Driver could hear the bald one yapping as they walked away. "His horizons expanded . . . that's choice, man . . . horizons expanded."

And then it was silent. Driver looked around. Gray steel lock-

ers lined the walls. Each locker was fastened by an identical com-
bination lock. White number on black dials. A worn wooden
bench ran down the center of the room, its once gleaming finish
nearly washed away, leaving irregular islands of shine adrift on a
sea of dull wood.

His attention slid toward the sound of running water in the
next room. He sat down on the bench and began to listen intently,
hearing each drop rhythmically followed by another, numbering
them in his mind as they fell. After a few moments, his ears began
to clear, as if he had come down from a mountaintop. Beneath the
persistent plopping he was able to hear the drops surrendering
themselves, gathering in the grouted joints as trickles before running down the drain. He closed his eyes and followed the water
down the grated hole. He saw himself swimming alone in the
damp blackness, using his hands to pull himself around the metal
corners, diving through subterranean culverts, sliding through
languid cataracts, until finally following the expanding cone of
light toward the smell of the sea and the cries of shorebirds.

When he opened his eyes on that afternoon nearly eight years
before, two Mexicans were standing in front of him, their perfect
blue shirts buttoned only at the collar, washboard bellies bare.
The one on the right wore a red bandana over his shaved head. He
had something tattooed on his chest in old English letters. The
one on the left had his hair pulled tight by a net, its nylon web
gathered in the center of his forehead like a fearful third eye. Bandana looked to his left and whispered.

Driver reached for his right shoe.

Bandana spoke. "No no, man. You gotta wait till we leave."

The Mexicans were elbowing each other, cracking up at what
they saw.

"Look at that thing," said Hairnet. "You got to put that thing
away, *cholo*. Got to put it away."

"*Madre de Dios,*" said the other.

Hairnet covered his mouth and looked away just in time to
see Driver fitting the dowel through the hole in the toothbrush
handle. He'd leaned over and whispered in his buddy's ear. They
both watched as Driver folded his arms across his chest, his hands
out of sight beneath his arms.

Kurtz was totally hairless. The lack of eyebrows made the
blue doll eyes seem loose on his face. He was nearly as wide as he
was tall, and his doughy white flesh filled the room with the smell
of camphor and stale sweat. His massive belly would have hidden
a normal cock. As it was, the fat fingers on his right hand flexed
as they stroked an erect appendage that looked more like a pipe
fitting than a penis.

He had a curious, high-pitched voice. "Hands and knees," he
said.

When Driver failed to move, Kurtz started shuffling his way. As
he drew near, Kurtz suddenly raised both arms to shoulder level.

"Gonna have to choke you down some, Mr. Navy."

At the last moment, Driver brought his right hand out from
beneath his arm and pistoned it toward Kurtz, who did what he
always did when somebody threw a punch at him. He ducked his
huge bald head and waited for the sound of broken bones to tell
him the fun was about to begin in earnest.

The plastic point of the toothbrush had been no match for
Kurtz's bald dome. The shaft bent on impact, numbing Driver's
arm, sending the point skidding over the sweaty surface, plowing
a bloody trench across the skull until it slid down the side of his
face, in search of softer flesh. The highly honed point finally
found ingress in Kurtz's right cheek, entering his mouth at a
forty-five-degree angle, skewering his tongue and pinning it to
the soft tissue of his lower jaw.

Kurtz went mad, throwing himself at Driver, butting him in
the face as he drove him into the wall hard enough to break three
of Driver's ribs.

At his resentencing hearing, Driver had been told he'd stabbed Kurtz another dozen times, including once through each eye. Not only that, but he'd supposedly stabbed one of the officers who'd tried to break it up. All of which had been news to Driver. He didn't remember anything past the point when Kurtz butted him back into the shower wall.

After fourteen days in the hospital, followed by sixty days of close confinement, he'd been summarily shipped to Meza Azul. Right next to Cutter Kehoe again. Old home week until they moved Driver to the punishment cell. And now, here they were.

"Hey," Cutter Kehoe yelled.

Driver pulled his eyes from the dead guard being dragged across the asphalt. He blinked several times and looked around.

"Don't be getting loopy on us now, Captainman. Got a lotta boys inside countin' on you to lead 'em to the promised land."

"Most of these boys are already in the promised land."

"How long you figure we got before they come for us?"

"Less than twenty-four hours. They won't let it go on for longer than that. It's bad for morale."

Kehoe bent his head toward the fallen guard. "They ain't gonna let that one go." He shook his head. "Bulls gonna kill my ass for sure, Captainman. They'll find somethin' . . . some reason why I got to die."

"Maybe. Maybe not," Driver said.

The words stopped Kehoe in his tracks. He had a half smile on his face as he ambled over and stood toe-to-toe with Driver. "You got somethin going?"

"Just an idea," Driver said.

"And what kinda idea might that be?"

"One that might get us the hell out of here before the army arrives."

"You don't say."

"It's a long shot."

"Always is."

"You do what I told you with them drivers?"

"I had somebody take care of it." Kehoe eyed him. "Why?"

"Let the linen supply driver go."

Kehoe opened his mouth, but Driver cut him off. "First, take everything out of the truck. Then hand him his keys and stick him behind the wheel. Give me a call when you've got him ready, and I'll open the front gate."

6

He looked away from the wavering water and wondered why he only imagined her in the mornings. Something about the flat water of dawn always brought Meg's face to mind, as if the first silver sheen of the day was forever devoted to her smile.

He pulled on the wet line, bringing the float over the rail and down onto his feet. Her childlike printing encircled the white plastic: SALTHEART, Seattle Wa. 206-933-0881. He kept at it, his breath steaming from his lips in the cold morning air as he formed a circle of line around the bucket at his feet.

When he looked back, she was still there, laughing now, floating on the shiny surface of the water like a mercury apparition. Corso shook his head and returned to the task at hand, hauling hard on the bright yellow line, taking up the slack until he felt the crab trap come loose from the bottom. He used his long arms to hand over hand the trap to the surface.

That's when he saw them coming. Working their way from cove to cove, checking every creek and estuary deep enough for a dinghy. A pair of those little Safeboat twenty-seven-footers they made over in Port Orchard. Homeland Security Boats. Coast Guard's newest toy, an aluminum-hulled, unsinkable boat, propelled by a pair of Yamaha 225s. Stable as hell at sixty knots. Rumor had it they'd ordered seven hundred of them at a hundred eighty-five grand a pop.

Corso pulled the crab pot into the dinghy, careful to keep the collection of slithering crabs and dripping metal out of his lap. The six captive Dungeness crabs had gnawed the turkey leg down to blue-tinged bone. One by one he checked the crabs. Four female, two male. Careful to grab them from the rear, where their pincers wouldn't reach, he threw the females over the side and dropped the males into the white plastic bucket in front of the steering podium.

The sky and the water were slate gray and slack. The surface was smooth as glass; here and there patches of fog slid along the surface like ghost ships. To the northeast, he could barely make out the Wescott Bay Oyster Company at the far end of the bay. He'd been buying a couple of dozen a day for the past week. Throwing them on the barbecue until they cracked open, then washing them down with cocktail sauce and a frosty Heineken. He shot a glance at the Coast Guard boat; just as he figured, they were headed his way. He heaved a sigh and picked up the crab bucket.

He'd been moored in Garrison Bay for a week. Other than emptying his crab pots and making his daily pilgrimage for oysters, all he'd done was write, sleep and eat. Crab omelets for breakfast, crab quesadillas for lunch and crab cakes and oysters for dinner.

Settling back into the seat, he eased the throttle forward. The prop pulled the stern down into the water for a moment, then, as Corso fed it more gas, began to lift the inflatable up onto plane. Corso pushed the throttle lever all the way forward and aimed the nose at *Saltheart*, floating, barely visible through the morning haze a half a mile away on the east side of Garrison Bay, just offshore of the English Camp.

During the summer months, Garrison Bay would have been thick with pleasure boats, but on this rainy November morning, with the kiddies back in school and the temperature in the middle thirties, *Saltheart* had the moorage to herself.

By the time he was halfway up the bay, the Coast Guard boat was running parallel to him, its bright orange paint job skipping along the gray water about twenty yards to port. A crew member stepped out on deck. He brought the red bullhorn up in front of his red face and rested it on his red life jacket. The electronic voice, shattered the stillness of the morning. "Cut your engine back and pull alongside."

Corso shook his head and pointed forward, toward *Saltheart* sitting at anchor a quarter mile away. The Coast Guard repeated the order. Corso repeated the gesture.

The crew member ducked back inside the cabin for further orders. By the time they sorted out what to do next, Corso had pulled the dinghy parallel to the swim step, tied off and killed the engine.

The Coast Guard boat was no more that ten yards astern as Corso climbed on board, secured the crabs and the dinghy and pulled off his black neoprene gloves.

"You Frank Corso?" somebody yelled.

Corso ignored the query. Instead, he knelt on deck and transferred the crabs from the bucket into an old topless cooler full of fresh salt water. He watched the two new crabs settle in. Watched how they fought for territory even within the featureless plastic domain of a cooler, thinking maybe there was some deeper truth to be found in the mindless battle for space, but not being quite able to put his finger on it. He didn't straighten up until he felt *Saltheart* twitch as somebody put his weight on the swim step. He got to his feet and looked down.

Wasn't the kid with the bullhorn; this one had himself a little gold braid on his cap and shoulders. He was about forty. Thick black eyebrows accented an angular face that looked like it had been assembled out of spare parts. The sight of Corso sent the eyebrows scurrying toward the center of his brow.

"You deaf or something?" the guy demanded.

"I don't remember inviting you on board," Corso said.

The guy laughed in his face. "We're the Coast Guard, man. We tell you to pull alongside, you pull alongside."

"I had crabs needed to be put away."

The guy sneered. "Under the provisions of the Patriot Act I could—"

Corso interrupted. "Don't even start with that shit. You want to check my paperwork or my gear, then go ahead. That's your legal right. Otherwise, I'll be up top cleaning crab."

The guy was nimble. He slipped a foot into one of the arched holes in the transom and hoisted himself on board in a single smooth motion.

Corso's first instinct was to grab him by the arms and pitch him overboard. He took a deep breath and restrained himself. "Okay, so I'm Frank Corso."

"You don't know what's going on, do you?"

Something in his tone brought Corso up short. "What's that?"

"In Arizona."

"What the hell are you talking about?"

The guy told him the *Reader's Digest* condensed version. "He shot the third one a couple of hours ago."

"Jesus," Corso muttered.

"I know it's a hell of a thing to ask of a man, put himself in jeopardy for the sake of people he doesn't even know." He raised his hands in frustration and let them fall to his sides with a slap. "People down there are hoping maybe if he sees you've showed up, maybe he'll stop. I'm supposed to tell you they don't expect you to go inside or anything, They just want you to show up and maybe talk to him. Something like that."

"And if I don't see this as my problem?"

The guy thought it over. "I guess that's between you and your conscience."

"I gave up guilt for Lent."

"My orders say it's up to you."

Corso ran a hand through his thick black hair. "My boat . . . ," he started.

"I'll personally take her back to your slip."

Corso nodded his thanks. "How am I supposed to—"

A sound in the distance stopped his thoughts. The noise was rhythmic and growing closer. More of a pop than a roar. Familiar. And then it was on them like a giant grasshopper, the helicopter pushing its way through the ceiling and settling down on the old British parade ground, scattering the ground fog like frightened children.

"The governor of Arizona's jet is waiting at Boeing Field," the guy said.

Corso checked his watch. "What time's he supposed to kill another one?"

"O-six-hundred."

"I need to change clothes. Come on inside."

The guy followed Corso into the salon. Stood there looking around while Corso navigated the three steps down to the storage lockers and the forward berths.

"Beautiful rig," the guy said.

"Thanks," Corso said from below.

"You live aboard full-time?"

"Yep."

"I always wanted to . . . you know, something like this . . . but you know, kids and such . . . and my old lady . . . I mean, there's no way in hell . . ."

"People do it with families."

The guy turned his back and changed the subject.

"What'd you do to this Driver guy where he wants you so bad?"

"I wrote a book about him."

The guy watched as Corso traded coveralls and long underwear for jeans and a black silk shirt. "Book must have really pissed him off."

Corso came back up the stairs into the galley. He pulled a black leather jacket from the nearest hook and put it on. "Actually, he was quite fond of the book."

"Then how come he wants to kill you?"

Corso barked out a sinister laugh. "Driver doesn't want to kill me. He wants to make sure his story gets told. That's my end of it."

"You're kiddin' me."

Corso signaled "Boy Scout's honor" with his fingers. "Honest." He pulled open the top drawer and grabbed his wallet, stuffed it deep into his hip pocket. "Listen, man . . . I don't want to rain on your Western hero motif or anything, but if I thought for one minute Driver was planning to off my ass, I wouldn't be going anywhere near that place."

The guy checked Corso for traces of irony and came up empty.

"When you get her back home, leave the lines loose," Corso said. "We've got some big tide shifts coming up here pretty soon."

"I'll take care of it."

Corso looked around, then drew a deep breath. "Let's go," he said.

7

"I thought Arizona was supposed to be hot," Melanie groused as she walked in a circle, hugging herself and stamping her feet to keep warm. The wind was everywhere. Seemed like whichever way you turned it was in your face. Melanie raised the collar of her coat and pulled her head in like a turtle.

On the roof of the satellite truck a pair of technicians engaged in the never-ending task of tuning and fine-tuning the dishes. "Not this high and not this time of year. Minute the sun goes down so does the temperature," one of them said. "Around here's got some of the biggest daytime to nightime temperature differences in the country."

"What're you, the weatherman?" his partner wanted to know.

Melanie gazed out over the barren landscape. Banks of portable lights had been brought in to light the perimeter, but the prison itself lay dark and silent. In the distance, the San Cristobel Mountains stood sentinel against the night sky, their jagged peaks offering the proceedings little more than a crooked grin. Another gust of wind swirled the desert dust, making Melanie's lips feel chapped and eyes feel heavy and full of grit.

"I'll be in my trailer," Melanie announced to the deepening

night. Her *trailer* was actually a forty-seven-foot mobile satellite unit designed to Melanie's specifications. Her agent had made it part of the last contract negotiation. As Melanie left the comfort of the studio less and less these days, they'd included the motor home merely so as to have something to jettison when negotiations got serious. Turned out, the network had given them everything they'd asked for . . . including the motor home. In the past five years, she'd used it less than a dozen times.

Tonight, however, she was glad to feel the warm glow of heat on her cheeks as she climbed inside and closed the door. She rubbed her hands together as she made her way to the refrigerator and opened the door. The usual. A fresh carton of half-and-half for her coffee, lots of bottled water and not much else.

She grabbed a bottle of water and walked over to the dinette, where she sat down in one of the deep, upholstered chairs flanking the table. She blew on her hands before lifting the phone from the cradle. Memory Dial 1. Home. She listened through several clicks, then through half a dozen rings before her own voice instructed her how to leave a message. She followed the recorded instructions. Wasn't until the beep sounded that she realized she had no idea what she was going to say. "Brian . . . er . . . it's me . . . I just wanted to . . . Anyway I'm here. Hope you had a good day. You can get me on my cell. Okay . . . see ya."

She sat back in the chair and took a deep breath. She couldn't remember anytime in the past thirteen years when she and Brian had left so much unsaid. When so many words had hung in the air at one time, so many confessions, admissions and epithets left to fester on the vine like overripe fruit. Her stomach felt like it had a hole in it. Her breath tasted of metal.

Brian had been gone by the time she set her bag by the door and returned to the back of the house to tell him she was leaving. She'd just begun to ponder the significance of his absence when the cab blew its horn from out front. She'd snapped off the TV on her way out. On the way to LAX she'd tried Brian's cell, but got nothing but voice mail.

She was halfway through the bottle of water when a knock sounded on the door.

"Come in," Melanie said.

Martin Wells poked his head in the door, then mounted the steps and came inside. "Fifteen minutes," he said.

"What's in fifteen minutes?"

"They shoot another hostage in fifteen minutes."

"I thought we were meeting with the prison people."

"They've got problems."

"What kind of problems?"

"National Guard problems."

"Such as?"

"Such as the fact that very nearly every combat-trained member of their National Guard is somewhere in the Middle East. They've still got a bunch of cooks and drivers and clerks here stateside, but that's about it."

"What are they going to do?"

"They've been trying to borrow soldiers from Nevada, but the governor of Nevada doesn't seem to be in a hurry to send his soldiers into anything where the opposition is as armed to the teeth as this."

"Are we set up and ready?"

Martin shook his head. "We're all sharing a CNN feed. Right now that's as close as we can get."

Melanie swallowed a mouthful of water. "Nobody's gonna tune in to see what they already saw on the news, Marty. We need something of our own."

"I got my people working on the Driver angle. He's the one shooting the hostages. Seems to be the leader of this thing. We're working on a full profile."

"So is everybody else. What else?"

"Rumor has it they've got tape of the moment when this Timothy Driver guy took over the prison's control module, which is like the *macher* of this whole prison. We're working on maybe getting a copy."

Martin liked to throw in occasional Yiddish words. Melanie figured it made him somehow feel more ethnic. Whatever.

"Working?"

"We're pushing on both ends. Freedom of Information Act on the front and we've got somebody who might be willing to cooperate on the back side."

"This somebody gonna come through?"

"Too early to tell." He made a conspiratorial face. "Source's got big-time money problems. We could be manna."

"Any idea what this Driver guy wanted with Frank Corso?"

"Nothing other than the obvious fact that Corso wrote a book about him."

Martin ran a hand through his thick salt-and-pepper hair. "You remember when we had him on the show . . . what was that . . . five, six years ago?"

"Women don't forget men who look like Frank Corso."

Something in her tone caught his attention.

"Everything okay?" he inquired.

"I'm fine," Melanie replied. "Only thing could be better was if we had something the networks didn't . . . some angle of our own."

"At home?" Martin pressed. "Everything okay with you and Brian?"

Melanie rose to her feet. "You spend as much time finding us an angle as you seem to want to spend inquiring about my private life and we'll be back on top of the ratings in a heartbeat."

Martin held up a hand of surrender, then brought it down and checked his watch. " 'Bout eight minutes," he said. "State cop said Corso is on the way. Didn't think he'd make it in time to save this one though."

"It's like the Roman circus," Melanie said. "Kind of makes you wonder if we're as civilized as we like to think we are."

"Civilized my ass," Martin said. "We're not civilized. We just created this little Disneyland of a world where we're on top of the food chain. We've taken the law of fang and claw and arranged it so the killing takes place offstage. All nice and neat so's we don't have to look at it. Dead cows come shrink-wrapped. Headless chickens were happy free-range fowl. Salmon are caught with hooks instead of being scooped up in nasty old nets. It's all a bunch of bullshit designed to make us feel better about ourselves."

Melanie walked forward, opened the cabinet beneath the built-in TV and pulled out a bottle of Dalwhinnie scotch. She read Martin's expression. "I'm just a little chilled," she said, pouring herself three fingers. "Trying to get a little blood flowing."

Martin Wells kept his face as blank as blank and as open as concrete. He pushed open the door and stepped out onto the first riser. "Come on. Bring it with you," he said.

"You'll excuse me if I skip the Christians and the lions today."

"Come on," Martin coaxed.

Melanie crossed to the refrigerator, found a handful of ice cubes and dropped them into her drink. "Close the door," she said. "You're letting all the heat out."

Martin gave a look and a shrug and disappeared into the night.

She waited a long moment, making sure he was gone, then brought the glass to her lips and took a substantial pull of the scotch, shuddering slightly as the liquor wound its way down her throat and came to rest as a warm puddle in her innards. The effect was sufficiently pleasant to encourage her to repeat the process.

With her free hand, Melanie, slid back the door in front of the TV and grabbed the remote control, before returning to her seat. She sat for a few moments sipping the scotch and looking out the window into the darkness. She aimed the remote at the TV, then changed her mind, pulling her cell phone from her jacket pocket instead, pushing the button for memory one . . . home . . . the phone rang eight times before her own voice came on the line and invited the caller to leave a message. She sighed and dropped the phone back into her pocket. Picked up the remote and turned on the TV. Moved up to forty-four, CNN. She took another sip of her drink and turned up the volume. *Dateline . . . Musket, Arizona.*

8

The helicopter pilot checked his watch. "You can usually see it by now. They must have turned the lights out."

"What time is it?" Corso asked.

"Four minutes to midnight."

Corso craned his neck and looked upward, out through the plastic roof at the glimmering carpet of stars overhead.

The pilot, whose monogrammed jacket proclaimed him to be Arnie, pointed with his free hand. "Bingo," he said. "That's gotta be it right there."

Corso squinted out into the darkness. All he could make out was a dull line of oddly spaced lights in the distance. "You sure?"

The pilot checked his GPS. "Gotta be," he said after a second. "Ain't nothin' else out here but jackrabbits and that damn prison."

Corso had his nose pressed to the plastic when, as if on cue, an area a mile in front of the helicopter lit up like a college football game. From two thousand feet above the desert floor, the banks of lights surrounding the prison yard formed a blazing bracelet of light surrounding the unadorned buildings, lighting the rolls of razor wire spiraling atop the chain-link fences like curls of steel smoke . . . making it possible to see the tiny figure in the blue shirt, walking a crooked line out onto the concrete.

"They're gonna shoot another one," the pilot announced. "Just like on the TV this morning. Goddamn."

"Put it down in the yard," Corso said.

"What?"

"Put it down in the yard."

Arnie made a rude noise with his lips. "You gotta be crazy."

"In between the guard and the building."

The guy waved him off. "No friggin' way. Maybe you got suicide in mind, buddy, but I got me a wife and three boys I plan on seein' again." He cut the air with his rigid hand. "I done my tour in 'Nam. That's the last chance anybody's ever gonna get to shoot up my ass."

"Put her down just long enough for me to hop out. Maybe we can save a life here."

Arnie rocked his head back and forth. "Ain't gonna happen."

"That's somebody's boy down there, Arnie. Just as easily could be one of yours." Arnie kept shaking his head. Corso kept talking. "That was your boy . . . what would you want us to do? Just sort of fly around up here until he was dead? That what you'd be expecting of us?"

"Aw, don't start that shit with me," Arnie whined. "You're startin' to sound like my old woman with all that guilt trip crap you're throwing around."

Corso kept his eyes on the ground, watching as the blue-clad figure walked slowly across the pavement, then stopped. "Come on, Arnie. Hurry up. Set this damn thing on the ground."

"You're one crazy bastard, you know that?" Corso made a resigned face and nodded, but Arnie kept talking anyway. "First some lunatic says he's gonna keep shooting people until you show your ass up at the worst goddamn prison in the country and you just haul off and agree to come on down, then . . ." Arnie sputtered a bit. "... and then you want me to put us down directly in the line of fire." He waved his free hand Corso's way. "You're one sick puppy. You know that? One goddamned sick puppy."

"You wouldn't be the first to think so, Arnie," Corso allowed. Arnie looked his way. "What?" Corso raised an eyebrow. "You want to live forever? I thought only women wanted to live forever."

Other than the slapping of the rotors, the cockpit was silent. Corso had to smile. The question of his apparent lack of concern for his own safety had been a major bone of contention in his relationship with Meg Dougherty and had, in a roundabout way, been at least partially responsible for her decision to end their often tumultuous affair. In the months since her departure, he'd had occasion to consider the possibility that she might have been correct in her assessment.

What he'd concluded was that he had as much regard for survival as anybody else. It was just that there were a number of other factors which, in his mind, held equal sway. He wanted to endure, just like everybody else, but it had to be on his own terms ... something he could live with when the smoke cleared.

"Aw goddammit," Arnie shouted above the noise. The helicopter started down with a lurch, spinning slowly as it descended, swooping low over a vast strung-out collection of television trucks, lifting every loose piece of dust and gravel from every nook and cranny as it made its way to the center of the prison yard, where Arnie swung the tail back toward the prison, offering as little target as possible to the shooters.

"Pop that belt, buddy," Arnie yelled as they approached the ground. "I want your ass out of here in a heartbeat."

Corso popped the harness and grabbed the door handle. In front of the copter, the guard stumbled forward, out of the radius of the rotor blades, shielding his face from the whirling collection of desert debris filling the air.

"Watch your head," Arnie yelled.

Corso gave Arnie the two-fingered salute, shouldered open the door and dropped the three feet to the ground. Corso used his jacket to shield his face as he bent low under the whirling rotors.

Inside the cockpit, Arnie reached over and latched the door, then began to ease the helicopter back into the night sky. "Crazy bastard," he muttered under his breath.

On the ground, the fading sound of the engine was accompanied by the insistent hiss of debris falling to the pavement. After another moment, both Corso and the guard straightened up and looked around through squinty eyes.

He was young. Not yet thirty. Skinny with an unruly shock of red hair, and at some point he must have been crying. He had a runny nose and a pair of telltale tracks running from his eyes to which the fine desert dirt had clung, lending a clownlike quality to his otherwise terrified face.

Corso wondered why a man with so much life in front of him would choose to spend his days locked up with the scum of the earth. Whether he was a sadist or a do-gooder or something in between, or maybe just a guy who really needed a job.

The air was cold and crisp. As the sound of the chopper faded from the sky, Corso heard shouts coming from over by the outer fence. He scanned the area until his eyes came to rest on the area just north of the main gate, where a camera crew waved their arms as they aimed their unblinking electronic eye his way. He turned his head.

What had to be the administration building stood forty yards away. An imposing three-story brick structure bisected by a round arch in the center of the building. In the blackness of the yawning arch, a flame flickered for long enough for somebody to light a cigarette.

The scrape of shoes pulled Corso's attention around. The guard had mustered a teaspoon of courage and was thinking about making a run for it. Corso shook his head.

"I wouldn't," he said. "You'll never even make it to the fence."

The guard opened his mouth to speak, but nothing came out. "I . . . ," he stammered.

"Stay behind me," Corso said as he turned and started toward the administration building. A third of the way there, Corso stopped. The guard ran into the back of him. "Not quite that close, kid," Corso said before turning and walking away.

At twenty yards, Corso could make out the shapes of three figures standing within the dark shadow of the arch. Corso adjusted course and aimed at the center of the shadow. A dozen strides and he could make out Tim Driver standing at the right, hands at his sides, watching in silence as Corso and the guard approached.

On Driver's right, a long-haired con pointed an assault rifle directly at Corso's chest. He dropped one eye to the sight and closed the other. Corso lengthened his stride. Below the gaping barrel, a thin smile worked its way across the guy's lips. Corso watched the finger tighten on the trigger. His throat began to close; breathing became a chore in the final seconds before Driver pushed the gun barrel aside, sending a three-shot burst of fire rocketing off into the night. Still holding the barrel, Driver said, "I didn't think you'd come."

The shooter snarled and jerked the barrel from Driver's hand. He was maybe six feet tall, with a full head of shoulder-length hair surrounding a narrow, angular face. Looked like the kind of guy you'd see panhandling on the beach. Except for the eyes. Corso had seen eyes like that before. Secret policemen in Haiti, Kurdish insurgents in Afghanistan and once in a while on the Nature Channel during Shark Week. The kind of eyes you crossed the street to avoid, the kind you hoped never to see staring out of a darkened doorway late at night. Especially not holding an automatic weapon.

"You knew damn well I'd come," Corso snapped. "What in hell was I supposed to do? Keep fishing while you shot people?"

Driver nearly smiled. "Tight ethical squeeze wasn't it? Sorry I couldn't leave you more wiggle room, Frank, but"—he aimed a palm straight up—"time constraints . . . you know."

The shooter moved the barrel and pointed the M16 at the guard, who began to wring his hands and pray out loud. The sudden sound of running water was soon explained by an expanding dark spot on the front of the guard's pants.

"Now look at what you made him do," Corso said to the shooter.

"Make you do worse, pretty boy," the man said with an air of self-assurance. "Wanna try me out?"

A snappy rejoinder caught in Corso's throat. Some deep-seated survival sense told him it was not the time. This was not the guy.

"No," he said in a soft voice. "Don't believe I do."

The guy's voice dripped with disdain. "There's always later," he teased.

"Believe I'll pass on that honor too."

The air seemed suddenly still and wet.

"Honor eh? You think it's an honor, do you?"

"Poor word choice," Corso offered quickly.

"Maybe," the guy said finally. "We'll see."

Driver nodded at the guard. "Bronko," he called to the third man, who now stepped sufficiently into the light to reveal a barn-sized specimen with what looked like a nine-millimeter handgun jammed in his belt. "Take him back where you got him from," Driver said.

Bronko made eye contact with Kehoe, as if to ask if it was okay to do as he was told. All he got in return was an insolent shrug, which he somehow interpreted as a yes.

"What about this faggot?" he wanted to know, nodding at Corso.

"He's part of the convergence," Driver said.

Another series of puzzled looks were passed. Finally, Bronko reached out a massive paw, grabbed the guard by the elbow and propelled him back toward the cellblocks with such force that the officer stumbled and nearly lost his footing.

Corso, Kehoe and Driver watched in silence as Bronko stiff-armed the officer across the yard, through a propped-open gate and into the darkness of an open doorway.

One floor above, the first level of the cellblock was alive with activity. At least a dozen gun barrels protruded from broken windows. With his eyes adjusted to the dim light, Corso could make out a nearly constant promenade of bodies inside the building. "Boys are getting restless," Kehoe said.

Driver ignored him. "They get that semi full of groceries unloaded?"

"Unloaded and damn near swallowed."

"Who'd you leave in charge of the truck drivers?"

"Forger namea Haynes."

"Have him let the semi driver go."

"Like the others?"

"Yes. Just give him his keys and tell him he can go. Call me when he's ready to roll and I'll open the front gate for him."

"Boys wanna grease the rest of them pigs we got rounded up downstairs."

"How many trucks we got left?" Driver asked.

"Nothin' but that tandem tanker rig."

Driver nodded. "You get done with that, you meet us back at the command pod."

Kehoe rocked on the balls of his feet. "You listen to me, Captainman. I ain't onea your fucking crew." He waved a hand toward the cellblocks. "Ain't none of these neither. Sometime tomorrow we gonna run outta food and things gonna get outright nasty around here. That happens you and your girlfriend here

gonna sure as hell wish you was someplace else. Not me or anybody else gonna be able to keep 'em offa you."

"We'll be gone by then," Driver said. Kehoe opened his
mouth to speak, but Driver cut him off. "The soldiers'll be coming in here after us just before dawn. They can't let this go on for
another day."

"The boys are ready for them," Kehoe said. "Motherfuckers
gonna find themselves in a hell of a fight."

Driver's face was carved from stone. "We'll see," was all he offered. "Let's get that driver on his way."

9

Governor James Blaine ran a hand halfway through his "presidential hair," then stopped. With his other index finger he pointed toward . . . toward . . . toward . . . he couldn't for the life of him remember the damn guy's name . . . so he freed his fingers from his hair and used both hands to fumble in his pants pocket until he came out with the guy's business card. The Randall Corporation. Dallin Asuega. Deputy Director of Security Operations.

"Mr. Asuega," the governor called.

Asuega raised his heavy eyebrows. "Yes sir," he said.

He looked too young to be a deputy director of anything more complicated than mowing lawns. Blaine had reached that stage in life where everyone looked too young and nothing was quite as good as he remembered it to be. Asuega couldn't be much past thirty. Dark-complected with a thick head of wavy black hair, far too "ethnic" to ever be considered "presidential." Some kind of South Sea Islander. A Samoan or maybe a Tongan. Something like that. Either way, he was a smooth unit in a good suit. Kept his answers to a minimum and his face as bland and unreadable as a cabochon.

"Have you seen the videotape? The one of this Driver fellow taking over the control pod?"

"No sir."

The governor turned to Elias Romero, who was at that moment trying to extrude himself through the wallpaper into the next room. "Can you cue that up again for us?" Blaine wanted to know.

Romero said he didn't think it would be a problem and reached for the phone.

"Iris. Could you please run the DVD again? We'd like to show it to Mr. Asuega." As Romero calculated the situation, Asuega's presence redistributed the blame somewhat, lightening his personal load and spreading the enmity to the Randall Corporation, where it rightly belonged. Meza Azul was, after all, their baby.

On the other end of the phone line, Iris mumbled a mouthful of unintelligible syllables before dropping the receiver with a *clank*.

"Iris?" Romero frowned and looked at the phone receiver.

"Coming right up, Mr. Romero," came the strained voice.

They stood for a long moment staring at the blank screen. And then another long twitchy moment passed. Romero's hand was creeping its way to the phone when the screen came alive with the sight of a solitary figure taking the last half dozen steps down the mezzanine before the central elevator. "Can you stop it there?" the governor asked.

Romero annexed the receiver and relayed the request.

"Tell me again," the governor began. "Tell me what it takes for a prisoner to be taken out of his cell."

Asuega deferred to Romero. "No prisoner ever leaves his cell without being shackled hand and foot and without an escort. In the case of most prisoners the escort consists of a supervisor and a correctional officer. In Driver's case, with his history of causing injury to prison personnel, he never leaves his cell without a three-guard escort. Two officers and a supervisor."

"And you're going to tell me this guy, shackled hand and foot, somehow managed to subdue three correctional officers." The governor looked from Romero to Asuega and back. "What are we talking about here? Houdini?"

"We don't know," Asuega said quickly. "All we know for sure is his cell door would never have been unlocked unless the officers felt certain he had successfully been shackled hand and foot."

"Sooo . . . explain it to me." The governor showed the ceiling his palms. "How could something like this happen in what is supposed to be the securest of the maximum security prisons?"

Romero cleared his throat. Asuega bailed him out. "We have to assume Driver somehow managed to slip his handcuffs. Nothing else makes any sense." A pair of nods indicated that all concerned were willing to admit the impossibility of a manacled man subduing three trained guards using only his feet. Before Blaine could ask another question, Asuega went on. "We also have to assume that through one ruse or another, Driver managed to lure all three of his jailers into the cell with him. Otherwise, the pod operator would surely have seen the commotion and taken emergency measures."

"We won't know until we get back inside and see the tape," Romero said.

"Inside the cell?" the governor looked confused.

"Mr. Driver was under video surveillance twenty-four hours a day."

Blaine paused and thought it over. "The lights never went out?"

"No," said Romero. "Never."

The governor stifled a shudder. "Really?"

"Yes sir."

"What do you call that sort of thing?"

"Extreme Punishment." Asuega said. "It's reserved for those who kill or injure prison personnel." Asuega read the revulsion on Blaine's face. "I assure you, Governor, the policy works as a serious deterrent. Compared to government-administered facilities, ours have an overall thirty percent lower rate of injuries to staff."

"How long has this Driver character been living under these conditions?"

"Four and a half years," Asuega said.

Again, the look of disgust on the governor's face gave his feelings away.

"Run it up to the elevator part," he said.

Romero relayed the request into the phone; on the screen Driver looked like a Keystone Kop moving up the cellblock at triple speed.

"There," said the governor. Driver's image had just inserted the electronic card into the elevator control panel and punched in that day's code. "Wait a minute now," Blaine prompted. "Stop," he said as Driver turned his back to the camera and hunched over.

"What's he doing there?" Blaine wanted to know.

"He's circumventing the fingerprint recognition system," Romero said.

"Not possible," Asuega said quickly. "Disabling it . . . maybe. Getting around the system . . . not a chance." Before Blaine could bombard him with more questions, Asuega went on. "Any damage to the hardware simply shuts the system down. Nobody goes up or down until the pod operator rearms the software."

"Then what in hell is he doing?"

"If I had to hazard a guess, I'd say he's probably using the system in the manner in which it was intended."

"I thought you said—" The governor stopped. A mixture of

confusion and horror plowed furrows in his forehead. "Are you suggesting . . . you mean like . . ."

Asuega jumped in. "The only explanation that makes any sense is that Mr. Driver is in possession of the security foreman's right index finger." He pointed at the screen. "Could we go on here?"

Romero said, "Let it run, Iris," and the picture once again began to move.

"Can you slow it down and back it up a little?" Asuega asked.

"Stop," he said after a moment. "Notice how carefully he's moving. As if he's folding something up, then putting it in his pocket." They watched in silence as the elevator arrived and Driver stepped inside.

They watched the last forty seconds. Romero and Blaine looked away for the last fifteen seconds or so. Asuega kept his dark eyes locked on the screen until the picture lapsed to static. "For ease of training, the control pod was designed to be as intuitive as possible," Asuega said. "To someone like Driver . . . trained in state-of-the-art electronics and control mechanisms, figuring out how to operate the prison's systems was no great problem. I'd be willing to bet he's already reprogrammed the software to recognize his own fingerprint."

As if he had the answer to an unasked question, a U.S. Army colonel threw back the door and strode inside. "My people will be ready in an hour."

"They've taken over the armory," said the governor.

The colonel sneered at him. "They got armor-piercing shells?" He didn't wait for an answer. "Any depleted uranium? Artillery? Air support?"

"Of course not," Romero answered nervously.

"Then they're in deep shit," announced the colonel. "I've got four hundred men who just spent the past nineteen months in Baghdad. They've been back with their families for less than a week, so it's safe to assume they don't appreciate this little exercise they're getting thrown into this evening." He stopped for effect. "I don't care what kind of peashooters those convicts have. We go through those gates"—he cut the air with the side of his hand—"they damn well better be ready for hellfire and damnation, 'cause that's what they're gonna get."

10

"Another day or so," Melanie Harris spoke into the receiver. The silence at the other end of the line spoke volumes. She tried another tack. "Maybe we could take a little time off. Go back to Michigan . . . visit your parents . . ." She stopped. The silence went on for some time before Brian's voice broke the spell.

"You're not hearing me."

"Of course I am."

"You know, Mel . . . you have the most amazing ability to hear only what you want to hear. It's like you've got some kind of built-in filter or something. Some device that doesn't allow anything negative to get in the way of the grand plan."

She sucked in a breath of air. Used the power to keep her voice modulated. "It's called focus, Brian. The ability to stay locked on something until it's finished."

"Unlike me, of course."

"I didn't say that."

"You didn't need to. It comes up every time."

"Not from me," she insisted.

"You know . . . I think you attend too many of those group-think meetings where everybody sits on their well-heeled asses nodding at stupid things. You forget what's it's like to just come out and say whatever you're thinking." Before she could speak, he went on. "You ought to try it now and again. It's a breath of fresh air. Listen . . . I'll show you. Ready?" He took a deep breath. "I'm sick to death of Hollywood and I'm going home to Michigan." She could feel his intensity over the phone line. "There. Did you hear that or should I say it again?"

"I don't need this right now."

"Would the 'right now' part of that statement indicate that there would be some other more convenient time to bandy this about?"

"I hate you when you're like this."

He laughed. "You don't pay enough attention to me to work up anything as strong as hate."

Melanie began to sputter. "I . . . I mean . . . how can you . . ."

The motor home's door flew back with a bang. The springs compressed as someone weighted the stair. Martin Wells bounced into the room with the kind of glee usually reserved for furloughed schoolchildren. In his right hand, he held a DVD in a plain white jewel case. The carefully combed lock of hair that usually lay plastered to his scalp had been blown straight up like a rooster's comb.

"We've got it," he announced.

Melanie pulled a smile across her face and covered the mouthpiece with her hand. "Could you give us a couple of minutes here, Marty?" she said in a strained voice.

Wells was too agitated to be so easily deterred. He shook the DVD. "Got the whole damn thing. Exclusive. Just us . . . nothing . . ."

Melanie raised her voice and cut him off. "A couple of minutes, Marty . . . pleeease."

When he failed to move, Melanie pointed at his head and

made a smoothing motion with her hand. Marty got the message, using both hands to steer the shingle of hair back into place, before stepping over and using the rearview mirror to check his efforts.

"For the time being, you can reach me at my parents' house," Brian said. "I get something more permanent, I'll let you know."

Unable to suppress it any longer, she heaved a massive sigh into the mouthpiece. "Come on, Bri, let's be reasonable here . . . I'm in the middle of a prison riot . . . I'll be home in a few days . . . we'll sit down and . . ."

Without warning the phone began to sing its solitary note into her ear. She sat for a moment in disbelief, words still on her lips, the phone still sweaty against the side of her head. She used her thumb and forefinger to massage the bridge of her nose before heaving yet another sigh and settling the receiver in its cradle.

"Everything okay?" Marty wanted to know.

She waved him off. He knew from long experience this was not one of those times when it was safe to press. He watched as she gathered herself.

"What is it you've got an exclusive on?" she asked.

"The takeover," he said tentatively. "The moment when this guy Driver takes over the prison."

"And how did we come into possession of this exclusive piece of media?"

"You don't want to know."

Melanie took him at his word and did not press the issue. She had long since resigned herself to the reality of her profession. Their job was to get the story and get it out to the public. Along the way, they sold ads for the program. The more popular the program, the more expensive the ads. What it took to get the story in the first place was very nearly a moot point. As long as the means weren't outright illegal or the story wasn't an outright fraud, they could skewer any other charges on the lance of "the public's right to know." Something in the way he stood his feet, however, caught her eye.

"No problem at all?"

He gave a semishrug and looked away. "The other end's a little dicey. Real need to know. Real small group of people who've been privy to the info."

"So?"

"So it's not gonna take 'em long to figure out who's wet on their end."

She eyed him closely and rolled a manicured hand around her wrist. "And thus by extension who's wet on our end."

"Yeah," he admitted.

"I don't like it," she said quickly. "We're not in a position to weather a lot of heat. At this point—"

"We're clean on it," Marty insisted.

Her face was skeptical. "How's that?"

"I had Jimmy make the connection," he said, naming one of the legion of assistant producers roaming the premises. "No other staff person was involved in any way. The show was never mentioned. This was strictly a cash-and-carry deal."

"You're sure the show wasn't mentioned?"

"Positive."

The way he'd described the situation, it wasn't possible for him to be sure beyond a doubt, but, in their business, factual leaps of faith were often required. She let it go.

"And if anybody comes looking for Jimmy?"

Marty's little boy smile crept over his face. "I sent him back to L.A. Gave him a week off." Before she could speak, he went on. "With pay," he added with a wink. "Kid's gonna take his girlfriend to Cancún."

She arched her eyebrows. "And this is worth all of that?"

"This"—he waved the jewel case in the air—"puts us right back on top of the food chain."

She pointed to the console. Housed inside were the TV set, the VCR, the DVD player.

"Fire it up," she said. "Let's see what you've got."

She gave the words all the positive energy she could muster. She'd been down this road before only to be disappointed. They hadn't had a true exclusive in a long time. Nothing that was worth the hoopla anyway. A couple of two-day leads on mediocre stories, but that was about it. After so many false alarms, she found it difficult to muster a great deal of enthusiasm for anything unseen.

The screen rolled once, then flickered to life. Melanie watched in silence as Driver accessed the control pod. At the point where Driver looped the piano wire around the guard's neck, she began to rise from the seat, pushing herself sympathetically upward with her arms, as if drawn on a string, until near the end, when her locked elbows braced her above the seat bottom and her red mouth hung open like a scar.

The screen rolled. She dropped back into the seat with a plop. "Jesus," she whispered. "Can we run that?" she asked.

"If we fuzz the face on the stiff, New York says we can put it on . . . as is." Marty checked his watch. "Maybe an insert on tomorrow night's show. All I need is the go-ahead from you and we'll pull the Norton piece. We can record you doing a lead and a follow right here and e-mail it to L.A. They'll take care of the rest."

Melanie leaned back in her seat. "It's pretty graphic," she offered. "We've never done anything quite that intense before."

Marty raised his hands above his head, brushing the low ceiling with the jewel case.

"Breaking new ground," he chanted. "Pushing the envelope." When she remained unconvinced, he went on. "Those forensic shows are always in the morgue these days, prime time . . . showing burnt dead bodies and such every night of the week."

Melanie shrugged. "Those things are simulated," she said. "Paint and rubber."

"What's the difference?" he wanted to know.

She thought about perhaps explaining the difference to him but immediately discarded the idea. Marty had been in Hollywood for so long that, like so many others in the business, the distinction between life on earth and life on the silver screen had been lost somewhere in the bargain. Didn't matter whether or not it was true. What mattered was whether or not it looked good on the screen and whether or not it put people in the seats, so to speak. "Good thing they don't put ratings on our private lives," she thought to herself.

She flicked a finger at the still-quavering screen. "This was real, Marty. You could feel it. There was something . . ." She searched for a word. ". . . something almost voyeuristic about watching it." She looked up at Marty. "Like I was watching a snuff film or something."

"We load the promos out there over the next thirty-six hours and we'll draw a bigger share than we've drawn in three or four years. No way we can keep this one in the bag. It means too much to all of us."

"What about the inside source? You as much as said the authorities are gonna know where this thing came from."

"Ya pays yur money, ya takes yur chances," Marty said, without so much as a hint of a smile. "Come on, babe." He was at his most sincere now. "We gotta run with this. It's now or never."

She let a long minute pass before she folded her fingers over her chest and gave him an answer.

11

The noise assaulted the ears like angry hornets . . . aloft, abuzz . . . fifty stations spewing a swarm of jazz, honky-tonk, speed metal, butt rock, rap radio . . . the shouts and grunts and groans, the talk and the twang and the tonsils rolling out into the air, where the concrete walls blended the bebop with the hip-hop, then bounced it back to the inside track where the homies and the hurt kicked back and relaxed.

They moved along the edges of the cellblock walkways, trying to separate themselves from the surrounding chaos. Driver and Kehoe were on either side of Corso as they slipped among the acres of broken furniture and burning mattresses littering the concrete floor. The air was acrid and oily. Smelled of piss and Pall Malls. Here and there, scattered knots of prisoners loitered. Some armed, some not. Mostly up by the front windows where they could keep an eye on the brightly lit perimeter and the front gate. At one landing lay a trio of corpses, all piled helter-skelter on top of one another, throats cut, bodies awash in a thick halo of dried blood.

Halfway down C Block, a hairy hand reached from the darkness of an open cell, caught hold of Corso's collar and jerked him backward into the darkness. Whoever it was smelled of old blan-

kets and wet sheep as he used his weight to drag Corso to the
floor, where it took all of Corso's strength to keep from being
yanked over onto his back. Corso struggled for all he was worth.
The guy moaned once and adjusted his grip before Corso heard
the voice. Kehoe's. Yelling.

"Hey. Hey. What the fuck you think you're doing? Get the
fuck offa him. You hear me, motherfucker. Get the fuck offa . . ."

Corso felt his attacker swipe at Kehoe with his free hand . . .
then, a moment later felt a deep shudder, followed by what could
only be described as a sudden loss of body tumescence, as if his
attacker had suddenly had the air let out of his balloon.

Three seconds later, the guy tilted sideways and fell to the
floor without a sound. Corso scuttled out from under and pulled
himself to his feet. Guy looked like some sort of caveman. Hairy
all over like an ape. Like, in his whole life, he'd never had a shave
or a haircut. Corso shuddered.

Corso was still trying to process what had happened when
Kehoe reached down and wiped the boning knife clean on the
dead guy's chest hair. One side of the blade, then the other. Real
nice and neat before he stuck it back into his pocket.

"One of those assholes can't get a hard-on less he can smell
shit," Kehoe said with a shake of the head. "Place is full of them.
Long as I been in these places I ain't never . . ."

And suddenly the air was filled with shouts and the slap of
running feet. "Here they come," someone bellowed.

Driver moved quickly to the opposite side of the walkway.
Through three layers of bars and steel grates, the area around the
front gate was roiling with activity. A phalanx of Bradley armored
vehicles rumbled just outside the gate. Along the main road a
seemingly endless procession of troop carriers discharged squad
after squad of foot soldiers.

"Shit," said Kehoe. "They're comin' for us with soldiers.
Party's over."

Driver shook his head. "Half an hour . . . forty-five minutes." he said. "It'll take them that long to get staged and ready."

"You got a plan, Captainman . . . I'm guessin' now's the time."

"Get the tanker truck. Bring it around between the buildings."

"You want I should bring the driver?"

"Just the truck. We'll fetch the driver later."

Kehoe started to amble off. Driver stopped him with a hand on the shoulder. He tucked a piece of paper into Kehoe's shirt pocket. "Keys for the oil truck and a bundle I put together . . . they're in the central elevator. Access code is in your pocket there." He took a deep breath. "You're gonna need this too." He reached into his pants pocket and pulled out a dirty piece of blue rag, stained here and there by some unidentifiable dark liquid. He offered the bundle to Kehoe, who kept his hands at his side for a long moment before finally taking it between his thick fingers. Something about the feel sent a question to his eyes. Kehoe set the package gently in the palm of his left hand. Using the tips of his fingers, he folded away the edges until a severed finger appeared in his hand. The cut at the butt end was rough and ragged. The fingernail needed cutting.

Kehoe pulled himself up to his full height and looked Driver in the eye.

"Just how iffy we talkin' 'bout here, Captainman?"

Driver held his gaze. "About as iffy as it gets," he said.

A tense moment passed before Kehoe pocketed the finger and began to jog back the way they'd come. Driver turned a quick right and started down the stairs.

Corso collected his wits and trotted along behind. "What's the deal?" he wanted to know. "What's so iffy?"

Driver threw a wolfish grin back over his shoulder. "Gonna see if maybe we can't get the hell outta here before the serious shooting starts."

Corso slid to a halt. "Hey now . . . ," he began. "A little prison

riot was one thing. You screwed me into showing up for that . . .
but you know . . . like some escape attempt . . . I'm thinking that's
maybe more than I bargained for."

Behind Corso on the walkway, a dozen armed prisoners
sprinted along the concrete. Scattered shots could now be heard
from every corner of the facility. Driver stopped and turned
Corso's way. "Okay," he said affably. "I can understand how
you'd feel that way, Frank. I was just trying to make sure my
story got told right, was all. Wanted to make sure everybody understood why I was doing this. How it was all coming together."
Driver grinned. "I'm a reasonable man, though. I'll certainly understand if you don't want to come along." He didn't wait for
Corso to make a decision. "I've got some errands," Driver said.
"You take care of yourself now," he said, throwing Corso a three-
fingered salute as he continued down the stairs.

Corso stood for a moment, listening to the building chorus of
gunfire. Somewhere above, another salvo of automatic weapon
fire was joined by another, then a third, until the scream of pro-
jectiles and the clank of brass swallowed every other sound.

Corso found himself taking the stairs two at a time, using his
long legs to erase the distance between Driver and himself. By the
time he pulled even, Driver was using his remote to open an outside door. "You can't just leave me in here, man," Corso said.
"These crazy fuckers will kill my ass in a heartbeat."

Driver paused to consider the statement. He fished in his
pocket pulled out an open pack of Juicy Fruit gum and, one by
one, unwrapped the slices and fed them into his waiting mouth.
"No doubt about it," he said after a moment. "You best not be out
and about when the shooting starts."

"What's that supposed to mean?"

"You could try to hide," Driver offered, his mouth wide and
wet around the gum. "Or maybe arm yourself." He held the door
open. Raised his eyebrows. "Coming?"

Corso stepped outside. The air smelled of smoke and steel. They were in a wide alley between the administration building and the short side of the cellblocks. Down in a deep well of darkness, in a spot where the searchlights held no sway. The crunch of broken glass beneath his feet took him back thirty years. Took him back to the old derelict cotton mill at Rasher Creek. The broken husk of another era, when sweat was king and labor was cheap. A rotting shell of a building whose windows had long since fallen victim to the stones of boys, where, in the heat of a summer day, one could find solace in the narrow, shaded alley between the mill and the creek.

Driver hooked the door open and hugged the darkness close to the building as he started off into the gloom. He talked as he walked across the manicured grass. "You could try to make a break for the front gate." Driver waggled a dubious hand. "Way I see it, that's way beyond iffy. Only real question is which side nails you first." He shrugged. "Or maybe give yourself up to the soldiers on their way in. You could explain to them that you're not really a con . . . that you're just in here on a lark." His lips formed the thinnest of smiles.

"This isn't funny."

Driver slowed. "I didn't plan on this, Corso. I didn't think they could put an assault together this quickly. I figured there'd be hours of dialogue. Threats and demands . . . that sort of thing, before anybody got serious. I figured we could have a couple of hours for an update. Things have changed." He waved a hand. "Maybe even a sequel." He paused and swallowed a thought. "I figured I could get you back out before the shooting started." He looked rueful. "Must be losing my edge."

Corso could feel the bile rising in his throat. The cold mantle of fear began to envelop him. "I haven't got a lot of options here."

Driver nodded his rueful agreement. "Your best bet is probably to find an empty cell, jam the door shut, pull the mattress over yourself and hope to God one of those Marines doesn't shoot your ass for fun." He nodded at the open door and the shaft of yellow light at the far end of the alley.

As if to aid Corso in his decision, another volley of small-arms fire erupted from the cellblocks above. When he looked back, Driver had a small black flashlight in his hand. He was bent at the waist, shining the powerful beam at the lock on what appeared to be the central back door of the Louis Carver Administration Building.

Corso watched as Driver fished a ring of keys from his pants pocket. Took him three tries to find the right key. He pulled open the door and inclined his head toward Corso. "What's it gonna be, big fella? You part of the problem or part of the solution?"

Driver stepped partially inside. Corso caught the door in his hand, looked around for a moment and followed the rapidly retreating shadow.

The electricity had been turned off in the building, leaving the hallways on auxiliary power, delineated by strings of small white lights at foot level like on an airplane. Green EXIT signs floated above occasional doorways as they made their way to the corner stairwell and started down.

12

Colonel David Williams stopped halfway to the office door as his mind tried to make sense of what he'd just heard. He pulled off his helmet and put it under his arm.

"What did you say?" As he hadn't seen who had issued the statement, he asked the question to the room. The guy with the hair. The one sitting at the extra desk closed his cell phone and opened his mouth.

"You'll need to do as little damage to the facility as possible," he said.

That's what he thought the voice had said. As the anger rose in his throat, the colonel started to speak but swallowed it. Instead, he turned to the warden.

"Who the hell is this guy?"

Romero looked embarrassed. He sucked air through his bottom teeth and ran a finger around his collar before answering. "This is Mr. Asuega. He's Deputy Director of Security Operations for the Randall Corporation."

"Ah," Williams said. "The folks who run this place. That figures."

The heels of his boots beat a slow cadence on the floor as he crossed to stand in front of Dallin Asuega. "Worried about your building are you?"

Asuega showed him an acre of teeth. "Meza Azul is a state-of-the-art facility," he said evenly. "The cost of replacement would be—"

The colonel cut him off. "Before you start in on the facts and figures, Mr. . . ."

"Asuega."

"Mr. Asuega. Let me make a few things clear to you." He hesitated long enough to ensure he had everybody's attention. "First off, you need to understand I don't give a hill of beans for your 'state-of-the-art' facility. The only thing on my agenda is the safety of the men under my command. If it takes razing the building to the ground to keep my men safe, I'll do it." Asuega raised a finger. Williams raised his voice. "Second, you seem to have failed to notice your 'state-of-the-art' facility is presently being run by the inmates. Leads me to believe that your 'state-of-the-art' systems must have left a great deal to be desired, so maybe you all ought to rethink your definition of state of the art."

Williams checked his watch. "It's twenty-two-forty," he announced. "We're going in at twenty-three hundred sharp. I'm going to have the first two Strykers put a salvo of fifty-millimeter cannon fire through that third-floor walkway where all the fire is coming from. Once those assholes figure out we can kill them right through the bricks, I'm guessing most of them will be feeling a whole lot less feisty."

He nodded at the assemblage. "If you'll excuse me," he said, before turning on his heel and marching from the room.

"You figure the boys will put up much of a fight?" Corso asked as they descended the stairs.

A harsh laugh escaped Driver's throat, the kind of studied

humor that gave sane men pause to wonder. "Hell no," he said. "Couple dozen of them may prefer 'death by soldier' to serving out their sentences, but . . . the rest of them . . . they're not soldiers. They're rabble. The scum of the earth. First heavy arms fire they see will send them scurrying back to their cells like lemmings."

They were at the bottom by then. Driver pushed his way through an unlocked door and suddenly they were in the modern version of a boiler room. Sans the boiler. All electronic gauges and digital readouts. Took Corso less than half a minute to see that Driver had been down there before. That whatever he was doing to the furnace was something he'd worked out on a prior visit. He watched as Driver manipulated the dials and gauges. Watched as he pulled the great wad of gum from his mouth, reached inside the service panel at the bottom of a heating and air-conditioning unit and slipped the gum into place. What the gum's function might be was lost on Corso.

Driver didn't bother to close the door. Instead he crossed the room to the far wall, to the cluttered desk, where he picked up the telephone receiver and set it gently on its side. Corso stepped in closer. Watched as Driver unscrewed the mouthpiece and began to pull wires loose. It was too dark for Corso to make out exactly what Driver was doing. Only that he was attaching the color-coded wires to one another in a fashion unintended by the phone's designers.

Satisfied, Driver screwed the cap back into place and set the receiver in the cradle. Corso followed along as Driver returned to the same set of dials and gauges he'd messed with before. He'd pushed only a couple of buttons when the hissing began. Deep and insistent like wind through a crack in the door.

And then that rotten egg smell and the beginnings of a painful heat in the lungs. Gas. No doubt about it. Natural gas was pouring out of the furnace at a prodigious rate, filling the room, causing Corso's eyes to tear and his lungs to stall.

Corso covered his mouth with his jacket, stood there with his eyes screwed shut, breathing the smell of himself as the gas folded itself around him. Driver took him by the elbow and led him back to the stairs. Closing the basement door behind them, Driver pulled Corso along as he climbed the stairs to the main floor and found their way outside, where they stood wheezing and wiping their eyes, until the sound of a diesel engine snatched them from their lethargy.

Kehoe was easing a tandem tanker truck around the side of the cellblock. Driver raised a hand and began to motion him forward. Come on, come on, until finally he stiffened his fingers and had him bring the big rig to a stop. He used his index finger in a throat-cutting sign. Kehoe shut off the truck, which now sat in the darkness hissing, and climbed down. "I don't know what you got in mind, Captainman, but it damn well better be quick. Those old boys out there look like they're about ready to go."

As if to reply, Driver pulled one of the tanker's delivery hoses from its bracket on the side of the truck, used the metal end to break the window in the upper half of the administration building's back door and pushed the hose most of the way through. "Don't just stand there, Cutter," he said. "Hook this damn thing up. We need to pump the front unit about two-thirds of the way out."

Kehoe's eyes narrowed. "Right into the building there?"

"Big as life," Driver said.

Kehoe didn't move. His face was hard as stone. "You know, Doc . . . one of these days we're gonna have to address this you givin' me orders thing." His face cracked into a smile. "But in the meantime, I sure like the way you think."

13

In the hours since Paul Lovantano had been dragged from the cab of his truck and locked in a cell with half a dozen other truck drivers, he'd come to believe his life might have turned out differently had he been subjected to this kind of treatment during his formative years. With the specter of death looming and with a little time to think, he'd come to a number of revelations concerning such matters as who he was and how he'd come to be driving a diesel delivery truck in bumfuck Arizona on the day a prison riot was destined to take place. Not coincidentally, he'd also come to realize that he'd managed to get through forty-four years on the planet without ever taking the time to sit and wonder about the choices made and the roads not taken. Like he'd just been along for the ride on the delivery of his life.

Wasn't like he was some sixth-generation redneck like some of the folks around here. Eking out livings cutting wood and working as handymen. Wearing the same winter coats until the fabric fell off their backs. Married to one of these hatchet-faced desert queens, so bony and brown they looked like overcooked chicken wings.

No . . . he'd had every advantage. Every chance to make some-

thing of himself. Like everybody else born and raised in Larchmont, New York, Paul had faced a fairly codified set of expecta-
tions. It was quite simple really. All that was expected was that he
graduate at the top of his high school class, ship off to Princeton
or Columbia, become a doctor or a lawyer or something spiffy
like that, then make it big in the Big Apple before bringing his
burgeoning family back to Larchmont just in time to take over the
family manse and shuttle the old folks upstate to Shady Rest.

He could see now that the difference between the success scenario and the situation in which he currently found himself was
predicated on a small number of ill-considered moments that had
sent his future spiraling out of control and left him adrift in the
dire straits of the present predicament.

It all started with knocking up Mary Ellen Standish in the
eleventh grade and then, as his parents had insisted, denying re-
sponsibility. He could see it clearly now . . . how something about
that particular subterfuge had gnawed at his gut every day for the
past twenty-seven years and how the experience had created
within him a sense of unworthiness, a sense he was doomed to
failure, a sense that he didn't deserve any better than he was
getting.

That feeling made it easy to get kicked out of Brown Univer-
sity after his father had pulled every string he could muster just to
get him admitted. Made it easy to take that trip out West the summer before he was scheduled to pick up the pieces at the local
community college. Made it easy never to go back. Made it easy
to marry Edith and then Sherry and Wanda June. To have half a
dozen kids floating around the Southwest somewhere. Kids
whose faces he couldn't conjure without the aid of a photograph
and whose names he'd never quite had straight. It went on and on.
One bad decision after the next until he found himself in his present position, sitting in a prison waiting his turn to die. That's how
he had it figured. Only way it made sense. They were taking them

out one at a time and shooting them. That's why none of them came back. Why he wasn't going to come back either.

So when the cell door opened for the fifth time, it was no surprise that Paul Lovantano's heart began to race. His mouth wanted to beg, but something inside of him would not permit it. Maybe that Mary Ellen Standish thing. Who knew?

The cell door opened with a rattle. The huge con had acquired what looked like an Uzi since his last visit.

"Let's go," he said. "Your turn now, buddy."

The smell of diesel hung heavy in the air. The rush of fuel flowing into the building nearly drowned the sound of the pump. Driver was up on top of the front tanker, pointing his flashlight down through the hatch into the tank. Most of the small-arms fire had stopped as the calm before the storm set in.

"Shit's gonna be knee deep in there," Kehoe said with a laugh. "We best hope nobody lights a match before we get outta here."

Driver looked up from what he was doing. "Turn the pump off," he said to Kehoe.

With the hum of the pump suddenly ended, a final spurt of fuel was followed by a short series of drips, then a short period of silence before a volley of gunfire and a series of screams echoed from inside the cellblocks. Sounded like somebody was begging for his life. Two more shots suggested the pleas had been in vain.

Kehoe heaved with both hands, sending the delivery hose through the hole in the door. "What's it gonna be, Captainman? Whatever the hell you got in mind for getting us the hell outta here . . . now's the time."

Driver walked to the passenger side of the cab, reached up, opened the door and dragged a tight bundle out onto the ground. He scraped up the tape end with his fingernail. The tape came away with a hiss; the bundle unfurled to reveal several pairs of bright blue coveralls, red rubber boots and helmets, black breathing masks. Driver sorted himself out a pair of coveralls and sat down on the ground, where he inserted one foot, then the other, before rising to his feet again and pulling the zipper all the way up to his Adam's apple. He looked over at Kehoe and Corso. "I found these haz-mat suits in with the rest of the guard equipment. We're gonna get inside that front tank there and ride it right the hell out of here."

A moment of stunned silence ensued. "Inside the tanker?" Kehoe asked.

Driver nodded, then smiled.

"Sittin' in diesel fuel?"

"Just about waist deep now," Driver said.

"That shit'll kill us."

Driver pointed to the bundle on the ground. "Not in these haz-mat suits it won't. At least not right away."

"What's that supposed to mean?" Kehoe demanded.

"It means that sooner or later the diesel is going to eat its way through the plastic. Either that or the filters on our breathing apparatus are going get saturated and we're going to find ourselves breathing diesel fumes in a closed environment. Either way, we end up dead." He shrugged. "Look on the bright side: they probably won't find us until whatever's left of us clogs up the pump system."

"How long you figure we got in there?"

"Couple of hours . . . three max."

"Jesus," Kehoe muttered. "This is your big deal fuckin' plan?"

"We been letting drivers leave with their trucks all day," Driver said. "Everybody should be used to the drill by now." He patted the side of the tanker truck. "It's a local company. If the driver's got a family, I'm betting he gets to them as soon as he can. If not, he'll want to get to his favorite bar and tell the story. Either way, I'm figuring he gets rid of the truck as soon as possible.

Minute he leaves, we get out and get up the road. It'll be a couple of days at least, before they get things squared away enough to know for sure we're missing."

"And if they decide to search the truck?" Kehoe asked.

"Only way to do that will be to get in there with us. I'm betting they're no more anxious to climb inside than you are." Before anyone could respond, Driver produced a black wireless phone. "Beside which," he said. "I've got a little surprise for them. Something to keep them occupied while we get some sea room."

He looked from Kehoe to Corso and back. "It's now or never, fellas. You're either coming along or you're staying behind. What'll it be?"

"Seems like all I get to choose is how I want to die."

"Must be your day for life-and-death dilemmas, Frank."

"You're out of your fuckin' mind," Corso said.

The glint in Driver's eye told Corso his assessment just might be correct. Kehoe was already in the suit, using the attached gloves to get the hood up, then fiddling with the mask and breathing apparatus Driver shrugged and began to help Kehoe with his breathing mask. "You're a grown man, Corso. Make up your mind."

As an answer, Corso sat on the cold ground and stuffed his feet into the coveralls.

"For a guy who had no intention of getting me into this mess, it's amazing how you came up with one of these suits to fit me."

Driver ignored him. Instead, he pushed a button and spoke into the wireless phone.

He said, "Roscoe."

"Yeah," came the reply.

"Bring that last driver down to his truck."

14

Paul Lovantano had never seen a sight so beautiful as that great big Texaco star on the side of his DESERT DISTRIBUTING rig, sitting there between the buildings, like a big silver liner just waiting to fly.

"Keys are in it," the big con said before kicking out the hook and slamming the door behind himself.

Unable to believe his good fortune, Paul looked around. The yard was empty. The sky above was the color of rolled steel and devoid of stars. The area along the side of the cellblock was ankle deep in broken glass. He moved slowly, as if expecting to be struck down by some unseen hand at any moment. He'd covered half the distance to the rig when several faraway pops ricocheted along the night air and suddenly the sky was alive with flares, arching their way high into the blackness, bathing the ground below in a quivering red light.

As far as he was concerned, whatever was going on with the flares didn't bode well. Some instinct told him to get out immediately, while the getting was good. He broke into a run, covering the remaining twenty yards with the speed of a halfback, grabbing the door handle, launching himself up onto the step and into the familiar confines of the cab.

Took him a full minute to get it running, then he was on his way. Sliding off the clutch harder and faster than he ever had before, feeling the wheels chatter on the concrete in the seconds before the rig got rolling. Spinning the wheel hand over hand as he brushed the front bumper along the far wall, making sure the tandem tanker had room to clear the turn, holding his breath as she swung around to face the front gate, hitting second gear, winding it up on his way across the yard toward the way out.

Two-thirds of the way across the yard the gate began to slide open. The smile on Paul Lovantano's face didn't begin to fade until he saw the armored vehicle motor across the entrance. Half a dozen soldiers rode in back like fleas on a dog, rifles raised, pointed at the windshield of the truck. Paul used one hand to downshift the truck and another to wave surrender out the window as he eased the big rig to a halt in the mouth of the gate. Just be his luck to get this far only to take one in the head from some nervous kid with an itchy trigger finger.

A sergeant hopped up onto the step and brought a black army-issue forty-five caliber automatic to bear on Paul's right ear. "Out" was all he said.

Paul left the rig running and popped the handle. As he began to slide across the seat, he heard the passenger side spring open and looked over his shoulder just in time to see another soldier step up into the other side of the cab.

He kept his hands high in the air as he hopped out onto the tarmac. The barrel of the automatic ground into the soft flesh of his ear, as somebody patted him down hard, came away with his wallet and flipped it open. Paul wanted to speak, to tell them who he was and how he wanted to get the hell out of here, but couldn't manage to spit it out.

The gun barrel left Paul's ear as the sergeant perused his ID and slammed the wallet against Paul's chest.

"Take it," he said.

Paul brought one hand down and grabbed the wallet, pressed it hard against his breastbone for a moment, then used the other to return it to his pants pocket.

He watched in silence as a soldier climbed on top of the rear tanker, popped the bolt on the hatch and peered inside. "Full," he reported to the sergeant, who nodded and motioned him forward. The soldier had just gotten to his feet and was making his way forward across the top of the cars when suddenly . . . out of nowhere . . . all hell broke loose.

Corso sat with his back against the front of the tank. He worked at keeping his breathing shallow, trying to pull as little air through the filter as possible. He was freezing. Chilled to the bone by the pool of diesel fuel that reached nearly to his armpits, he looked to his left, toward Kehoe, who was covered nearly to his neck and beginning to shiver.

Wasn't until he swiveled his head back around that he saw Driver was up and moving, bent at the waist and sliding along with great deliberation. He held a phone in one gloved hand as he slid his feet carefully across the bottom of the truck until he was directly beneath the partially open hatch.

In slow motion, Driver pushed the phone's antennae out into the open air. As Driver pushed the first button, the keyboard lit up green. Corso winced and pulled his hands into knots. Before his brain could begin to process the possibilities, however, the earth gave a sudden violent shake, then a second, and a roar before a shout from outside worked its way inside the tank.

Driver was on his way back toward Corso and Kehoe when the truck's engine raced and they began to move. The fuel sloshed back and forth in the tanker, at one point completely covering his clear plastic face panel. Corso closed his eyes and tried not to breathe.

• • •

Paul Lovantano watched the soldier get to his feet and begin to walk along the top of the rear tanker, then suddenly throw his hands out for balance, wobble once and fall headfirst toward the pavement below. Paul's exhausted mind had just begun to register the fall and the fact that the front hatch was ajar when he experienced what he would later describe as "one of those lightning things." One of those moments when the air seems to stand still as the nostrils twitch at the acrid odor of cordite, in the seconds before the sky is ripped apart by sudden thunder.

In this case, however, it wasn't thunder. Or lightning or any other natural phenomenon. It was the administration building trying to take off like a rocket ship. Paul watched openmouthed as a bright blue flame lifted the brick building completely from its foundations. Within two seconds, the building had divided in two. One half was sinking in upon itself, falling back toward a roaring pit of fire, no longer blue, but orange and smoky as it poked its dirty fingers higher and higher into the sky. The other half of the building was airborne, blown upward and outward by the force of the blast, tracing fiery fingers across the night sky in all directions.

The sergeant pushed Paul toward the open door of his rig. "Go. Go," he shouted. "Get that damn thing out of here."

15

They put her on the roof. Up there with a microphone and a Japanese camera operator who had mastered the art of shooting her upper torso while, at the same time, looking up her skirt. The original plan had been to tape a lead-in for the takeover segment. The idea was to get her high enough off the ground so they could shoot out over the top of everybody else, leaving only Melanie and Meza Azul in the frame, creating the illusion that they were the only people on the job.

As was often the case, what had seemed like a nice low-key, low-tech idea had turned out to be a nightmare. First of all, Melanie's lead-ins and promos nearly always began with her striding confidently onto the set looking for all the world as if she'd just slammed the cell door on yet another lawbreaker. On the motor home's roof, however, she was forced to stand absolutely still. Not only was there a danger of inadvertently stepping off the roof and falling the eight or so feet to the ground, but the sheet metal beneath her feet rumbled ominously with even the hint of movement.

"Let's try it again," Marty Wells shouted from below.

Melanie adjusted the microphone on her lapel, heaved a sigh

and nodded at Yushi the cameraman, signaling she was ready to start. Before she could begin her recitation, however, a series of loud pops suddenly filled the air. Melanie turned away from the camera in time to see several arcs of light speeding up into the sky. Wasn't until they reached the apex of their flight and burst into flame that she realized they were flares.

As the balls of orange light began their slow descent back to earth, Melanie Harris turned back toward the camera and rolled her wrist quickly over itself. The red light on the front of the camera appeared as Yushi began to shoot.

"*This is Melanie Harris for* American Manhunt." She swept an arm across the sky. "*We are coming to you tonight from Musket, Arizona. From outside the front gates of the Meza Azul Correctional Facility, where for the past eighteen hours, a prison riot has put the facility in the hands of the inmates and put at risk the lives of more than a hundred and sixty prison personnel who are presently being held hostage by some of the most dangerous criminals in the United States.*"

Melanie sneaked a quick peek down at Marty Wells, who was smiling for all he was worth and bobbing his head up and down like a bobblehead doll. "*As we speak, the tense standoff seems to be reaching a new stage as National Guard units prepare to storm the prison.*"

At that moment, another, deeper growl reached her ears. She turned in time to see a Texaco tanker truck come rolling out from behind the building, elbowing around the sharp corner like some kind of segmented beetle. "*What we would seem to have here, ladies and gentlemen, is the release of yet another tradesman.*" As the prison's gate began to slide out of the way, she looked into the camera with an intense gaze. "*All day long, for reasons known only to themselves, the inmates have been releasing those delivery drivers who were unlucky enough to have been trapped inside when the riot began.*"

She half turned back to the prison yard, where the soldiers had parked an armored vehicle across the mouth of the gate; the Texaco truck was pulling to a halt as the flares found their way back to earth and extinguished themselves.

"As has been the case all day, authorities are conducting a thorough search of the vehicle, both underneath and up above." Although Yushi's upward angle prevented him from taping anything on the ground, Melanie was confident that the ground unit was getting the shots of the driver being dragged from the cab of his truck. *"Here comes the driver,"* she intoned. *"They're checking him out."* A moment of silence followed. She watched as the driver lowered his hands. *"The authorities seem to be satisfied about the driver and are now checking out the truck itself."* Again she assumed the other unit was getting the shots. *"As you can see . . . ,"* she began.

Later reviews of both the video- and audiotapes would reveal the basement windows of the Louis Carver Administration Building imploding as the impending gas explosion sought sufficient oxygen for the conflagration to follow. A second later, a great *whoosh* roared through the surrounding air as an inferno of bright blue flame took the building in its grip and tore it free of its foundations, lifting the entire structure a full foot in the air before opening its hand and allowing those parts of the building not reduced to flying rubble to settle back into the cauldron of flame.

The blast wave took but a second and a half to cross the yard. Next thing Melanie Harris knew, she had been knocked from her feet, thrown facedown on the roof of the motor home by the sheer power of the explosion.

A heaviness in her feet and ankles told her that the lower third of her body was hanging over the edge of the roof. She scuttled forward like a crab, using her knees and elbows to propel her to safety. The hail of dirt and bricks and glass had just begun when Melanie rose unsteadily to her feet. Across the roof, Yushi sat

openmouthed, breathing hard, staring dumbly down at his upturned palms. Half a brick bounced off the roof with a *boom.*
Yushi looked up. A single rivulet of blood had escaped his right
nostril, crossed his lips and now dripped from his chin.

"Roll it," Melanie shouted his way.

He dusted his palms on his sides and put his eye to the
viewfinder.

*"You've seen it for yourselves, ladies and gentlemen. A mas-
sive explosion has rocked . . . no, rocked can't be the word . . .
has . . . an explosion has totally destroyed . . ."* Another substantial
piece of debris shook the motor home, obliterating whatever
Melanie said next. By the time the camera stopped bouncing up
and down, she had regained her poise and had once again become . . . *"Melanie Harris broadcasting live from Musket, Arizona, for* American Manhunt.*"*

At ground level, the technicians had the camera rolling again.
"The National Guard is going in," she chanted. *"The first two armored vehicles are moving quickly across the prison yard. And
then another pair and another."*

A wall of soot and flame rose from the carcass of the administration building, nearly obscuring the cellblocks. Sirens approached in the distance. A loudspeaker blared orders but
Melanie could not make them out. She watched in stunned silence
as the lead pair of Strykers came to a stop about forty yards in
front of the cellblocks. Melanie let the pictures speak for themselves, a trick she'd picked up from sports announcers.

The lead Strykers began to rake the building with heavy
machine-gun fire. Above the roar of the flames and the clatter of
the machinery, shouts could be heard from within the cellblocks
in the moment before the Strykers' back hatches began to rise in
unison and the soldiers hidden within began to step out onto the
ground and sprint toward the building. Melanie had the odd
thought that the troop carriers were a lot like the story of the Tro-

jan horse in the way they discharged their hidden cargoes. Next thing she knew, she was talking.

"The assault has begun in earnest, ladies and gentlemen. The armored vehicles are now deploying their troops. As we speak, the first soldiers have breached one of the lower doors and have entered the prison." She hesitated. The prison yard was full of double-timing soldiers, trotting along, using the armored vehicles for cover as they hurried their way across the debris-strewn pavement. Melanie felt the blood rising in her cheeks, almost as if she were down there with a rifle. She rolled her wrist at Yushi again.

"This is real-time action from American Manhunt. *Melanie Harris coming to you today from Musket, Arizona, where . . ."*

16

"Damage?" Dallin Asuega sputtered. "What damage? We're not talking about damage here, for christsakes. We're talking about the whole damn building being . . ." He searched for a word, then forced himself to say it. ". . . gone. Twenty-three million dollars and it's gone. Vaporized, then burnt to a cinder." He threw a hand in the direction of the prison. "Probably another twenty million or so damage to the cellblocks." He paused, as if overcome by his own words. "And that's just structurally. God only knows what kind of damage has been incurred to the interior."

Asuega threw a quick glance at the TV monitor. CNN must have hired a helicopter. The sound of the rotors could be heard above the voice-over. "Clop clop clop . . . *high above Meza Azul Correctional Facility, where units of the Arizona and Nevada National Guards . . .*"

"Turn that damn thing off," Asuega demanded.

Iris Cruz lifted an eyebrow, as if to ask Warden Elias Romero if she should comply with the directive. Like most men, Elias liked to think of himself as inscrutable, but she could read him like a lunch menu. He was in a full sweat. Almost as bad as when she pressed him hard about dumping his wife. He was trying to figure how all of this was gonna come down on him. Typical. He met her eyes briefly, then an almost imperceptible movement of his head told her to turn off the volume but leave the picture in place.

From a thousand feet above the prison yard, the picture showed a trio of fire trucks pouring high-pressure cannons of water at the smoldering pile of debris that had once been the Louis Carver Administration Building. The camera panned out, revealing row after row of prisoners lying belly down in the yard, arms handcuffed behind them with those white plastic cinch strips. Stark naked . . . every one of them, all of them with their faces turned to the side and their butts pointing up at the sky. Didn't matter that she'd turned down the volume. The closed-caption function took over and the words appeared on the screen anyway. It was all Iris Cruz could do not to laugh.

Apparently, Mr. Asuega felt differently. His face was turning the color of an eggplant as he watched the flickering images dance across the screen. It was as if they were hypnotized. Standing around with their mouths open reading the little white words as they popped up on the screen. Iris didn't bother to try reading. The words always came too fast for her anyway. She brought the back of her hand to her mouth to hide her mirth.

And then the blue shirts appeared, coming out in twos from the doors, with their hands waving high in the air like children at play. Rows of soldiers, guns at the ready, trotted alongside the blue shirts, prodding them forward, forming a nearly solid line between the blue shirts and the naked prisoners.

"They rescued the hostages," said Elias Romero.

"Thank God," somebody whispered.

"How many?" another voice asked.

"Why have they got their hands up?" Asuega asked. "It makes them look like they've done something wrong." He pointed at the screen, where the camera had panned back far enough to show the blue-clad men and women being lined up against the fence. Hands on the chain link. Feet spread out behind like the cops are always making people do. Asuega was incensed "Look. What are they doing? Why are they lining them up like that?"

Nobody answered. They stood there in the sun-washed room watching the little box with the picture of the guards coming out of the cellblocks two by two like calves out of a chute, then lined up against the fence. The line seemed to go on forever, until finally the color changed to white.

"Kitchen crew," somebody said.

And then gray. "Maintenance and Sanitation," Romero offered. His big round face split with a smile. "Looks like they got most of them," he said hopefully. When he closed his eyes and allowed a silent prayer to find his lips, for a moment Iris liked him again. She got over it as soon as he started to talk "We better start making phone calls," he said. "We don't want anybody finding out about their loved ones from the television."

A hum of agreement rolled around the room.

"Iris . . . ," he started. She was about to cross the room and whisper in his ear. Tell him that they couldn't be calling anybody at home because they were all out there on the access road, behind the barricades and the soldiers, waiting to find out what had happened to their loved ones; but she never got that far because the door banged open.

Colonel Williams had a black smudge on one cheek and a bloody knuckle on his left hand. He threw his leather gloves into his helmet and stuffed the helmet under his arm. His thick sandy hair was soaked with sweat. He gave the room a curt nod, sending several drops of sweat cascading from the tip of his nose. He ran a sleeve across his face, caught himself and stopped. "I need personnel files," he announced. "Anything official with a photograph."

Asuega stepped forward. He pointed at the TV. "What's this?"

"That's *my* men doing *your* job," Williams said. "Case you haven't noticed, we got your hostages back for you."

"How many?"

"That's what we're trying to find out." He turned his gaze to Elias Romero. "The files?"

Romero shrugged resignedly. "They were kept in the admin building." He pointed at the TV set and shrugged again.

Williams gave a short bark of a laugh, as if to say "wouldn't you know it." Before he could decide what to do next, Asuega stepped right up in his face.

"Why are our personnel being treated like common criminals?"

"Because some of them probably are," the colonel answered. "I've just rescued twenty more people than supposedly were missing, and I'm betting some of them are convicts. Ergo, nobody's going anywhere until I'm damned well sure everybody's who they say they are."

"I can get shift commanders down here," Elias Romero volunteered. "I can get Human Resources to help out." He nodded Iris's way. "My assistant, Ms. Cruz, and I know most of the staff. We could—"

"Get it rolling," the colonel said. "We can do the IDs from the other side of the fence. Soon as we're sure who we've got we can process them out and get them home to their families."

He turned his attention toward Dallin Asuega. The television image had reverted to the streams of water being directed toward the fiery remains of the admin building. The image seemed to jog the colonel's memory.

"Mr. . . . ." He paused again. This time with a glint in his eye.

"Asuega."

"Mr. Asuega. I relayed your contention to the fire chief."

"What contention was that?"

"The contention that my men must somehow have been responsible for the destruction of your building."

"And?"

"And he wishes me to inform you that the building was destroyed as a result of a natural gas explosion combined with significant amounts of an undetermined accelerant, quite possibly diesel fuel."

Asuega unhinged his jaw to speak, but the colonel beat him to it. "I believe his exact words were 'thousands of gallons.'" He paused for effect. "He said you should call his office if you have any questions."

Whatever Asuega had to say, he kept to himself.

17

Numb to the bone, barely able to flex his fingers, Corso leaned back against the front of the tanker with his eyes closed so that he wouldn't see the waves of diesel fuel sloshing back and forth inside the tanker.

Seemed like they'd been inside for hours when the truck drew to a halt for the fourth time. Then started again, drove a short distance and stopped again. Ten seconds later the diesel shut down and everything went silent.

Driver switched on his flashlight. Held up a "take it easy" hand. They waited. Seemed like days before Driver crawled over to the hatch, reached up with a gloved hand and pushed it all the way open, careful not to let it bang. The purple rays of the overhead lights glimmered on the wavering pool of fuel as Driver maneuvered one shoulder and then the other out into the night air. The sound of dripping diesel fuel ricocheted through the tank as he thrust himself up and out of sight.

Unable to force himself to his feet, Corso crawled forward on his knees. By the time he reached the hatch, Kehoe had come around and was trying to push him out of the way. Corso mustered the last of his strength, shook off Kehoe's clutching hands and got to his feet. He got one shoulder out on his own. Driver pulled him the rest of the way out.

They were parked inside a fenced truck yard. A dozen mercury vapor lights showered the area with artificial luminescence. Forty yards away, a red neon sign in the window of a dilapidated white shack blinked OFFICE over and over into the night. On the roof, clumsy six-foot letters spelled DESERT DISTRIBUTING. The erratic light of a television set bounced around the interior of the building.

The diesel fuel had left Corso slick and slippery. He had to lie flat on his belly and hang on with both hands to avoid sliding over the side. He watched as Kehoe was birthed from the belly of the beast, one awkward movement at a time.

Again, they waited. Again it seemed like hours before Driver was satisfied they hadn't been seen, before he got to his hands and knees and began to crawl along the top of the tanker, moving slowly toward the rear, bridging the gap between the tanks, until finally he was all the way at the rear of the rig, where a stainless-steel ladder was welded to the back of the tank. No more than a foot separated their plastic face shields as Corso lay on his belly and watched Driver reverse himself and climb down onto the ground.

Then Corso and finally Kehoe descended, until the trio stood together at the rear of the truck. Took the better part of five minutes for them to free one another from the suits. Despite their best efforts, a trickle of diesel fuel here and a few drops there found their way up sleeves and down necks.

Driver retrieved the pile of gear from the ground, clutching it against his chest with one hand. He nodded toward the flickering light coming from the office. "See who's in there," he said to Kehoe. "Find out what he's driving. It'll be best if we have the keys."

Kehoe put his hand in his pocket and disappeared into the

darkness along the far side of the truck. "Lace your fingers together," Driver said. "Give me a boost."

Corso did as he was told. "That lunatic is gonna murder whoever's in there," Corso whispered through clenched teeth.

Driver raised one foot into Corso's proffered hands. "Makes him feel better about himself," Driver said with a grunt. "Makes him feel superior." Driver wiggled. "Higher," he said.

Corso put all his frustration into it, lifting Driver high enough so he could put one foot on Corso's shoulder. Took Driver half a minute to stuff the gear down the hatch, into the tank and jump to the ground. As if on cue, a shriek poured out of the office . . . then a second, followed quickly by a low, gargling moan, plaintive and resigned, the kind of noise a person makes only once.

Corso felt his throat constrict. "I don't want any part of this," he said. He cut the night air with the side of his hand. "I'm done. I'm bailing out."

Driver threw an arm around Corso's shoulder. The gesture seemed almost fraternal until Corso noticed the black automatic in Driver's hand. He rubbed the front sight gently across Corso's cheek. "I think you better stick around for a while, Frank," Driver said with a sigh. "We've got a couple of days head start. I've got things I need to do, so I'd really hate to see anything get in the way of that." Corso opened his mouth to speak, but Driver cut him off. "I know. I know," he said. "You'll lie low until they figure out we're gone." The barrel caressed Corso's cheek again, rubbing back and forth. "I trust you, Frank. I really do. You tell me you're not going to compromise our position . . . I believe you." Again he tilted his head toward the office. ". . . but my friend Kehoe there . . . he's a most untrusting fellow, and I just can't see him wanting a loose end like you floating around, if you know what I mean."

Corso pulled himself out from beneath Driver's arm. "Guy's a stone killer, man. He snuffs out lives the way other people change their socks."

Driver nodded his agreement. "Prison breaks doth make strange bedfellows indeed," he said. He reached for Corso again, but Corso stepped away.

"The guy I used to know didn't stand around and let some maniac do his killing for him," Corso said. "The guy I wrote a book about had a sense of honor, a sense of pride. He was a good man caught in a bad situation. He—"

And then the barrel of the automatic was jammed hard against his lower jaw, forcing the words to die in his mouth. Driver had his nose about an inch from Corso's. "That guy saw the reflections," Driver whispered. "Saw the light from the reflections." Something in his own words seemed to calm him. "You live in front of a camera twenty-four hours a day, seven days a week. Never seeing anybody else. Never talking to anybody else. Having people watch you brush your teeth, watch you take a shit . . ." Driver's breathing had gone shallow. His eyes held a gleam Corso had never seen before. "You either see the convergence or you die there on the tile."

"The convergence?"

"I don't expect you to understand."

"Does Cutter see the convergence?"

"Only thing Kehoe and I have in common is the fact that neither of us is going back inside alive."

The sound of approaching feet stopped him. A moment passed before Kehoe stepped around the corner. "Got us a beater pickup, camper and all," he announced. "I cleaned up after myself. Put the geezer who owns it in the back. That way we won't have anybody looking for the truck right away."

Kehoe turned his feral eyes Corso's way. "What about this faggot?" he asked. "Way I see it, we got no need for this motherfucker anymore."

"I need him," Driver said quickly. "I got something I need to do, and I need him to tell the story."

Kehoe thought it over. "What's this thing you got about tellin' your story, Captainman?" he asked. "You thinkin' you some kind of hero people wanna read about?"

"Everybody wants to tell their story," Driver said.

"Not me," said Kehoe. "Other folks wanna talk about me when I'm gone . . ." He waved a hand. "Fuck it. Let 'em talk all they want."

"Let's get out of here," Driver said.

Corso started to move. Kehoe stopped him dead with a hand on his chest. Corso looked down. The hand was so big it looked like it must have belonged to a much larger man "For now you comin' along," Kehoe said. "You twitch . . . you fart . . . you do anything to make me nervous"—he hesitated for effect—"and your ass is dead. You understand me? Story or no story. Captainman or no Captainman. You do anything but what we tell you and you're dead."

The overhead lights hissed. Corso nodded his understanding.

Kehoe turned and left. Corso followed along, with Driver bringing up the rear.

Beater was the right word for the pickup. An old Chevy from the early seventies. All the hubcaps gone. Once blue paint had oxidized to a dull satiny patina. Big old cab-over-camper. A caveman camper, its friendly Neanderthal logo looking down in horror at the trio standing at its back door.

Driver clapped Corso on the shoulder. "Got a driver's license, Frank?"

Corso said he did.

"Nice and easy then."

18

Morning flickered like a flame. A spark alone in the darkness, then, as if it had lost courage, suddenly gone, before showing itself again, as two and three and four, until the sparks became a full-fledged fire and the outline of the San Cristobel Mountains stood sentinel in the east, grinning wild and crazy like some jagged jack-o'-lantern in the sky.

Corso squinted, reached up grabbed the mirror and pointed it straight down. Nobody'd spoken for an hour. The interior of the truck smelled of men and motor oil.

The glint of sunshine pulled him from his waking dream. Somewhere in his mind's eye, he'd been riding in his father's battered Chevy pickup, rolling along Route 74 on a hot summer's day with the windows down and the thick air blowing around the cab like an overheated hurricane. He'd been watching his farther's hands on the steering wheel. The hands . . . broken and twisted by the North Koreans until they looked like ancient roots, like his real hands had somehow been left behind in that POW camp, buried in the same cold grave as whatever humanity and kindness he might once have posessed. A single tear rolled down Corso's cheek, He wiped it away with his sleeve and glanced to his right, where Driver and Kehoe slept.

The sights and sounds of freedom had mesmerized Driver and Kehoe, reducing them to a state of slack-jawed awe as they'd rolled west across the desert in the gathering light. The sun at their backs and the movement of Corso's hand seemed to stir them from their stupor.

"Where the hell are we anyway?" Kehoe asked.

"About fifty miles east of Phoenix," Corso answered.

Driver stretched. "What's the gas situation?"

"Just over a quarter of a tank."

"I'm hungry as hell," Kehoe said.

Driver reached over the seat back, tapping Corso on the ear with the barrel of the automatic. "How much money have you got?"

Corso thought it over. "Not more than a couple of bucks," he said. "I've got a bunch of plastic, though."

Kehoe rolled his neck. "Good. Let's stop and get us some—"

"No plastic," Driver interrupted. "We start using plastic, they'll run us down in a heartbeat. We need to do business in cash."

"Which we ain't got," Kehoe added.

"Then I guess we better get some," Driver said.

"Whatta you got in mind?" Kehoe asked.

Driver considered the matter for a minute. "As I see it, the two things we need most are guns and money. For where we're going, those two can't be beat."

"*Send lawyers guns and money.*" Kehoe sang the tune. "*The shit has hit the fan.*"

"And where are we going?" Corso inquired.

"You mean geographically or philosophically?" Driver asked.

"I'll settle for either."

"East and straight to hell." He looked at Kehoe. "What about you? You going some place in particular?"

Took Kehoe a minute. "Ain't thought about it. Only thing I

made my mind up about was I didn't want to die inside. Just as
soon die like a bitch in the road as end up in one of them new
wood boxes they put 'em in." His eyes glazed over for a moment.
He seemed to be staring at something far over the horizon. "Ain't
nobody waitin for me or nothin'. Hell, I been down a long time.
'Cept for nine months I was out in eighty-four, I been inside for
the better part of twenty-five years. Anybody give a shit about me
probably dead by now." He looked from Corso to Driver. "I ain't
headed anywhere in particular. I just wanna make a hell of a lotta
noise on the way out."

"A noble calling," Driver said. And then they went silent
again.

A series of crumbled buttes showed themselves in the bright-
ening sky. The two-lane road lapped out in front of the truck for as
far as the eye could see. The terrain would never make *Sunset* magazine. No Monument Valley vistas. No regal saguaro cactus pointing the way to heaven. No tiny desert flowers waiting for morning
to show their delicate petals. No. This was no-man's-land. The land
God never got around to finishing, or maybe the land he'd used up
before moving on to greener pastures. Broken land, falling in upon
itself in a series of gulches and gullies, separated by discarded ap-
pliances, burnt-out cars and pathetic patches of trash-littered
mesquite.

A tandem semi came hurtling at them through the semidark-
ness, lights dimmed, engine roared, fracturing the air like an east-
bound freight, its blast sending the old truck rocking on its
springs, rendering its occupants short of breath and speechless.

"Fucker," Kehoe spit.

Quarter mile ahead, a road sign announced FLINT . . . 1 MILE.

"Stop. We can throw whatever cash you've got in the gas
tank," Driver said. "Maybe use the facilities."

"I surely need to drain the vein," Kehoe announced.

The sign read MAD MIKE'S CAFE, HOME OF THE THUNDERBIRD

BURGER, a one-story shack added on to so many times it looked like a lumber truck had been involved in a pileup, and this was the result. An eye-level window ran the length of the building. Stools along the counter. Booths along the front wall. Half a dozen gas pumps outside. Chevron. One regular, one high-test, four diesel. Three cars and a pickup were nosed into the weeds hard against the building. Another five or six big rigs were spread out across the expanse of gravel to the north of the café. Looked like most of them were cooped up for the night.

Corso nosed the pickup close to the regular pump. Two dollars and ten cents a gallon. Corso got out and frisked himself. Came up with six dollars and fifteen cents in cash. Driver and Kehoe stepped out onto the gravel, where they stretched and groaned and looked around, while Corso tried to get the pump to work.

"Be back," Kehoe announced.

Kehoe was most of the way to the front door when Corso finally caught sight of the faded little card taped to the pump.

"We've got to pay first," Corso said.

Driver walked to the far side of the truck, where he checked the safety and transferred the automatic from his pants pocket to the front of his belt, which he tightened a couple of notches before patting his shirt down over the front of himself.

"Nobody trusts nobody anymore," Driver lamented.

Melanie Harris used the back of her hand to hide a yawn. Right at the end, her ears popped, causing her to wonder how long they'd been stopped up and whether she'd missed anything important as a result.

Marty Wells ran one hand through his thinning hair while patting Melanie's shoulder with the other. "Looks like the party's over," he said.

As usual, Marty was the master of the obvious. The prison yard was nearly devoid of life. Only the firefighters remained, standing vigil over the steaming pile of smoke and refuse that had once masqueraded as the Louis Carver Administration Building.

The ranks of once-naked cons had been stuffed into bright orange coveralls and returned to their cells, a few kicking and screaming, but mostly under their own power, escorted back inside by pairs of burly Arizona State Patrol officers.

The hostages had first been separated from the eighteen or so cons who were found to be secreted among their number. After that, a consensus of prison officials, fellow workers and loved ones had been required for release. Wasn't long before the sounds of tearful reunions rose in the predawn atmosphere.

The media rumor mill was reporting prisoner casualties at somewhere in the low one hundreds and National Guard casualties as zero, but nothing official had been released and probably wouldn't be until midafternoon.

"I'm headed for the motel," Marty said, "Nothing going on here."

"Been a long time since I stayed up all night," Melanie offered.

"We got some great footage."

"Nothing everybody else hasn't got."

"Are you forgetting the other?"

A shiver ran through her.

"I didn't tell you, did I?"

"What's that?"

"Networks' not gonna wait till Wednesday evening. They're gonna run it as a special edition tonight."

She looked wan and haggard. He made a mental note to have a word with makeup and wardrobe, then did what he always did at times such as this: tried to cheer her up. She saw it coming and looked away.

"Got some new material on the way," he said.

"Oh yeah?"

"Same source as the other."

"Something a little less morbid, I hope."

"Everything they've got on this Driver guy."

She stifled another yawn. "I don't catch a few winks I'm gonna look like the Bride of Frankenstein tomorrow," she said.

He made it a point not to agree. "See you later," he said.

She stood in the fresh light and watched him walk away, wondering how he managed to keep his optimism. How he managed to keep from drowning in the drek.

When no lightbulbs came on, she grabbed the handle and stepped up into her trailer.

19

Six minutes before nine on a bright desert morning. Parked in a self-service car wash diagonally across the street from Crosshairs Guns and Ammo. FINEST INDOOR SHOOTING FACILITY IN THE GREATER PHOENIX AREA THE SIGN PROCLAIMED.

Driver was using the wand to spray water on the windshield while they waited for Kehoe to return from casing the place.

"Just so we're clear, Frank. You do anything to mess this up and I'll put one in your spine," Driver said.

"I don't want any part of this," Corso insisted.

"Don't fuck it up."

"Come on, man."

"Did you hear me?"

Corso was working his way up to another plea when Kehoe came skipping back across the street. "Two of them," Kehoe announced. "They came together. Parked out back by the loading dock. Both of them packing heat on their sides."

"One of them probably runs the range while the other works out front," Driver theorized.

"Place got alarms up the ass," Kehoe said. "Coupla big bells on the outside of the building. Probably a silent too."

"We're going to have to be quick and dirty," Driver said. "In and out in three or four minutes tops."

"With nobody left behind to be pushing buttons," Kehoe added.

The words turned Corso's stomach upside down, sending the scald of bile to his mouth, causing his head to spin for a moment. He braced himself on the fender of the truck and shook his head in an attempt to clear his vision.

"She looks like she's gonna be sick," Kehoe said.

"You let me worry about him," Driver said.

"Be a lot easier we just off his ass and put him in the back there with the other one."

Driver nodded at the building across the street, where the CLOSED sign in the front door had just been flipped to OPEN. "Here we go," he said, pulling the truck door open. "Park it out back. We'll walk around."

Corso hesitated. "Why don't you just let me—"

"Get in," Driver said. "I'm not going to tell you again."

Wasn't until Corso ran the windshield wipers that he noticed the jungle scene painted under the letters on the front of the building. Some guy in a Ramar of the Jungle outfit aiming a rifle at a charging elephant. Flame coming out the barrel. Elephant cringing from the impact. All very bwana.

Corso dropped the truck into drive and crept out of the stall. Morning in the Valley of the Sun was in full swing. A solid line of traffic whizzed by on both sides of the road. Semis and Sonatas, horses trailers and Hondas, all hurrying to and fro. Took several minutes of nervous waiting before Corso could send the pickup bouncing out over both lanes and into the gravel parking lot beyond. Loose stones popped beneath the tires as Corso wheeled the truck along the front of the building, then looped around back, sliding to a stop next to a green Cadillac STS parked at one end of the loading dock.

Corso tried to hang back but Driver wasn't going for it, urging him forward with a tilt of the head, then falling in behind the taller man as they made their way along the side of the store. The sun was bright to the eyes and warm to the cheek.

"He asks for ID you give it to him, Frank."

"I've got a felony conviction."

A bitter laugh escaped Kehoe's throat. "Well ain't you just the dangerous dude."

"Just give him the ID, Frank. He asks you anything, you give him an answer."

"What am I gonna . . . ," Corso began.

"Just make up shit, Frank. It's what you do for a living." Driver clapped him on the arm. "Can't fail, my man. It's all coming together. The notes are all in place."

A quick glance over at Kehoe said he didn't have a clue either, but by that time, they were on their way up the front stairs, leaving their unspoken questions to flee like bystanders.

A harsh buzzer sounded as they pulled open the door. Behind the counter, a big redheaded guy in a black T-shirt straightened up and took them in with a rolling gaze. His hair was thin on top, combed straight back, leaving his freckled scalp to shine in the overhead lights. The expression on his face suggested he had a toothache.

Something in their demeanor immediately set him on edge. Corso slowed his pace only to have Driver bump him from behind, forcing him closer. Kehoe fanned out to the right, over toward the cases with the handguns. The guy squared his shoulders.

"Help you fellas?" he inquired.

"Thought I'd . . . ," Corso stammered. "Thought I'd buy my brother a gun for his birthday."

The black T-shirt had a logo. Same bwana picture as on the outside of the building. Crosshairs on top of the picture. Guns and ammo underneath. He hooked his thumb in his belt, leaving his fingers a scant few inches from the handle of the holstered automatic on his right side. "What sort of gun did you have in mind?" he asked.

"Oh . . . I don't know . . . maybe . . ."

"This one right here," Kehoe said from across the room.

Kehoe kept tapping on the glass countertop with his finger as the guy moved slowly around the room, keeping the counter between the trio and himself, keeping his hand close at the ready. Somewhere along the way, he must have pushed a button or maybe stepped on some lever or something because the door to the shooting range opened and what at first glance seemed like his body double stepped into the room.

Took Corso a minute to realize the second guy was considerably older than the first. Maybe old enough to be his father. Same red hair and stocky build. Same pained expression on his face. The man stood holding the thick sound-insulated door ajar as the younger man moved past him, over to where Kehoe stood looking down into the case like a kid at a bakery window.

"You've got expensive taste in guns," the younger man said. "That's a Colt Python Elite. Three-fifty-seven. Stainless steel with a four-inch barrel. Lotta people would tell you it's the finest handgun in the world."

"Lemme see it," Kehoe said.

"Eleven hundred dollars right out of the box."

Kehoe waved an impatient hand. "Lemme see it," he said again.

"I'm gonna need some identification and a credit card."

A strained silence settled over the room. The two guys passed a quick "just as we thought" look. Another bump from Driver sent Corso fishing for his wallet. Moving as slowly as possible, he pulled out two pieces of plastic and dropped them on the glass countertop. The younger guy used his left hand to pick them up.

He fanned them with this thumb and forefinger and brought them up close to his face.

The sight of an American Express Gold Card and a valid Washington driver's license stopped the tension from escalating further. It was like everyone took a deep breath at once. The younger man finally pulled his thumb from his belt and used it to open the back of the cabinet. Five seconds later Kehoe had the revolver in his hand. He spent the next minute or so hefting the piece and aiming it here and there.

"I wanna shoot it," Kehoe said finally.

They passed another look. Older shrugged slightly and stuck out his hand, palm up. Junior shuffled over and dropped the license and card into the upturned palm. Kehoe was once gain swinging the gun to and fro as if he were playing cops and robbers.

Senior held up the AMEX card. "Mind if I run this through the system?" he asked with a thin smile.

Corso returned the shrug. "Go for it," he said.

The guy took two steps to his left and swiped the card through one of those countertop card readers. One electronic beep later and the tension in the room dropped another couple of notches. "There's a two-day waiting period in Arizona, Mr. Corso."

"No problem," Corso said.

Senior thought about it for a long moment and walked to junior's side. "You help Mr. Corso here with the paperwork. I'll take Mr. . . ." He looked over at Kehoe.

"Cutter," Kehoe said with a wide grin. "Mr. Cutter."

Elder passed behind younger and made his way to a spot directly across the counter from Kehoe. He held out his hand. For just a flutter, it looked like Kehoe wasn't going to hand over the gun. Like maybe he was going to bring it upside the guy's head or something and all hell was going to break loose right then and there.

But no. One strained beat and Kehoe slid the revolver into the guy's hand. He watched in silence as the guy opened a drawer in the back of the cabinet, came out with a box of cartridges and a brown rag, which he used to wipe the gun's shiny surface clean.

"Right this way," the guy said, inclining his head to indicate that Kehoe should make his way over to the gate in the center of the room. Her buzzed Kehoe through, then the two of them disappeared into the shooting range. The door hissed to a close.

Younger ambled over to the cash register, reached down and came out with a pair of forms. On the way back, he pulled a pen from his pants pocket, scooped the gold card and the driver's license from the counter and handed all of it to Corso. "Gonna need for you to fill these out," he said. "I don't know what the law is in Washington, but somewhere along the line here, your brother's probably gonna need to register the gun for himself. That's the way it is here anyway."

Corso stuffed the AMEX and the ID into his jacket pocket and began to fill out the forms. Name, address, number of years at above address, Social Security number. Two lines down was the question about whether you'd ever been convicted of a felony. He skipped that one and moved on.

"Just passing through?" younger inquired.

"Staying with some friends in Scottsdale," Driver said.

They started jawing on the weather next. Worked their way through that on to how America was going to hell in a handbasket because of liberal politicians.

Corso was a third of the way down the second form when the guy's hand leapt from the counter like a scalded rat. Must have been something like the way certain animals can sense an earthquake in the moment before it actually happens. Whatever was going on in the shooting range hit younger's senses like a runaway cattle car. Younger's head snapped toward the back of the store in the same instant his hand hit his gun butt. Driver must have already had his piece in his hand, ready to rumble, because in the second it took the gun to clear the guy's holster, Driver had gotten a round off.

The slug took younger just under the right ear, found some serious inner resistance and ricocheted out through the top of his head before continuing up to the fluorescent light above, where it exploded the tube and sent the shade to rocking violently back and forth.

Back at ground level, the younger guy's automatic went off before he got it all the way up to level, getting off one round on his way down, sending a nine-millimeter bullet through the back of Corso's left hand before disintegrating the glass counter below, sending a shower of blood and broken glass streaming to the floor with a bright clatter.

Corso reeled away with a hoarse bellow. Holding his wrist and screaming at the heavens, he staggered across the room. In his peripheral vision, he caught sight of Kehoe, grinning like a madman as he came back into the store, revolver in one hand, canvas bank bag in the other. "We hit it big, Captainman," he shouted

Corso dropped to one knee, rested his torn hand on the other, as Driver began to pull weapons from the racks behind the counter. "Whatta you want?" he asked Kehoe.

Kehoe shook the shiny revolver in the air. "Got everything I need right here."

"Get all the ammo you can find."

Corso's vision swam and he went black for a moment. He was awakened by a bout of vertigo before he could topple all the way over onto his side. When he opened his eyes, Driver was pushing something soft and black into his face.

"Wrap this around your hand."

When he didn't respond, Driver said it again.

If the smell of sweat hadn't been enough to tell him what it was, the hunter and elephant logo certainly sufficed.

20

Elias Romero slapped the desktop with the flat of his hand. The action sent a bead of sweat rolling down over his cheek and onto his thick neck, where it surfed the wrinkles before disappearing beneath his collar. His voice was a hoarse whisper. "If they didn't get it from you, then where in hell did it come from?"

Iris Cruz appeared to ponder the question. "How am I supposed to know?" she said evenly. "You had me give copies to the governor's office and to the corporate people. Maybe the TV people got it from one of them." She wagged a manicured finger in the air. "You got no cause to be treating me this way. I ain't done nothing wrong."

"Why would corporate or the state leak a thing like that? It's their worst damn nightmare. The last thing on earth they want on the boob tube."

"You tell me," she said. "I ain't no mind reader." She gestured toward the next room. "The governor's office got more leaks than an old bucket. You said it yourself, bunches of times." She cut in the air with the side of her hand. "Maybe you ought to go ask *them* about it."

Romero raised his hand for another assault on the desktop,

but it wasn't to be. Iris stepped right up into his chest. "And don't you be raisin' your hand to me neither," she said. "I ain't some dog you think you can scare off with all your noise. You got no damn right to be accusin' me of nothin'. You remember that. No damn right."

He opened his mouth to speak, but she cut him off. "I got a union," she said. "You saying I done something wrong, maybe we better take it up with them."

She tried to keep smug off her face but was unsuccessful. The Meza Azul Classified Employees Union, of which she was a dues-paying member, held great sway with management. Not like they were in bed together or anything. Quite the contrary. Management hated them like hell. They'd fought the intrusion of the bargaining unit every step of the way. And lost. Every step of the way.

What she knew from being on the inside was that the amount of time and energy required to fight the union on small matters was considered by the Randall Corporation to be unworthy of the time and effort. Unwritten company policy was that skirmishes with the union were to be avoided at all costs.

Elias Romero showed his mud shark smile. The one that looked like the grill of a fifty-seven Chevy Bel Air. "Come on now, baby," he entreated, "we ain't got no reason to be . . ." He reached out to put a hand on her shoulder, but she brushed it aside.

Her voice rose. "And don't be startin' that baby stuff with me neither," she said. "You keep accusing me of what I ain't done . . ."

"Come on now, baby."

She didn't hesitate. "I'll put your business in the street, Mr. Elias Romero. Swear to God I will. You think I been telling folks stuff . . . I'll tell 'em for real. Tell 'em about us. Tell 'em how Mr. Respectable been droppin his pants on my floor for the past year and a half. Tellin' me how he was gonna dump his skinny wife and—"

"Whoa, whoa now, baby. Take it easy. Don't go running off on no—"

"I ain't gonna end up pushin' tacos, Elias. Ain't gonna end up like my sister. You hear me: I worked too long and too hard. I ain't gonna—"

The door to the conference room snicked open. The governor's press attaché, Gil Travor, stuck his bald head into the room. The muted roar of a crowd slipped in through the crack in the door. Travor's senses immediately picked up the air of tension in the room. He wrinkled his brow and looked from Elias to Iris and back. "You ready?" he inquired.

Travor's bald head disappeared, leaving the door ajar. Elias Romero fingered his necktie a couple of times and started for the opening. He flicked his black eyes her way. Iris put on a haughty gaze, folded her arms across her prominent prow and turned her back on him. She was glad he was suffering. Made up some for all the lies he'd told her. For some. Just some. She was glad he'd been picked to do the press conference. Shit rolls downhill they'd told him. It's *your* prison. *You* get out there and explain the leak. Bastard deserved it. He closed the door behind himself as he left.

He mounted the dais and began adjusting the microphone upward. Goddamn thing was set up for a midget. Somebody's idea of humor. Iris maybe. The thought of her threat sent a shiver down his spine. His wife, Constance. She couldn't find out. Period. End of story. That cat got out of the bag . . . shit . . . no telling what might happen there.

He could feel beads of sweat forming around the roots of his hair. What with the riot and all, he had no doubt. Any further scandal would surely get his ass out the door. Hell . . . he might be on his way out already.

The scrape of a hundred shoes and the clatter of television equipment failed to drown out the booming thud that roared from the sound system when the microphone came loose from the stand, leaving Elias Romero standing before the crowd with the mike in his hand like a lounge singer. Took him a full two minutes to get the damn thing attached to the stand again. Even after all of that, he had to bend hard at the waist to get his mouth anywhere near the mike. He wanted to curse and kick the stand over, but restrained himself.

He was on his own. Asugea and the corporation people had gone into the cellblocks to have a look around. The governor and his people wanted no part of anything might make them look bad, so, other than Travor, they were nowhere to be found. He was about to be a one-man news conference.

He looked up and found himself gazing into a sea of unblinking electronic eyes and expectant faces. They were all there. CBS, NBC, ABC, CNN, MSNBC. The whole nine yards.

He turned away long enough to clear his throat and then began.

"Ladies and gentlemen," he said.

The cameras began to whir. *"I'm going to read a brief statement, after which I'll take a few questions. As I'm sure you all understand, we're still quite busy securing the facility and will need to keep this as brief as possible."* A buzz of cynicism ran through the crowd. Elias Romero ignored it and forged on. *"As of this morning, the facility is completely under control. All inmates are back in their cells and normal prison functions have been reinstated."* He pulled a handkerchief from his pants pocket and mopped the back of his neck. *"A preliminary count . . ."* He paused for effect. *"A preliminary count indicates that a total of fifty-seven people were killed during the incident."* The buzz got louder. *"Fifty inmates and seven staff members, one of whom apparently died of natural causes."* The buzz had become a roar. Romero held up a restraining hand. *"I want to emphasize that these figures are preliminary and that final tallies will not be available until later this afternoon."*

By the time he finished, the buzz in the room sounded like an airplane was about to land. First question was from the CNN reporter. "Can you confirm, Mr. Romero, that the film clip aired last night on the ABC program *American Manhunt* was genuine?"

He was determined not to outright lie and figured the best he could do was keep it short and sweet. "*Yes,*" was all he said before calling for another question.

"The inmate in the clip," the question began. "Is that inmate accounted for at this time?"

Romero took a deep breath. The words nearly stuck in his throat. "*No. At this time, he is not.*"

The buzz reached airliner levels. "How many other inmates are unaccounted for?"

"*We have several bodies which . . . ah . . . due to the level of damage, are going to require forensic identification.*"

"But you don't believe any of them is this . . ." The AP reporter checked his notes. ". . . this Timothy Driver."

"*No. I didn't say that. I said, we won't know until the forensic examinations have been completed.*"

"Is Driver the only inmate believed to be missing?"

"*I didn't say he was believed to be missing. As I said,*" Romero began to show his exasperation. "*As of this morning . . .*" He hesitated, waiting for the roar to subside and then held up a moderating hand. "*I want to emphasize . . .*" He raised his voice. "*I must again emphasize . . . until the forensics people are finished there is just no way we can give you an accurate accounting.*"

"Can you give us some idea how this Timothy Driver managed to escape his cell and literally take over the prison?"

"*No we cannot,*" Romero said.

"Our sources tell us Mr. Driver was under twenty-four-hour video surveillance. Surely you should be able to—"

Romero interrupted. "*It appears Mr. Driver may have managed to erase the tape loop used to record activity in his cell.*"

"How could a prisoner . . ."

Romero anticipated the question. He'd been waiting for it. *"Mr. Driver is not your run-of-the-mill convict, Mr. Blitzer. He has two master's degrees. One from the Naval Academy in advanced warfare techniques and another from Harvard in electrical engineering. He's a highly trained professional and thus capable of things . . . outside the realm of other convicts."*

Romero squelched a smile. He'd wanted to get the words *thus* and *realm* into his answers regarding Driver. Sounded real high tone and articulate. "Is it true he's been trained as a Navy SEAL?"

"Yes. San Diego. Nineteen ninety-four."

From the back of the room. "But he was never deployed as a SEAL."

"You'd have to ask the navy about that."

Elias Romero nodded at the crowd. *"If you'll excuse me . . . ,"* he began, as the roar of shouted questions engulfed the room. Before the assembled multitude had a chance to settle down, Romero ducked to his right, stepped down off the dais and disappeared back through the door from which he'd entered ten minutes earlier.

He leaned heavily against the inside of the door, closed his eyes and took several deep breaths. "Iris," he said. No answer.

He opened his eyes. The makeshift office area was empty. He cursed. Seemed like that damned woman was always missing these days. No doubt about it. Things settled down, things got back to normal . . . sure as hell, she was gonna have to go.

21

Driver smoothed on one last piece of adhesive tape, then dropped the scissors and the rest of the roll onto the bed. "That's gonna have to do," he said. "You just keep eating those ibuprofen. That's as good as it's going to get."

Corso sat with his bandaged hand in his lap. The slug had gone completely through the back of his hand and exited the center of his palm. He'd nearly passed out when Driver had poured hydrogen peroxide on both sides of the wound and cleansed the interior with a cotton probe. The throbbing pain in his hand had caused his arm to go numb. A handful of Aleve had dulled the pain somewhat but only enough to keep him from crying out. What he needed was a doctor, but that wasn't going to happen anytime soon. He got to his feet and made his way over to the other bed, where he first sat, then, leaving his feet on the floor, let himself down onto his back in stages.

They were holed up in the Palm Garden Hotel and Casino, a crumbling remnant of the days of Bugsy Siegel, about five miles north of present-day Las Vegas. A peek out the back window, out over the Dumpsters and the half dozen junkies who called the area home, revealed the new skyline of the Strip barely visible through the omnipresent desert haze.

Kehoe had lobbied hard for the brighter lights. The Bellagio or the Luxor or something like that. They'd come out of the gun shop with the better part of eleven thousand dollars and the cash was burning a hole in Kehoe's pocket. Driver had reasoned that the bigger, fancier hotels were going to have larger and more effective security forces and that their best bet was to find someplace on the skids, someplace where security was perhaps playing second fiddle to the power bill. After much wrangling, they'd settled on the Palm Garden, a four-story pink stucco structure wedged between an Arby's and the North Vegas Animal Hospital. Bludgeoned by a merciless sun and swirling winds, the paint was peeling so quickly it sounded like rain.

With Driver behind the wheel, they'd driven the three hundred miles from Phoenix without stopping, hitting the outskirts of Vegas just after three-thirty in the afternoon. The digital sign on the bank announced seventy-four degrees. Then a happy face. Then seventy-four degrees. Corso sat slumped in the middle seat, holding the T-shirt tight around his hand. While Driver went inside and got them a pair of adjoining rooms, Corso and Kehoe sat in the cab of the truck watching the valet parking attendants, listening to their chatter as they scurried to and fro across the parking lot.

Before settling in, Driver had visited the strip mall up the street. Half an hour later, he'd returned with a pair of black Nike gym bags, groceries, painkillers and first-aid supplies. After carefully cleaning Corso's wound, he'd bandaged the damaged area with professional expertise.

While Driver was gone, Kehoe, who'd taken over the room, had gotten busy on the phone. The hooker had arrived about five minutes after Driver returned. About the time Corso had stopped moaning and groaning over Driver's ministrations, the damp sounds of carnal commerce began to seep into the room from next door.

"Kehoe ever wears himself out . . . you can be next, if you want."

Corso shook his head. "Not my cup of tea."

"If you're afraid of catching something . . ."

"There's that for sure . . . but that's not it."

"Yeah . . . ," Driver said. "Me neither."

"I availed myself a couple of times when I was a kid," Corso said. "It just didn't feel right to me. Like I was stealing money from the poor box or something really shitty like that. Different strokes, I guess."

"I never have," Driver said. "All those navy towns and shore leaves and somehow I could never bring myself to . . . you know."

"Probably for the best."

"I always imagined what my mother would think."

Corso checked Driver from the corner of his eye, looking for signs of irony in a guy who'd just been party to innumerable deaths yet was concerned about what his mother might think about him getting his knob polished. If he was kidding, he wasn't letting on.

On the TV a graphic announcing an imminent police bulletin rolled across the bottom of the screen. Thinking it was about them, Corso picked up the remote and adjusted the volume. Not so, though. Cut to a press conference in Shep, Texas. Multiple murder suspects Harry Delano Gibbs and his eighteen-year-old girlfriend, Heidi Anne Spearbeck, had been apprehended in northern Nevada and now awaited the results of an extradition hearing, scheduled for the following morning. Seems Gibbs, having had his marriage proposal rebuffed at gunpoint by Heidi Anne's father, Sheldon, had returned several hours later to dispatch the old man with a single bullet in the head, before running off with his daughter.

It was a week before Sheldon's decomposed body was discovered by a fertilizer salesman who'd stopped by for a visit. By that time, Gibbs and Spearbeck had already cut a wide swath of crime and killings across the Southwest, leaving a grocer and his wife dead over what authorities figured to be no more than sixty-five dollars, killing Texas Ranger Wade Ott Rufin as he attempted to arrest them at a motel in Vici, Oklahoma, and holding more than seventy customers at bay as they robbed the Pig and Pancake Truck Stop way out in the panhandle by Guymon, Oklahoma. In addition to these confirmed atrocities, the pair were now suspected in another half dozen equally grievous felonies.

Sheriff Mace Walker of Harris County, Texas, wanted everyone to know it was safe to go outdoors again as the pair had been brought to bay, that justice had prevailed and that peace reigned once again in the land.

"Heartwarming," Corso said.

Driver pointed at the television. The graphic on the screen read Musket, Arizona. Meza Azul Correctional Institute. Driver grabbed the remote from the end table and turned it up louder. The new graphic said the guy in the brown suit was one Dallin Asuega, an executive of the Randall Corporation. While Driver fumbled with the volume control, the screen split in two, Asuega on the left, Kehoe's mug shot on the right. Then Corso and Driver. They laid it out. The whole nine yards. Life stories. Criminal records. Armed and dangerous. Do not attempt to apprehend. Back with more after . . .

22

Melanie Harris surveyed Main Street, Musket, Arizona, and shuddered. "Anybody ever finds me living here," she thought, "they should put a bullet in my head." Everything in that single-story fake adobe look. Built around a little town square, flagpole and all. Except that's probably not what they called it in Arizona. Probably had some tongue-rolling Spanish name. The oversized American flag popped and snapped in the stiff, swirling breeze.

Marty was up the street somewhere meeting their contact. Getting more info. Stuff they presumably could use on this week's show. She hoped it was good. Not as gory as last night's tape but something hot and exclusive. The number of calls she'd fielded from the network told her they were more popular than they'd been in a long while. In Hollywood, you could always judge your status by the number and quality of people who belatedly returned your calls.

In the far distance, out beyond the greenery of the park, out beyond the cookie cutter housing development, out where the desert sought every day to reclaim its sovereignty, a dust devil whirled madly about the sky, brown and menacing, full of loose

dirt and desert debris. It twirled and snaked over the ground, taking this, leaving that, as it made its way west across what she was
told was once a vast inland ocean.

She pulled her phone from her pocket, thumbed it on and
waited to see what service was going to be like. Three lines. Way
better than back at the prison, where she'd tried several times but
had been unable to establish a connection. She pushed nine, then
autodial. The phone rang six times before the voice said. "Hello."

"Helen, it's Melanie."

"Oh." The phone company was telling the truth. You *could*
hear a pin drop. Melanie grimaced at the phone. The reception
told her Brian's mother had wasted no time taking sides. Not that
she'd ever been on Melanie's side. No . . . they'd never gotten
along. Freud would have had a field day. Classic case of Mommy
competing with the wife for the son's affections. Add to that the
fact that people of Helen Martyn's social standing don't welcome
incursions from army brats like Melanie Harris and you had what
could be charitably described as fourteen years of mutual for-
bearance.

Melanie kept her voice cheery. "Brian there?" she inquired.

Helen hesitated. "Oh . . . I don't know . . . uh . . ."

And then Melanie heard his voice in the background.

"Your wife," she heard Helen say.

A minute passed before Brian came on the line. "Hey."

"Hey yourself."

"How's the weather in Arizona?"

"Windy. What about Michigan?"

"Dad says you're all over the tube."

"How is he?"

His timing told her something was amiss. "He's getting on.
His memory's not what it used to be. He forgets things these
days."

A moment passed, neither of them willing to use the "A"

word. Brian changed the subject. "He says the show's getting a lot of press."

"We're on a bit of a roll. What about you?"

"I've been so busy I haven't even got my bags unpacked yet."

"Busy with what?"

"You know; settling in. Catching up on old times. That kind of thing." Another voice could be heard in the background. A woman's voice. Not Helen.

"Who's that?" Melanie asked. She heard his intake of breath.

"Patricia," he said. "Patricia Lee . . . you remember Patricia don't you?" Melanie used her voice training to keep her tone neutral. "I remember," she said. How could she forget? Patricia had been Brian's high school sweetheart. The girl he'd been expected to marry. Her father was a state appellate court judge. All very incestuous you know. At least until Melanie appeared and gummed up the plan.

"What's she doing there?" Melanie asked with a bit more of an edge in her voice than she would have preferred.

"She's helping me find an apartment."

"Oh really?"

"She's in real estate."

"Still married to Larry?"

"Harry, and no. They got a divorce four years ago."

"Somehow I could have guessed."

A strained silence settled over the connection. "So anyway," Brian said after a long moment. "You kinda caught me on the way out."

"I can be home in a few days." The words were out of her lips before her brain had a chance to censor them. "We could maybe—"

"I'm not coming back to California, Mel. Not now. Not ever. Not gonna happen. Place never felt like home to me anyway. I always felt like I was on a bad vacation."

"Brian please . . . we could—"

"Please," he said. "Listen, Mel, I understand. You're a big TV star and all. No way you can give it all up for a life as a lawyer's wife in Grand Rapids, Michigan. I don't blame you." When she didn't respond, he went on. "We're just too different from each other. We want different things."

"We didn't used to."

"That was a long time ago. Before Samantha. Before everything."

"Yeah," she said softly.

"I ran into Stan Rummer yesterday," he said, naming another old high school chum. Another lawyer. She remembered then, and her heart froze in her chest. "Mr. D . . . I . . . V . . . O . . . R . . . C . . . E, Detroit." she spelled it out like his obnoxious TV commercial used to. "Stan still trading in human misery is he?"

"We need to talk, Mel."

She felt him squirm. "So talk."

"Not now."

Patricia's voice rose in the background.

"Tell her to shut the fuck up."

He paused and gathered himself like he always did when she swore. "Listen . . . I gotta go."

"With her?"

"I told you. I'm looking for an apartment."

"Brian," she said. "Maybe . . ."

A dial tone told her the conversation was over.

Melanie Harris pulled the phone from her ear, used her thumb to turn it off, then dropped it into her jacket pocket.

The dust devil had disappeared from view. She wondered whether it had gained speed and whisked off to parts unknown or whether it had simply run out of steam, uncoiling to an ignominious stop, dropping its collected contents back to the desert floor to await the next thrilling ride in the sky, maybe a million years hence.

The wind rose, flapping her collar, plastering the coat to her chest. She reached up, as if to hold a hat in place, and squinted her eyes so hard she was blind. On the inside of her eyelids she could see the interior of Brian's parents' house, straight out of Ethan Allen. All very traditional. Full of oriental carpets and warm wood. In her mind's eye it was always decorated for the holidays, with Christmas music playing, with bows and red ribbons everywhere and the biggest Christmas tree they could fit through the double doors holding court in the living room.

When she opened her eyes, Marty Wells was a hundred yards away, walking briskly in her direction. The wind had again lifted his careful comb-over from his head. She could tell from his stride. He thought he had something special.

"Good?" she asked.

"Better," he said, grabbing the handle and pulling open the motor home's door. He used a thick red folder to shepherd her inside. The air inside was still and old. Marty used his free hand to pat the shingle of hair back into place. "Get this," he said with a wink. "This all started with what they said was a medical checkup for this Driver guy. Right? That's how he got out of his cell and how this whole thing started."

"So?"

"So . . . it wasn't medical at all. It was a psych appointment."

"Really."

"He'd been exhibiting disassociative behavior."

"Like?"

"Losing it. Not knowing who he was or where he was. Going into loud diatribes with himself." He tapped the folder with his forefinger. "He was losing his mind. That's why they were taking him to see the shrink. They were afraid he was going nuts."

"And nobody's got this but us?"

"Nope."

"And we can prove this?"

"Absolutely."

"Cause I don't want to be doing a Dan Rather here, Marty."

"We've got everything. All the paperwork. Everything."

"And the source?"

"The source's got enough money to disappear. I spent damn near the whole fall budget on this and the video."

She raised her eyebrows.

"Don't worry about it. We're hot right now." The twinkle returned to his eye. "You heard the numbers?"

She shook her head.

"We pulled a seventeen share last night. Third highest rating of the year. Only the Super Bowl and the *Survivor* finale had a bigger number. They'll find us some more money, believe you me they will."

"That explains the calls I've been getting from network all morning. People I've been trying to get ahold of for a month."

"We've been reborn," Marty announced. "I'm going to ask for a 'Special Edition' to go on tomorrow night."

"Think they'll go for it?"

"They'll wet their pants."

"We can reuse a lot of the stock prison stuff."

"Plus whatever we get from the press conference this afternoon."

Marty moved quickly forward, slipping into the driver's seat and starting the engine.

"Let's get it on tape," he said.

Somehow, she couldn't get the sound of Christmas music to leave her head.

23

Elias Romero was late and greatly agitated. On his way home to change his suit, he'd found Iris Cruz sitting in her red Toyota Camry . . . parked diagonally across the street from his driveway . . . sitting there big as life for all the world to see. With his hands shaking and his pulse pounding in his ears, he'd stepped on the accelerator and sped all the way to the end of the street and turned right.

Iris stayed a semidiscreet block behind him as they ran all the way to the end of Linda Vista Boulevard, out past the last of the houses, out to where they'd paved it and put in sidewalks and driveways, in case, sometime in the future, they needed to build more houses. It was nothing but desert with driveways. Kinda eerie like some sci-fi flick or something. Like the giant ants had eaten up everything and moved on.

Reaching the back of the cul-de-sac, Elias Romero swung his Lincoln Town Car in a wide arc and stopped, facing back the way he'd come. Iris pulled up alongside. Their windows slid down simultaneously.

"What the hell is the matter with you?" Romero growled. "You come to my house? You—"

She cut him off. "I need to talk to you," she said.

"We got ways. You got no cause to be coming to my house."

Iris's eyes narrowed. She could feel her anger and indignation rising in her throat like molten metal. "What? You afraid that skinny wife of yours gonna find out. Afraid she gonna find out you been droppin' your pants on my bedroom floor."

"Hey now . . . don't be startin' that stuff with me. What we did is between you and me. We agreed."

"What we agreed was that you was leaving that bitch and we was gonna be together." When he didn't reply, she prodded. "Well didn't we?"

Romero started to bluster but changed his mind. He lowered his voice. Started talking like he did in bed. "Hey now," he soothed. "They's a lotta things goin' on right now. We get past all of this . . . you know, back to normal—"

"Don't you dare," Iris interrupted. "Don't you dare start that shit with me, Elias Romero. Don't you dare dis me like that. Bad enough I listened to that shit once. Now you tryin' to feed it to me again. What kind of idiot you think I am?"

Romero sat for a moment. The breeze soothed his overheated cheeks.

"What do you want?" he said finally.

"I'm taking my sick leave, my comp time and my unused vacation days . . . I'm going back home for a while."

"Mexico?"

She nodded.

"Chasin' that husband of yours."

"Got nothing to do with Esteban," she said. "Esteban's a weakling and a loser. Couldn't take being dishonored by the gringos. I don't need him no more neither. I just had enough of all of this. I need to get away for a while."

"Don't matter anyway," he said. "All that's going on here . . . there's no way I can cut you that much slack. Hell, Randall would lose their minds if I . . ."

She raised her voice. "The paperwork is on your desk. Sign it. You don't want me and your precious wife having a little conversation, you just sign those damn papers."

"Don't be threatening me, woman," he said.

"You didn't fool me for a minute, Elias Romero. I knew what you was coming round for. You just like all the rest of them."

"If you knew, baby," he mocked, "how come you so pissed off?"

"I'm pissed off 'cause you let me believe it. 'Cause you know a woman is ruled by her heart and you watched me forget myself and you didn't say nothing. My heart wasn't as important to you as your dick was."

"Ain't nothing is," he said with a wicked smile.

"That's the sad part, Mr. Elias Romero. Hearts don't matter to you 'cause your sorry ass isn't even got two percent of the milk of human kindness. You're pathetic, that's what you are."

Before he could reply, her window slid closed. He began to sputter at the tinted glass, but by that time, she'd dropped it in reverse, backed up, swung past his fender and roared back they way they'd come in a cloud of dust.

Elias Romero spent a minute and a half cursing and strangling his steering wheel. With a sigh, he checked his watch, swore again and put the car in gear, headed for town.

The parking lot for the Musket Community Center was overflowing. Seemed like every remote satellite truck in the country was sitting out there with its blind white eye pointing at the heavens. Inside, the place was jammed to the rafters with reporters.

With the prison's administration building little more than a pile of rubble, the community center was now the only place within fifty miles big enough to hold a press conference. He'd had to park at the far end of town and walk down.

By the time he slid into position on the dais, Asuega was already finished offering the Randall Corporation's deep, abiding sorrow to the loved ones of those killed in the riot and the corporation's sincere regrets that an incident such as this had taken place at all. He was now assuring the audience that all practices and procedures would be reviewed with an eye for strengthening security at what was already America's premier maximum security prison. He paused for a moment, shuffled his note cards and began again. *"As of this time, a total of three people remain unaccounted for."* A buzz of anticipation rose from the crowd. *"Two inmates and one civilian."* The buzz got louder. *"Inmate number nine nine three six four. Clarence Albert Kehoe. Imprisoned in the State of Mississippi in nineteen seventy-eight for killing three people in a bar fight. Found guilty in nineteen eighty of killing another prisoner and sent to a maximum security prison in Walla Walla, Washington, where he again killed a fellow inmate. Suspected in the deaths of four other inmates and deemed a habitual offender, Mr. Kehoe was finally sent to Meza Azul Correctional Facility in nineteen ninety-seven and housed in the Special Containment wing."* Asuega looked up at the sea of cameras. *"Mr. Kehoe is to be considered armed and extremely dangerous."*

Asuega waited until the volley of shouted questions subsided and continued. *"Inmate number one o nine five six three. Timothy Haynes Driver. Found guilty in King County, Washington, of two counts of aggravated murder. Serving two concurrent sentences of life without the possibility of parole. Assigned to Walla Walla Penitentiary, Mr. Driver assaulted and blinded another inmate during his first week of incarceration. During the course of the incident, Mr. Driver also seriously wounded a correctional officer. In nineteen ninety-eight, Mr. Driver was sent to Meza Azul and contained in the Extreme Punishment section of the Special Containment wing. Mr. Driver is considered to be armed and extremely dangerous."*

This time he kept talking, forcing the reporters to keep it down if they wanted to hear. *"As many of you recall, Mr. Driver's chief demand was the appearance of one Frank Corso. No middle name. Mr. Corso wrote a best-selling novel about Mr. Driver. Unfortunately, Mr. Driver made good on his threat to murder a correctional officer every six hours until Frank Corso was delivered to him. Mr. Corso entered the facility at midnight on the day before last and has not been in any type of communication with the outside world since that time, at least not to our knowledge. Mr. Corso's role in this incident is unknown at this time."*

Asuega neatened up his file cards and half turned to the row of dignitaries lined up behind him. *"At this time I'd like to introduce Special Agent Ronald Rosen from the Phoenix office of the Federal Bureau of Investigation. Special Agent Rosen will fill you in on the current state of the search for these three . . ."* For the first time he fumbled for a word. *". . . for the missing,"* he finally blurted.

Rosen was a stocky specimen in the standard FBI gray suit. His thick black hair was cropped close to his head. His eyebrows joined each other on the bridge of his nose. He thanked the crowd for nothing in particular and began. "I'm going to keep this brief," he said. "In conjunction with police departments in a seven-state area, the Bureau is now conducting an all-out manhunt for the three fugitives. Although our investigation is in its initial stages, we have reason to believe the three escaped Meza Azul Correctional Facility in the back of a delivery vehicle." When the buzz in the room threatened to swallow his statement, Rosen waited calmly for it to subside. "At this stage of the investigation, it would be counterproductive to provide specific details. Suffice it to say we have strong reason to believe that this was their method of egress from the prison."

Rosen gave the crowd a minute to chew on the information, then continued. "We have further reason to believe these fugitives were responsible for a double homicide that took place this morning in Phoenix." He held up a quieting hand. "At this time, we wish to strongly caution the public not to interfere with these fugitives in any way. Mr. Driver and Mr. Kehoe are serving life sentences without the possibility of parole. They have absolutely nothing to lose by any of their actions whatsoever. Anyone who thinks they may have spotted these fugitives . . . please dial the number at the bottom of the screen. We have set up a special hotline for the purpose of dealing with leads in this matter."

He paused. Shouted questions filled the air. He pointed at the AP reporter.

"Yes sir," he said.

24

Driver rose from the bed, walked to the adjoining door and knocked three times. The stream of grunts and squeals and groans that had been leaking through the wall for the past twelve hours finally stopped. After a minute the door opened wide enough for Kehoe's head to pop through the crack. Driver pointed to the TV, where three mug shots and the phone number for the FBI hotline filled the screen.

"I think we better get out of here," Driver said.

Took Kehoe a while to realize what he was looking at. Once he zoned in on the screen a crooked smile crossed his face. "I expect you're right," he said. "Gimme a few minutes." He turned to the other room. "Best find your drawers, darlin'. This here party is definitely over."

"Aw sweetie," she could be heard to coo.

Whatever she said next was lost among the rustling of bedclothes.

Driver turned to Corso. "Get your stuff together. You can stow it in the ammo bag." He disappeared into the bathroom for an instant and reappeared with an armload of towels. In a matter of two minutes he'd broken both guns down, wrapped the vari-

ous component pieces in towels and packed them in the larger of
the two Nike gym bags. By the time he got the ammo arranged in
the other bag, Corso was ready. He handed Driver everything except the bottle of Aleve, which he emptied into the inside pocket
of his jacket before tossing the empty bottle into the trash can.

Kehoe came bursting back through the door. "What'd they
say on the tube?"

Driver told him.

"Shit," said Kehoe. "I figured it'd take 'em a whole 'nother
day."

"Me too," said Driver.

"Probably means they made the truck."

"Yes. It does."

"We gonna have to do somethin' about that."

"Yes. We are."

Kehoe cast a glance at Corso. "Let's kill this faggot motherfucker and be done with that shit."

Driver steeled himself. "I need him," he said.

"I'm sicka draggin' him around. His ass is dead."

His hand plucked the boning knife from his pants pocket.
Driver jumped between the two men and grabbed Kehoe by the
wrist with his left hand. His right jammed the barrel of the automatic hard against the underside of Kehoe's chin. They stood, hip
to hip, arms aloft shaking like crazy, gazing into each other's feral
eyes. "I need him," Driver said again. "Either that or it all ends
right here in this room."

For a second, everything was in doubt. Who was going to live
and who was going to die was settled in silence, as gleaming silver
dust motes floated through the shaft of sunshine coming through
the parted curtains. Tendon by tendon the death grip relaxed,
until each man took a hasty step back. Driver dropped his right
hand, stuck the automatic in his belt. Kehoe kept the knife steady
at waist level. Both men were gulping air.

The hot blood filling his cheeks reminded Corso of a day when he was sixteen years old. The day when everything changed forever. Long and lean, he'd nearly attained his adult height of six-foot-six, when his father, angry that they were out of beer, reached out with those claws he called hands, grabbed the young Corso by the throat and pinned him against the wall, in just another angry outburst in a steadily increasing series of such acts of violence aimed at both Frank and his mother.

Looking back, as Corso had so many times, the day was like any other day. Nothing special, except that something broke inside of Frank Corso that morning, and without thinking, he grabbed the gnarled, nicotine-stained fingers clutching at his throat and bent them all the way back until they made a noise like snapping twigs.

A great roar erupted from his father's innards as he staggered backward, cradling the maimed hand against his chest. His bloodshot eyes looked up just in time to see his son's fist on its way toward his face. The impact drove him to his knees on the kitchen floor, where his broken nose steadily dripped blood onto the worn linoleum.

Frank and his father never spoke another word.

"I need him for closure," Driver said. "It's the only way I can bring it all the way around. The only way the journey matters is if the story is told."

Kehoe shook his head in disgust. "You was in that punishment cell too long, Captainman. They done fried your brain in there, you know that. You don't make no goddamn sense sometimes."

Driver flinched at the words. His eyes rolled farther back into his head than anatomy suggested was possible. He suffered a brief fit of shaking before coming to grips again.

He rubbed his eyes like a man waking from a deep sleep, pointed at the two black bags on the bed. "Take the little one," he said. "We'll keep Corso here between us and just mosey right out the front door."

"We can't be drivin' that truck no more."

"No shortage of cars out there. We'll just requisition one."

The plan seemed to satisfy Kehoe. "Let's go," he said. "We get the fuck outta here, we'll talk about his ass again."

Driver pulled open the door. Kehoe strode out carrying the ammo bag in his left hand. Corso fell in behind Kehoe with Driver bringing up the rear. The carpet was so bright and busy with color, you could have slaughtered a hog on it and nobody would have noticed. They marched to the trio of elevators at the end of the hall.

The clang and clamor of the casino assaulted their ears as they stepped from the elevator car. The Dollar Drinks Promotion was working. The casino was jammed full of low rollers, senior citizens and the kind of sad sacks indigenous only to Vegas, sitting there on their wrinkled asses, one-pound coffee cans in their laps, sitting in front of slot machines pulling those handles for all they were worth, counting their lives in quarters through a thick, blue haze of cigarette smoke.

The bells and the whistles, the flashing lights, the shouts of the winners and the curses of the losers followed them down the long central aisle toward the front door in the distance. Corso began to slow. Driver nudged him forward.

The crowd in front of them began to part like the Red Sea as one of the casino cash carts was being wheeled up the aisle by a pair of security guards. God knows how much money was on its way to the counting room and the vaults beyond.

Another pair of guards trailed along behind, making no bones about their intent, hands on their gun butts, narrow eyes sweeping back and forth across the room, looking for any poor soul sufficiently desperate as to impede their progress.

Corso stepped aside to allow them to pass. Driver had the automatic pressed against Corso's side as they leaned against a slot machine to make room for the gleaming steel cart.

As the cart drew parallel, Corso stepped out into the gap between the cart and the pair of guards trailing along behind.

Driver grabbed at his jacket but Corso backpedaled away. Their eyes met.

"Half an hour," Corso said. "I'll give you half an hour."

Driver growled with rage and reached for his belt. Corso cringed. Seemed like the scene would surely end right there and then. Like the last sound he was ever going to hear was going to be the flat crack of gunfire. The last sight muzzle flashes. The last smell gun smoke.

Corso snapped a glance to the right, looking for a place to dive. Nothing but a little alcove barely big enough for the slot machine and the ancient woman pulling the handle. When he switched his attention back to Driver, Kehoe had stepped into the breach, putting his back between Driver and the passing parade.

The nearest of the rear guard started for Corso. He'd unsnapped the safety strap on his holster. "Move it, buddy," the guy said.

Corso showed him both hands and stepped into the alcove, tripping over a purse and nearly losing his balance. The woman smelled of lilacs.

"Sorry," Corso said.

"Gwnagetout ahere," said the old lady at the keno machine.

On his way by, the guard fixed Corso with his most baleful stare. Corso kept his hands in sight as the cart continued up the central aisle.

"I'm tellin' you, buster," the old woman rasped, "get lost."

Corso peeked out into the aisle. Driver and Kehoe were nowhere in sight. He held his breath. Took his time looking around, then stepped fully out into the aisle and craned his neck. Gone . . . both of them. When he turned back, the old woman was missing too.

He resisted the urge to run and instead followed along in the wake of the cash cart until he got to a serious casino thoroughfare, where he turned right, then right again, and left, trying to lose himself among the hoard of blackjack and craps gamblers.

His chest felt like he hadn't taken a breath in an hour. He inhaled half a dozen times, then took another moment to compose himself. For the first time in nearly two days, he wondered what he looked like. The thought caused him to run his hands through his hair and make adjustments to his clothes.

He was about to consider what came next when a powerful hand clamped onto his shoulder. He stood paralyzed, waiting for the soft sound of the knife puncturing his coat, the prick of the sharpened tip on his skin and the feeling of cold steel as it entered his body. He tried to shout but nothing came out. His mouth hung open as he turned his head.

25

"The logo's crooked," Melanie said.

She was right. The American Eagle looked like it was battling a strong wind.

"Goddammit," Marty yelled. "Fix that friggin' bird. You got any idea what it cost to FedEx that thing from L.A.?"

"Are we supposed to guess?" asked Sheldon, the stagehand who'd flown in with the eagle. "Is this like the jellybeans in the jar kind of thing?"

"Me first. Me first," taunted another. He brought a single finger to the cleft in his chin. "Nine hundred fifty bucks."

Marty thought about opening his mouth but changed his mind. They were in a race against time, trying to turn the Musket Community Center into a replica of the *American Manhunt* set in Santa Monica. Bad enough they had to borrow a desk from the local real estate office. In just over an hour, people were going to begin arriving for the purpose of turning the room into a bake sale for the local Cub Scout troop. No time for banter.

The makeup people were smoothing Melanie's hair around the mike cord. The lighting crew were taking a final reading, shouting numbers at the impromptu control board they'd set up out in the center of the space.

"Time to do it people," Marty shouted above the din. "Unless you want old ladies with brownies walking onto the set, we better get going."

"Oooh, brownies," said Sheldon. "I like 'em gooey."

"Why am I not surprised," Marty growled.

Sheldon arched an eyebrow. "Careful now," he chided.

Marty smiled and turned to Melanie. "You ready?"

She gave him the okay sign with her fingers.

"Places," Marty yelled.

The lights dimmed, leaving Melanie and the desk and the logo alone in the glare. Her eyes followed the green lights on the lone teleprompter. *"Good evening, ladies and gentlemen. I'm Melanie Harris."* Saucy tilt of the head. *"Welcome to another Special Edition of* American Manhunt.*"*

A five-second vamp on the theme song and a camera pan gave Melanie a chance to arrange her notes and Marty time to switch cameras. Melanie counted to five in her head, adjusted her focus to the right and waited for the light to change from red to green.

"Once again, this is Melanie Harris with a special Tuesday night edition of American Manhunt, *live from Musket, Arizona, scene of this week's prison riot where fifty inmates and seven staff members lie dead in America's the most violent and deadly prison uprising ever."*

Back to front-on camera angle. *"If you joined us last night, you saw the spine-chilling beginning of this prison uprising as inmate number one o nine five six three, identified as Timothy H. Driver, a multiple murderer from the State of Washington, murdered the operator of the prison's control pod and took over the prison. For those members of our audience who were unable to join us last evening, we are going to run the clip at this time. Because of the graphic nature of this footage extreme parental caution is advised."*

Marty made the "cut" sign across his throat. Everyone relaxed.

"Bad enough we ran it last night," Melanie groused. "I don't see why we needed to air it again."

"If you got it, flaunt it," Marty said without taking his eyes from the monitor. He raised a hand and began to count with his fingers. "Five, four, three, two, one." His hand dropped like a guillotine.

"*With that ghastly act began a thirty-six-hour period of chaos and death at Meza Azul Correctional Facility,*" Melanie said in her voice of doom voice. "*Late yesterday afternoon, prison officials reported that three persons were missing from the penitentiary. Two inmates and one civilian.*" Melanie read the names and bios.

Marty's screen was filled with photos of Driver, Corso and Kehoe.

"*As of late this afternoon, The Federal Bureau of Investigation and the State Police in a seven-state area are conducting an all-out manhunt for the three fugitives.*" Lapsing again into her voice of doom, she read the standard admonition to the public regarding the armed and dangerous status of the missing men. "*Stay tuned to* American Manhunt *for exclusive information on Timothy H. Driver, the man who instigated the most deadly prison riot in U.S. history, then managed to disappear like smoke from what was advertised to be the most secure super-max correctional facility in the country.*"

Cut to commercial.

Melanie sat back in her chair. Makeup rushed forward, dabbing here, patting there.

"You going ahead with that copy?" Marty asked.

Melanie nodded.

"We're going to hear about it."

"I know," she said.

"Network's gonna go ratshit."

"I know."

"Places," Marty intoned.

Again he counted down from five to zero.

"*Welcome back to* American Manhunt, *ladies and gentlemen.
For tonight's special edition,* American Manhunt *has obtained
exclusive and until this time, confidential information regarding
the mastermind behind the uprising and subsequent escape. Initial reports from prison authorities alleged that Mr. Driver escaped from his cell during preparations for a routine medical
checkup.* American Manhunt, *however, has obtained documents
proving beyond a shadow of a doubt that Mr. Driver was being
removed from his cell as a result of having demonstrated irra-
tional and disassociative behavior over the previous five and a
half weeks.*"

Melanie allowed a pregnant pause, then continued. "*What fol-
lows, although not graphic in the manner of the earlier footage,
nonetheless possesses an upsetting quality that may not be appropriate for some of our viewers.* American Manhunt *recommends
extreme parental caution.*"

Marty watched intently as the scene switched to the interior
of the prison. Split screen. One picture from far up in the corner
of Driver's cell, the other taken through the bars from the outside.
Driver paced the length of his cell like a caged animal. His sandals
and orange coveralls could be seen neatly arranged on the narrow
bed. He wore only a pair of brown prison-issue underwear. His
body was pale but fit to a degree attainable only by someone with
a great deal of time on his hands. His voice sounded as if he was
preaching to hundreds of people in a huge room.

"Everyone contributes," he shouted. "If not in one way, then
in another. You don't have to agree. It doesn't have to be okay
with you. From the bears to the tiniest of insects. A part for
everyone and everyone for his part. Nature cannot be subverted.

The plan cannot be altered in any way. It's molecular. Beyond the realm of man because it's perfect and man is not. Acres of concrete and the weeds will find the smallest crack. No matter . . ."

Marty continued to watch the monitor as Driver ranted and raved for another forty seconds. He used his fingers to count down from five, then pointed at Melanie.

"*What troubled us here at* American Manhunt *was the question of how a fine mind like that of Mr. Driver, a Harvard graduate no less, how an incisive mind such as he possessed could be driven to madness by incarceration, when so many other inmates manage to maintain their sanity over considerably longer periods of time.*" She gave the audience time to join in on the wondering, then continued. "*The answer lies in the privatization of the American penal system and a positively medieval process called Extreme Punishment. Stay tuned.*"

"I can hear the phones ringing already," Marty said.

"Nobody deserves what they did to him."

"Lot of our viewers are going to disagree."

Another countdown to the final segment. Three, two, one . . .

Melanie went through it all. The Randall Corporation. The eight-by-eight white-tiled cell. The unblinking white lights. The cameras. Twenty-three hours a day in a fishbowl. No radio, no TV, one visitor once a month. The early signs that Driver was losing his mind and how the signs were ignored for the sake of profit. A call for an investigation of conditions in all Randall Corporation institutions and an immediate end to Extreme Punishment cells. By the time she finished, Marty's face was locked in a permanent wince.

Cut to commercial, then back to Melanie.

"*This is Melanie Harris for* American Manhunt. *Join us next time when* American Manhunt *again turns up the heat on the criminal plague permeating our nation. As of this week,* American Manhunt *and our millions of viewers at home are responsible for the arrest and successful prosecution of nine hundred and seventy-nine dangerous criminals. Let's add these guys to the list. Let's find these three before the authorities do.*" She offered a twisted smile and pointed at the camera. "*Until next time,*" she intoned.

Marty dropped his hand with a slap.

26

"You sure your friend ain't forgot about you?"

The kid was under twenty, dressed in black pants and a crisp white shirt with SKYWAY VALET SERVICE stitched on the shirt pocket.

"I'm beginning to wonder myself," said Driver with a wan smile. "He said he'd be right back."

A silver Mercedes coupe slid to the curb. The kid abandoned his post at the key kiosk and hustled around the front of the car to get the door. "Afternoon, Mr. Abrams. How are you today?"

Mr. Abrams was a big beefy specimen with a pockmarked face and a diamond pinky ring as big as the Ritz. He slipped the kid what looked like a ten-dollar bill and started up the stairs as if his feet were sore.

"You gonna be going out again today, sir?" the kid inquired, as he pocketed the cash and pulled open the car door.

"Going to Jersey to see my kids in the morning," the guy said. "You can put it in long-term if you want."

"Thank you, sir."

He stood holding the car door open, looking for one of his

two helpers. A minute later a blond kid with bad skin and a wrinkled uniform came running out from among the parked cars with a set of keys circling his index finger.

Key kid held the Mercedes' door open as Blondie slid into the seat. "Put it in long-term," Kiosk said. "He's not going to be needing it for a while."

Driver casually raised one hand above his head, as if he were stretching. Across a hundred yards of parked cars and asphalt, Kehoe stood in the mouth of the parking garage. Overhead, the clouds above were threatening to make way for the sun. Kehoe threw Driver a two-fingered salute and stepped out of sight, into the dark mouth of the garage.

Driver watched the silver Mercedes skirt the five acres of parked cars and disappear into the garage. A red Chrysler convertible pulled up. And then a blue Chevy Malibu.

The kid let the drivers come to him. Filling out tickets and trading them for the car keys. By the time he finished the second car, Blondie was jogging his way across the lot.

"Where in hell is Bobbie?" Kiosk demanded.

"He's on break," the kid said, handing over the keys to the Mercedes. "I think he went to Arby's."

"Well hurry up, man. We can't have them piling up out here."

"D forty-three," the kid said.

Kiosk wrote it down on the ticket, stepped inside the little booth and pulled open the double doors of the key cabinet. Driver was no more than three feet behind him as he hung the keys from a brass hook in the interior. Top row, second from the right end.

"Guess I should go looking for my friend," Driver said. "Probably better take my bags with me in case I find him." He held out a five-dollar bill. As the kid stepped to the front of the booth and bent to retrieve the two Nike bags, Driver lifted the set of keys from the hook and soundlessly slipped them into his pants pocket.

"Feels like you got lead in these things," the kid said through his teeth as he set the bags on the sidewalk. "Sure as hell wouldn't want to be carrying them too damn far."

"Good exercise," Driver said with a laugh.

A pair of quick good-byes and Driver was on his way across the lot, winding back and forth through the maze of cars, parked nose to nose at angles. Overhead, the clouds threatened to split into rays of sunshine. By the time he reached the mouth of the garage, Kehoe was jogging down the ramp in his direction. He stopped and put his hands on his hips. He was out of breath.

"You get the keys?" he wheezed out.

Driver patted his pants pocket. "Right here."

"Silver Mercedes?"

"That's the one."

Kehoe grinned. "It's up on the roof."

"Let's went."

Three minutes later, they crested the ramp and stepped out into the suddenly bright sunshine. Both men's faces wrinkled to a squint. Kehoe indicated they should take a left, then a quick right. The Mercedes was backed into the slot. Driver pushed the keyless entry button. Kehoe slipped around to the left and dropped into the passenger seat. He craned his neck and watched Driver open the back door and set the Nike bags in the floor cavities behind the seats. Any questions he might have had were immediately answered by the rush of zippers, the snap of metal parts, and the quiet sound of skilled hands assembling well-oiled weapons. He watched in silence as Driver loaded both guns and laid them out across the backseat using the towels to cover them. The Nike bags he dropped on top of the towels.

Kehoe nodded his grim approval. "Where we headed?"

Driver got in, fastened his seat belt and turned the key. The engine sprang silently to life. "Nearest beauty parlor," Driver said

Kehoe folded his arms across his chest and scowled. "What's that shit about?"

"We need a makeover."

Special Agent Rosen dropped the file folder on the desk. "Kehoe hasn't had a letter or a visitor in the better part of seven years."

Somebody gave a low whistle. "Talk about being alone."

"You go down for life without, the phone calls taper off."

"We followed up on everybody who's been in touch with him, no matter how long ago," said a younger FBI agent in a chocolate brown suit. He began to leaf through a sheaf of paperwork held together by a black spring clip. "His mother, Gladys Alma Kelly, stopped writing in eighty-five. Died of congestive heart failure in eighty-six. She was forty-nine. His half sister, Dorsey Anne Clements, was shot and killed outside a bar in Lake Ponchartrain, Louisiana, in nineteen ninety. The case remains open." He rustled the papers again. "The only visitor he's ever had was a guy named Harvey Gerald Raynes. Visited him twice in ninety-two and twice in ninety-three. His letter in ninety-eight was the last one Kehoe ever got." He pulled it out and slid it onto the table for anyone who might be interested. The big guy with the square head and the Arizona State Police uniform picked it up for perusal. "Raynes was a cellmate of Kehoe's from his days in the Mississippi system. He went down again in ninety-nine for armed robbery and aggravated assault. Was beaten to death by a fellow prisoner in November of ninety-nine."

He pointed his palms at the ceiling. "That's it."

"What about this Corso character?"

"Corso's a famous writer. Been on Leno half a dozen times. More or less a recluse. Lives on a boat. Moves around so the press can't keep track of him. His tax return for this past year shows he made just over three million after taxes. He's got quite a bit of family in south Georgia. We've got people on the way and wiretaps ready as soon as they arrive, but I wouldn't hold my breath. He keeps in touch, but hasn't been there in the better part of ten years. We've got the Seattle office working his ex-boss at the *Seattle Sun*. One Natalie Van Der Hozen. Wiretaps are probably not going to be forthcoming. We've already been denied twice."

"Why's that?" Rosen asked.

"Lack of probable cause," said Brownsuit.

Rosen shook his head. "That whole Pacific Northwest is a pain in the ass that way. And Driver?"

"That's our best bet. Gets a constant stream of letters from his mother in Prineville, Oregon. When he first went down he got letters from shipmates and other navy personnel, but those quit after a couple of years. Nowadays it's only his mother."

"How we doing on that front?"

"The Portland office is working with both the Oregon State Police and the locals. We've got a local wiretap warrant and will have people on the scene within the next couple of hours."

Rosen nodded his approval. "Good," he said. He turned to the state policeman. "What are we doing to protect the highways and byways? These skells have already killed a couple of merchants. We need to bring them under lock and key as soon as possible."

"We've got state and locals in a seven-state area on the lookout for a nineteen seventy-nine Ford pickup truck with a Caveman cab-over-camper. Oregon plate number AET874. We believe the vehicle was stolen from the service yard of Desert Distributing, down the street here in Pauling, Arizona. The yard security man was reported missing by his wife. The truck is missing from the yard. Luminal shows traces of blood on the guard shack floor."

Rosen began to rifle through the morass of paperwork spread

about the table. "Where've I heard that before? Desert Distributing." He dropped one pile and picked up another. "Here," he said. "The cons let six locals and their delivery trucks go unharmed." He began to read. "Mesa Laundry and Uniforms, United Grocers, Arizona Linen Supply." He tapped the page with his fingernail. "Desert Distributing."

The room was silent. "Gotta be how they rode out," Rosen declared. "Find that truck. Comb every inch of it."

The state cop was already halfway to the door when Rosen's voice brought him to a halt. "Inside and out," Rosen added. "Check inside those damn tankers."

Brownsuit got to his feet and straightened his jacket. "The press?" he asked.

"Nothing," Rosen said. "Investigation in progress. Pursuing a number of leads. Nationwide manhunt. That's it."

27

Corso held his breath and inched his head around. He'd always been a guy who looked the other way when the doctor gave him a shot, so he sure as hell didn't want to catch the glint of the blade as it started toward its journey for his heart. As a guy who didn't figure to die in bed, he'd often imagined his final moment. The second in which he knew it had gone to shit and the jig was all the way up. Penetration seemed to be the constant motif, be it a bullet plunging its way to his heart or an ice pick through the eye; the imagined final nanosecond of his consciousness always began with the tearing of his flesh and always ended with a sudden shudder and a final fade to black.

Black as the hand on his shoulder. Seemed like everybody in this town had a pinky ring. Corso moved his eyes up the arm until he was looking into as hostile a pair of brown orbs as he had ever seen. "You been bothering Mrs. Gravley?" the voice asked.

"What?"

"You been bothering Mrs. Gravley?"

The hand on his shoulder turned Corso to the left. That's when he saw her. The old woman. The one who'd been sitting at the slot machine. Still holding a blue Maxwell House coffee can half-full of quarters. "That's him," she said, pointing at Corso. "Guy was all over me like a cheap suit."

"I stumbled," Corso said. "I fell into her."

"He groped me," the old woman said. "Grabbed my knockers."

"I fell into her. That was it."

When the death grip on his shoulder eased. Corso stepped out from under the hand. The guy wore a greasy red sport coat with a badge attached to the front pocket. Casino security. He brought his face close to Corso's and sniffed a couple of times, then leaned away. "I'll take it from here Mrs. Gravley," he said. "You go on back to your machine. I'll come round and check on you later."

"Somebody probably got my machine by now."

"They's lots of machines, Mrs. Gravley."

He listened patiently as she launched into a tirade about how the machine was just about to pay off. How she was going to have to start all over again on some accursed new machine, which would surely suck her dry.

They stood amid the clang and clamor of the casino and watched her waddle away.

"Used to be a showgirl in one of the big casinos. Years ago. Way back when," the guard said. "These days she gets a little bit too much caffeine and all of a sudden every man who passes by is trying to get into her pants." He shook his big head in amusement. "Probably was a time when it was true."

"Time flies," Corso said.

"Ain't it the truth," the guy said with a chuckle.

"I was hoping maybe you could do me a favor."

"What's that?"

"Call the FBI."

Gone were the shoulder-length brown hair, the Fu Manchu mustache and the perpetual Harley-Davidson scowl. Kehoe now stood clean-shaven in front of the beauty shop mirror, using the palm of his hand to test the collection of short black spikes rising from the top of his head. "Cut yourself on this shit," he offered with a grin.

"You're a new man," Driver said. "Even your own mother wouldn't recognize you."

"She'd kick my ass she saw me like this."

The beautician slid out from behind the counter and handed Kehoe his change and an electric blue jar of hair gel. "You look great, honey. Gals gonna be all over you like ugly on an ape."

Driver was unable to satisfy himself as to the specifics of the beautician's gender. A creature with outsized breasts and a five o'clock shadow was heretofore beyond his experience and was causing him a great deal of confusion. Although he had never considered the matter prior to that afternoon, he had come to realize that gender was one of the first things with which his nervous system came to grips when confronted by an unknown fellow creature and that an inability to classify a fellow *Homo sapiens* according to gender seriously unhinged his basic manner of dealing with people, leaving him addled and unable to proceed.

Driver's head was shaved bald and polished to a shine. A week's worth of scruffy beard was trimmed to look intentional. The effect was dramatic. Like Kehoe, he bore scant resemblance to the photo on TV.

"Where you boys headed?" she/he wanted to know.

"Around," Driver said. "Gonna bring it all around."

She/he gave her gum a quick crack. "Well drop me a line when you get there." The idea set her/him off laughing. She/he bent at the waist and cackled. ". . . Lemme know when you get there," she/he howled.

Kehoe's hand was on the way to his pocket when Driver took him by the arm and started him toward the door.

"Thanks for everything," Driver said over his shoulder as they slipped out the door.

"That motherfucker a boy or a girl?" Kehoe asked, jerking his arm free of Driver's grasp.

"What's it matter?" Driver asked.

"I don't kill women," Kehoe said.

Driver laughed. "Nice to meet a man with standards."

"Gotta draw the line somewhere."

Driver stifled a strong desire to laugh. "Has it ever occurred to you that murder may not be an acceptable problem-solving technique?"

"It's always worked for me, man."

Driver kept moving toward the car; Kehoe reluctantly followed along. A fierce desert sun had taken over the sky, painting the winter air with a faint coat of warmth and scattering the clouds like frightened sheep.

Driver popped the locks and they both got in. Kehoe belted himself into the passenger seat, threw one last scowl at the House of Hair and looked over at Driver.

"Where in hell are we headed anyway?" he demanded. Before Driver could respond, he went on. "And don't be givin' me any more of that circle shit neither. I'm talkin' about a direction or a place or somethin' real like that."

Driver started the silent engine and dropped the car into drive. "North."

"What for?"

Driver wheeled the car out into traffic. "I gotta see my mother one last time."

"And she's like where?"

"North."

Kehoe nodded his understanding to discretion. "She write you?"

"Yeah."

"Cause they gonna sit on anybody you been in touch with."

"I know."

"They're probably there already."

Driver managed the thinnest of smiles. "Not a chance."

Kehoe studied him. "You sure . . . ain't you?"

"Yeah," he said. "I'm sure."

"How's that?"

"Probably best I keep that to myself."

"Probably is."

"What about you?"

Kehoe thought it over. "We get that far, I'm thinking about trying to get my ass into Canada."

"Why's that?"

Kehoe's laugh was short and brittle. " 'Cause they're for sure gonna find some way to burn us for those guards, Captainman. They'll make it a federal rap or something. They'll make shit up if they gotta. They gonna want to off our asses for good."

"And Canada won't send you back unless the feds agree not to give you the death penalty."

"That's it, baby."

Driver began to sing in a rich baritone. *"North to Alaska. Go north, the rush is on . . ."*

28

"We through?" Corso asked.

Special Agent Rosen abandoned his chair and walked over to the window. He stood with his hands on his hips gazing down at the city below. They'd spent the first two hours in a windowless interrogation room on the sixth floor of the Federal Building in downtown Phoenix. About the time Corso's story began to check out . . . after they found the stolen truck in the casino parking lot where he'd said it would be . . . after they found the hazmat suits floating around inside the tanker truck, found the hotel room and the casino security guard, they'd moved the show up two floors to the corner conference room where they were now. Rosen leaned back against the window and made heavy eye contact with Corso.

"How's your hand?" he asked Corso.

"Better," Corso said. "Thanks for the professional repair work."

"And you've got no idea where they may be headed."

"None," Corso said. "Kehoe claims to be alone on the planet and Driver just rambles on and on about fish and grizzly bears and blowflies and whatever else crosses his mind."

"But he's lucid some of the time."

"Whenever he needs to be."

"You think he's faking it?"

"He's real hard to read. Maybe that's what happens when you lock men up in white-tiled cells and leave the lights on twenty-four/seven."

"He ever mention his mother?"

"Not when I was around."

Rosen ran it all through his circuits again. The younger agent picked at his cuticles. The stenographer kept her hands still and her face blank.

After an anxious moment Rosen said, "You're free to go, Mr. Corso."

Corso got to his feet. Rosen looked back over his shoulder at the ground below.

"I hear you shun the press, Mr. Corso."

"Same way I shun hyenas and rattlesnakes," Corso answered.

"Well you best put on your sneakers then, because every reporter in the known world is downstairs waiting for you to come out."

Corso crossed the room to Rosen's side. He looked down and heaved a sigh.

"We could take you out through the garage."

Corso shook his head. "I've had my fill of government hospitality for the day."

They watched as Corso moved to the door in four long strides. He pulled open the door, stepped into the breach and fixed each of them with his gaze before disappearing from sight. Rosen picked up the phone receiver and poked out a code.

"Mr. Corso's been released," he said. He listened for a moment, his gaze sweeping the carpet. "Send her in," he said finally.

"I figured you'd keep Corso for a couple of days," said the younger agent.

"Feels to me like he's leveling with us." He shrugged. "Anyway . . . we need him again, we'll find him again."

The door opened. A young woman in a gray business suit entered the room, closing the door behind her. Despite the faint pinstripe and the fine tailoring, the suit was unable to hide the nimble vitality of her figure. She'd been a member of the U.S. bronze medal volleyball team during the last Olympics and the muscles in her long legs rippled beneath the fabric as she took a seat at the far end of the conference table.

Rosen raised his eyebrows.

"The Portland office has a bit of problem," she said in an even voice.

"Such as?"

"Such as . . ." She sorted her words. "So far . . . it doesn't seem, at this point in the investigation . . . it doesn't seem as if Driver's mother lives anywhere in or near Prineville, Oregon."

Rosen folded his arms and frowned. "Really?"

"Yes sir."

"Her letters are all postmarked from there."

"Yes sir."

"How big a place is it?"

"Not very sir. It's out in the high desert behind Bend. Folks out there either work in wood products or they mold rubber at the Les Schwab tire plant."

Rosen rolled a hand over his wrist. "And they've . . ."

"They've got the locals and the staties involved."

"They check the private mailboxes?"

"Forensics is examining every postmark meter within fifty miles, trying to find out which one stamped the envelopes."

"Are all the marks the same?"

"Quantico says they are."

His thick eyebrows met in the center of his face. This was supposed to have been the slam dunk section of the manhunt.

That's why he'd assigned the task to Special Agent Westerman, hoping to create a bit of early career success for her and thus spur her on her way up the Bureau's somewhat old-school promotion ladder. She was a capable and well-trained young woman who had endured the low-key sexism of the Phoenix Bureau Office with grace and good cheer and thus, as far as Rosen was concerned, was deserving of a career kick start.

"So," Rosen said, "what do you think?"

"I'm thinking that maybe she's very rural. Way out in the sticks somewhere, where she doesn't have much contact with other people. I'm thinking that they'll find her as they widen the circle."

"And if they don't?"

"Then we'll have ourselves a mystery sir."

The crush of bodies brought out the worst in him. He made it halfway down the tunnel of cameras and microphones and tape recorders before somebody hit him in the face with a camera. From that point on things got ugly. He shoved the offending camera hard enough to bounce it off the face of the operator, breaking his glasses, sending him staggering backward into the melee, where he tripped and fell among the morass of feet and legs. His cries for help rose above the shouted questions and the crush of bodies.

Corso cursed under his breath and continued to swim his way through the crowd. The plan had been to outwalk the media. He had long legs and liked to stretch them. News teams were set up to do their business within a confined area. They needed plugs and cords to operate. Out past the reach of technology, they were worse than useless.

This, however, was going to be a problem. He'd exited the building at the back of a cul-de-sac, leaving him adrift in a sea of

question-shouting, microphone-waving humanity, without hope
of a cab or even the vagaries of evening traffic to use as a buffer.

He pulled his chin up to avoid a handheld tape recorder. The
evening sky was a deep blue. The lights of the city had swallowed the stars. The noise of men and their machines filled the
air like a swarm of hornets. Corso bit down hard and pushed
forward.

He used his hands to move people out of the way. On the far
side of the enclosure, parked between a pair of FBI forensics wag-
ons, a huge brown-and-white motor home squatted along the
curb with its front door hanging open.

Corso recognized her right away. Melanie Somethingorother
from the *American Manhunt* TV show. He'd done a segment five
or six years back when he still needed to tour books. She crooked
her arm and beckoned him her way. And then did it again, more
urgently this time.

Corso picked up his pace and dropped his shoulder. Like a
bowling ball he ricocheted his way across the expanse of pavement. As he approached the motor home, she backed inside, holding the door open as she slipped from view.

Corso felt his weight rock the motor home on its springs. A
clank of the door and the click of the lock and silence settled like
a breeze. He looked around but failed to take anything in. Running both hands through his thick black hair, he took a deep
breath.

"That's worse than a prison riot," he said.

She laughed. Rich and deep, the sound brought a smile to
his face.

"You'd be the guy to know," she said.

Corso moved to the center of the coach. Looked around.
"Spiffy," he said.

Melanie shrugged. "It's been sitting around the ABC lot for

years," she said. "My agent negotiated for it, but I've never really used it much before."

Corso bent at the waist and peered out from between the curtains.

"Does this thing go? I mean, like is there a driver or something?"

She wrinkled her creamy brow. "What do you mean driver? I'm the driver. What kind of thing is that to say? You're gonna be like that, you can get back out, Mr."

Corso showed his palms. "Sorry. Didn't mean to offend. I can be really dumb sometimes."

Her expression said she agreed. "Where do you want to go?"

"Anyplace but here."

She moved the beige curtains, exposing the windshield and side windows, then slipped into the driver's seat. "Airport?"

Corso thought about it. She started the engine.

"Howsabout Scottsdale?" he asked.

"Where in Scottsdale?"

She backed up until she felt a small thump of resistance, crimped the wheel hard to the right and eased away from the curb.

"The Phoenician," Corso said. "Take me to the Phoenician. It's a resort on Scottsdale Road."

"I know where it is."

A dozen photographers backpedaled in front of the moving motor home, trying to take shots through the windshield. She tooted the horn and raced the engine. She accelerated. The paparazzi peeled off like ocean from the prow of a ship.

"At least you've got good taste in hotels," she said as they slid into southbound traffic. "You gonna hide out, that's the place to be doing it."

"I'll buy you dinner. There's a restaurant in the hotel named . . ."

"Mary Elaine's," she finished. "Great joint."

Corso slid into the passenger seat and buckled up.

She threw a sideways glance in his direction. "Good taste in restaurants too," she said with a smile. "It's a wonder some clever woman hasn't snapped you up by now."

He turned her way. "Who says somebody hasn't?"

"Your reputation precedes you, Mr. Corso."

29

"Nice your mom's still writing you letters," Kehoe said.

As promised, they were heading north. Sliding along under a slate gray sky, radio playing one of those gloom-and-doom preachers you only find in the middle of nowhere. Out on the eastern horizon, a line of storm clouds dropped forks of silver lightning, probing the ground here and there, as if searching for sinners.

"Lotta guys go down . . . you know the family hangs in there for a while . . . does the best they can . . . writes and visits and sends shit . . . but you know man, life goes on. People die. Others gotta get on with their lives. Can't spend the rest of their days draggin' some con along behind them like some old anchor. Somebody else comes along. Get a fresh start maybe. New names in a new place where people don't look at 'em funny. Can't hardly blame 'em for movin' on."

He wasn't expecting a response. Driver had been in never-never land ever since they stopped for food and gas a couple of hours back. Kehoe pulled down the vanity mirror and looked at his new hairdo for something like the fiftieth time.

For the first time, he heard thunder in the distance and turned toward the sound. The storm was running them down from the east, coming hard along the prairie with a wavering curtain of rain leading the way. Another hour of daylight, tops.

He was watching the approach of the storm out of the side window when, out of nowhere, Driver spoke. "My mother never gave up. Never will. As long as both of us live, I'll always be her son, and she'll always be on my side. Doesn't matter what I may have done. She'll find a way it wasn't my fault. Find a way to blame somebody else. That's part of being a mother as far as she's concerned."

"Be nice to have somebody like that," Kehoe said. "Hell, my family come apart before I ever even showed up. Long as I can remember I was getting sent from my mother to my father to my grandma Jean to my aunt Sophie. Whoever was out of jail at the time and had a roof." Kehoe settled down in the seat and began to work his teeth with a toothpick. "My old man was one of those types believed a good beating was a cure for just about everything. Beat a little religion in ya. Beat the devil out." He chuckled. "Tell you what though . . . you sure as hell didn't want to come home from school and tell my old man anybody else beat your ass . . . no sirree . . . you either come home the winner or you best not drag your ass home at all."

"Where's he now?"

"Don't nobody know," Kehoe said. "Walked out of his favorite bar in Greenville, Mississippi, one night and ain't never been seen since. I was twelve. I waited a few days until the peanut butter run out and called my aunt Sophie. She come down from Tennessee and picked me up."

"What about your mother?"

Kehoe thought it over. "She had a bad heart. Just never had the strength it took to be raisin' children." he said. "Wore out way before her time. Sophie used to say Gladys was too good for this world. Always seemed to me like it was the other way around, like the world was just too much for her or something. No sooner would I get there and she'd be sending me back where I come from." Kehoe shrugged and went back to his toothpick.

Raindrops . . . those big silver tears that run along the edges of a storm began to hurl themselves against the sheet metal. Looked like liquid mercury bouncing off the hood, then a clap of thunder right overhead, a trident of lightning right in front of the car and the storm, pouring down out of the sky like a waterfall, swamping the wipers, reducing visibility to just about nothing.

"Like a cow pissin' on a flat rock," Kehoe shouted above the din.

Driver slowed the car to a crawl, inching along in the right lane, wipers slapping like crazy until, five minutes later, the deluge was gone, moved on off across the high desert, heading west at a hundred miles an hour.

Kehoe worked his gum line with a toothpick. Dislodging a morsel, he gathered it with his lips and spit it down onto the carpet. "Had me a whole nother meal there," he commented. When Driver failed to respond, he shot a quick glance in that direction. Driver had gone back to perusing whatever inner landscape his mind had invented to keep from going all the way crazy. "Hey," Kehoe called. No response. "Hey," again.

Driver turned his face Kehoe's way. Watching Driver's eyes return from never-never land was like watching a slot machine click to a stop. Three lemons.

"Whatcha need?"

"What I need is to take a leak. Sign back there says there's a rest area a coupla miles ahead."

The last drops of rain, the rear guard of the storm, fell from the sky, then it was silent again. And then the sign . . . REST AREA ¾ MILE . . . State of Utah, Route 191, little picture of a beehive. Busy busy, these Mormons.

Driver lifted the turn signal lever and eased off the highway. A thicket of shrubbery separated the rest area from the highway. Wiry desert plants they didn't have to water.

Place wasn't much and what there was was damn near deserted. A pair of concrete block bathrooms and four picnic tables. On the left, an elderly couple was repacking the back of a blue Volvo station wagon. On the right, an enormous Worldwide Moving van was angled across a bunch of parking spots. Driver backed the car into a slot and turned off the engine. "One at a time," he said. "You go first."

Kehoe opened the glove box and pulled out the shiny Colt revolver.

"Just in case," he said with a wink, as he stuffed it into his belt and pulled his shirt down over it. "You never know who you're gonna meet in these public shitters."

Driver got out with him. He stood next to the Mercedes stretching his arms and back, watching Kehoe cross the tarmac in that leg iron shuffle of his. The sound of an engine starting pulled Driver's head around. The couple in the Volvo were loaded up and leaving. He watched the old man back up, wheel hard to the right, and creep off toward the highway entrance ramp.

When he turned back, a guy in a white T-shirt and a gray Stetson hat was headed his way. One of those highway jockeys with a big gut and no ass, pushing a pair of spit-shined cowboy boots over to the side of the moving van, where he grabbed the long silver handle and pulled himself up into the driver's seat.

The howl of the starter split the gloom, then the engine burst into life, sending a dark pair of plumes rolling from the silver diesel pipes. Driver heard the hiss of the hydraulic clutch and the slip and shudder of the tires as the big rig began to roll. He watched as the yellow-and-white globe painted on the side of the truck passed before his eyes. Heard the driver make his first shift, then, in an instant, lost all interest in the truck, as the final set of wheels rolled by and he could now see what had been hidden by the moving van. His breathing became rapid and shallow. His body began to tingle.

A Nevada State Police cruiser was nosed into the handicapped
slot closest to the bathrooms, no more than twenty feet from
where Driver stood. The last flattop hairdo in America sat behind
the wheel. A young woman sat leaning forward in the backseat.
The windows were down. He could hear her plain as day.

"When it's my turn, you gonna stand there and watch me pee?
What kinda pervert are you anyway? They teach you how to be a
pervert at cop school? Huh do they?"

The cop threw an exasperated look at Driver and went back
to staring straight ahead. Driver reached in through the open window of the Mercedes and unlocked all the doors, then pulled
opened the rear door and pretended to busy himself with something inside. The girl was still running her mouth, but Driver had
tuned her out. Suddenly, a loud bang forced Driver to look up.

The door to the men's room had been thrown back against the
building. Another Nevada State policeman was engaged in a spir-
ited wrestling match with a guy in blue jeans and a black T-shirt.
Connected at the wrist by a pair of handcuffs, they whirled and
twirled and flailed about as both men sought to gain an advantage
on the other.

Flattop was out of the car in a flash. As he loped toward the
melee, scratching at his holster, the wrestlers went down on the concrete sidewalk with a thud. The cop came out on top, but the other
guy was quicker; he hooked a leg around the cop and jerked him
down to the ground, where the grunting and cursing reached a
crescendo as each man used his free hand in an attempt to deliver a
crippling blow.

From there on, like they say, timing was everything. The second cop arrived just as Kehoe stepped out of the men's room
door. Forty yards away, Driver saw it come down. He wanted to
shout. To tell Kehoe to just keep walking. It happened too fast
though. Way too fast. Confronted by a pair of cops and a life-and-
death struggle, Kehoe acted on instinct; he went for his gun.

Driver watched as Kehoe beat the cop to the draw, getting off
a single round, catching the cop square in the chest, forcing the air
from his lungs and sending him staggering backward, as if he'd
been hit in the sternum by a sledgehammer. The officer was
whooping for breath and kneading his chest with both hands as he
reeled across the pavement toward the police cruiser.

Soon as Kehoe figured out the cop was wearing a vest and
wasn't going to be dead anytime soon, he sent a couple of rounds
after the staggering lawman and started running toward the Mercedes at full speed. Driver reached under the towels and came out
with the Mossberg twelve-gauge. He grabbed a handful of shells
and covered the distance between the Mercedes and the State Police cruiser in a dozen quick strides, arriving just as the wheezing
policeman threw himself into the driver's seat and grabbed the
radio.

In the instant before his thumb engaged the TALK button,
some primal instinct told the cop to take a quick glance to his
right. Must have looked like a sewer pipe, that enormous, gaping
mouth of a shotgun pointed at the side of his head in the split second before the powder expanded and the roar and the flame followed the plastic wads out the barrel into the air. His eyes were
big as quarters. He was reaching for his gun and calling for his
savior when the thirty or so lead pellets packed inside the shotgun
shell blew his head to mist, sending a mass of hair-covered detri-
tus rocketing out the side window like a scalded cat.

The girl was screaming now, low down in her vocal range, almost like a roar. Nothing you could make sense of, but not in terror either. Something like excitement accompanied her cries into
the darkening sky, but Driver had no time to listen.

Up at the restroom, the cop had gained the upper hand and
was now kneeling on his prisoner's back as he exchanged gunfire
with Kehoe, who had flattened himself on the ground and was
using one hand to steady the other as he squeezed off high-

powered rounds, several of which had plowed irregular holes through the bathroom's concrete-block wall.

Fighting for his life, the cop was so focused on Kehoe he lost track of Driver. Let him get within forty feet before the boom of the shotgun tore him apart. Last thing he saw was Driver pulling the trigger at every stride aiming at whatever the Kevlar vest didn't cover. The cop fell over backward in a heap, twitched a couple of times and was still.

By the time Driver got there, the cop was dead and the guy pinned beneath him was squirming like a fish on a riverbank, trying to get out from under the corpse. Driver grabbed the dead cop by the front of his shirt and pulled him over to the side. The guy rolled over a half turn and got to his feet.

He was young, under twenty-five, with fine almost girlish features and a pompadour worthy of Elvis himself. Wasn't till he reached up to run a hand through his fancy hair . . . wasn't till then he saw the handcuffs were still connected to both his right arm and to the left arm of the cop, except that arm wasn't connected to the cop's body anymore.

"Holy shit," he said, lifting the severed limb from the ground. He stared down at the arm swinging from his wrist, turned pale and for a moment looked like he might puke. He started to bring his right hand to his face, thought better of it and used his left to wipe his brow.

At that moment the girl in the cruiser began to holler. "Harry," she yelled. "Get me outta here, Harry."

For his part, Harry was in something of a quandary. While his heart was clearly with the young woman in the patrol car, his arm was still attached to the cop's. He took a step toward the cruiser, decided he didn't want to arrive with an extra appendage and instead dropped to his knees, using his unencumbered hand to go through the cop's pants pockets, patting here and feeling there until he came out with a small ring of keys. Took him three tries to find the right one, but he finally managed to get himself separated from the long arm of the law, just about the time both Kehoe and Driver had reunited and reloaded their weapons.

"I'm comin', honey," he shouted into the gathering darkness.

Kehoe and Driver hurried along in his wake, scanning the deserted rest area as the love birds staged a tearful reunion in the backseat of the patrol car.

"I saw them on TV," Driver said as they hustled along.

"Doin' what?"

Driver filled him in on the details. The rebuffed Harry putting one in her father's ear. The crime spree across Texas and Oklahoma. Extradition back to Texas. Everything he could remember from Vegas.

Kehoe gave a low whistle. "Texas ain't no damn place to be killin' people, Captainman. Those crackers'll drop the pellets on you in a heartbeat."

Out on the highway, an eighteen-wheeler backed down on its gears, sounding for all the world like it was going to pull into the rest area, before shifting up again and continuing on into the darkness. "We better make tracks," Kehoe said.

Harry had extricated his beloved from the backseat by then and was assuring her that everything was going to be alright. Heidi Anne was a high-strung-looking girl in a pair of tortoiseshell glasses and matching hairband. While by no means classically beautiful, Heidi Anne's vapid blue eyes and voluptuous contours held sufficient promise to explain a murder or two on her behalf. By the time she was inclined to take Harry's word for the viability of their situation, Driver and Kehoe were approaching the Mercedes.

They came sprinting over hand in hand. Stood there like waifs at a bakery window.

"We gotta get out of here," Harry said. "Me and Heidi, we . . ."

"I saw you on TV. I know who you are," Driver said.

"Then you know why we gotta get outta here."

"Texas is a very unforgiving state."

Kid bobbed his hairdo up and down. "So howsabout it?"

Driver shrugged. "Take the cruiser."

"We won't get ten miles in that thing."

"Not your problem," Driver said evenly. "Should have thought of that before you wasted her father."

"That old fuck got exactly what he deserved."

"Sure of that, are you?"

"Damn right I am."

Over the kid's left shoulder, Kehoe had moved in close to Heidi Anne and was looking her over like a lunch menu.

"What do you say, Cutter? We give 'em a ride or not?"

Kehoe gave it some consideration. "They was wanted any-place but Texas, I'd say leave 'em," he said with mock sincerity. "But . . . Texas . . . you know . . ."

"Honor among thieves and all that?"

"Whatever you say," Kehoe said.

Driver laughed. "I'll take that as a yes," he said. With his laughter still in the air and the smile lingering on his lips, Driver put the barrel of the twelve-gauge right between Harry Gibbs's eyes. "I'd stay real still if I was you, boy," Driver whispered.

Kehoe picked up on the sudden tension and tore himself away from the lovely Heidi. "Problem, Captainman?" he asked.

"Pat our young friend here down for me will you, Cutter? Last I saw that cop in the car over there, he had a piece. Seems it's gone missing."

They found it in Harry's boot, a nice compact little Browning nine-millimeter.

"You'll excuse me now, boy, if maybe you're not the type I want sitting behind me with a nine in his shoe."

The kid was smart enough to keep his mouth shut.

"Her too, Cutter," Driver said. "Make sure she's clean."

Kehoe reckoned it was a filthy job, but he was willing to take it on. For the sake of modesty, he walked her around to the far side of the Mercedes. Harry surely wanted to bend over and look through the cars windows, but the shotgun on his forehead kept him at rigid attention. Took four minutes and a series of giggles before Kehoe came up with the dead officer's Mace canister. Heidi assured everyone it was strictly for protection. Harry told her to shut up.

30

The attendant scanned the car rental agreement with his little handheld computer. A moment later, a tongue of paper emerged from the mouth of the machine. The guy tore it off and handed it to Special Agent Rosen, who carefully folded it and slid it into his wallet.

Special Agent Westerman stood nearby holding her briefcase in one hand and Rosen's in the other. The roar of jet engines hovered in the night air. She turned her head in time to see a Southwest Airlines passenger jet rising from the runway.

They were on the roof of the parking garage at Phoenix International Airport. Rain was in the air, one of those desert soakers that fills the arroyos in a heartbeat. Everyone could feel it.

"Thank you for choosing Hertz," the attendant said as he closed the trunk with a bang, but by that time, Rosen and Westerman were halfway to the elevator.

"So?" Rosen said.

"So we pinpointed the information leak, sir."

"Where?"

"The warden's personal secretary. A woman named Iris Cruz."

Rosen said he remembered her. The elevator car arrived; they stepped in and rode it to the bottom floor. Food and gifts. Rosen checked his watch. "Let's get some coffee," he suggested.

They found a table over by the Burger King franchise, did their little dance about who was going to Starbucks for coffee, then, when Westerman returned, settled in.

"How do we know it's her?" he asked.

Despite her best efforts, Westerman could feel the blood rising to her cheeks. "She and Warden Romero had a little something going on the side. Cruz had been telling people Romero was going to leave his wife and marry her. Looks like it didn't turn out that way."

Rosen raised a thick eyebrow, sipped at his coffee. Westerman continued.

"Once the bloom was off the rose, she peddled the stuff to *American Manhunt* for something like seventy thousand bucks, then took Alaskan Airlines flight ninety-eight from Phoenix to Guadalajara yesterday morning."

"A well-earned vacation," Rosen quipped.

"No sir. She made arrangements to have her furniture shipped."

"Ms. Cruz had quite an eye for an exit."

"Yes sir."

"Not much to come back to."

"Seventy grand goes a long way in Guadalajara."

"Especially since Asuega and Romero got fired this morning," Rosen said.

"It's worse that that, sir."

"What's worse than that?"

She gave him a twisted grin. "Romero doesn't know it, but he's about to get served with divorce papers this morning. Seems the scorned Ms. Cruz sent his wife a letter on her way out of town. According to our information, Ms. Cruz thoughtfully included a number of compromising photographs."

Rosen blew air across the top of his coffee. "You're right, Agent Westerman. That's worse. Take it from a man who's been thusly served. What else?"

Westerman took a deep breath. "So we've got our mystery, sir. The letters come from the Prineville, Oregon, post office. We've got a clerk who remembers seeing the letters and a match on the postmark machine. Quantico ran the DNA on the stamps, compared it to what we got from Driver's prison blood samples. It's either a mother or a father or a sibling. Since the father's dead and he's an only child . . ."

Rosen's eyes were hooded. His nose was in the coffee cup.

"That leaves the mother. It's her. Five hundred million to one, Quantico says. No doubt about it."

"So?" he said again.

"So she's got somebody in Prineville mailing them for her."

"Which tells you what?"

"Which tells me we need another field of inquiry if we're going to figure out where Driver's headed."

A couple more sips of coffee jogged something in Rosen's mind. "How long have the letters been coming from Pineville?"

"Prineville," she corrected. "Hang on." She rummaged around in her briefcase and came out with a sheaf of papers, used her thumb and forefinger to move through the pile backward. "Since ninety-seven," she said. "Before that she was like a camp follower. Hawaii, San Diego, Bangor, Washington, Bremerton, Washington, Long Beach, California. Wherever her son was stationed, that's where she moved to."

"Some devotion."

Westerman raised her eyebrows in agreement. "I guess."

"Almost scary."

When Westerman didn't disagree, Rosen posed a question. "Why's a senior citizen like his mother need a mail blind?" He was almost talking to himself. "I mean it's not like they're hard to organize. We do it all the time for witnesses, for undercover officers stuff like that. Why does somebody's mother need one?"

"No idea," Westerman admitted.

"And who showed her how to do it?"

Because she hated admitting she didn't know, Westerman kept silent.

"Shit," said Rosen, slamming the cup down hard enough to send coffee spilling out over the rim. "What year was it Corso wrote the book about Driver?"

Westerman pulled yet another file from her briefcase. Then another and a third.

"Ninety-seven," she said. She looked over at Rosen, who was cleaning up his mess with paper napkins. "So you're thinking . . ."

"Find Mr. Corso," he said. "Don't pick him up or anything. Just find him. I'll bet dollars to donuts Corso—"

He never got it all the way out. His pager went off. He pulled the unit from his belt, eyeballed the text message, then pulled his cell phone from his inside jacket pocket.

"Rosen here," he said after speed dialing. He listened for the better part of two minutes, said, "You're sure," and listened again before hanging up.

"We've got two officer fatalities. Southern Utah. A pair of Nevada Staties who were transporting those Texas teenagers . . ."

"Gibbs and Spearbeck?"

"Yeah. Both cops shot dead at a rest area in Utah. Gibbs and Spearbeck conspicuously missing."

As if that weren't bad enough, she could tell there was more. "And?"

"And Clarence Kehoe's thumbprint was found on both the sink and the flush handle in the men's restroom."

Her mouth hung open. She didn't care. "They're sure?"

"Hundred percent."

• • •

Corso used his napkin to wipe his lips. He thought about throwing it on top of his plate but remembered where he was and changed his mind. Instead, he folded it twice and placed it to the right of his unused coffee cup, all nice and neat-like.

"What flavor was that sorbet again?" Melanie Harris asked.

"Clementine."

"Which is?"

"Darling."

She laughed again. "Really."

"I have no idea. I just ordered it so you'd think I was sophisticated."

"You *are* sophisticated."

"Comes from spending lots of other people's money."

She staged a mock toast with her decaf coffee. "To life's little joys."

"That's my acid test for when something is way too expensive," Corso said.

"What's that?"

"When my publisher is paying for it, and I *still* object to the price."

She nodded knowingly. "I take it you didn't grow up with things like clementine sorbet."

His turn to laugh. "I grew up in Georgia. Macaroni-and-cheese was considered haute cuisine where I came from. What about you?"

"I'm meat-and-potatoes Michigan. The closer to Sunday you get the better the cut of meat. That's about as fancy as it got."

Corso raised the last of his aperitif. "We've come a long way, baby."

Her eyes suddenly grew serious. She made no move to join his toast. "For the better you think?"

He shrugged. "Sometimes I wonder."

They'd allowed two hours between the time they'd checked in and when they'd agreed to meet for dinner. The results were impressive. Melanie had come up with a particularly striking version of what women generally refer to as a "little black dress." Either she'd called in the show's makeup department or the people from the spa had spent the past couple of hours in her room. Whatever . . . she was easily the best-looking woman in a room full of good-looking women.

Corso's situation had been more dire. The clothes he'd arrived in had survived a prison riot, a shoot-out, a cross-country flight to avoid prosecution and a couple of nights as pajamas. Oscar, the concierge, had assured Corso he'd get everything dry-cleaned and shipped back to Seattle. In the meantime, he sent one of his minions down to Fashion Square with Corso's measurements in hand. A hour and a half and three grand later, Corso was outfitted with a black silk shirt, a black cashmere blazer and a nice pair of gray slacks suitable for dinner at Mary Elaine's. For occasions less formal, Oscar had provided a couple pair of jeans and two black silk T-shirts. Apparently, Oscar also enjoyed spending other people's money.

Corso surveyed her disconsolate face. "Something I said?" he inquired.

She waved him off. "I'm a little off my feed lately."

"You're on every channel. How bad can it be?"

"I meant personally," she said, staring down into her coffee.

Silence settled over the table like a cloak. Across the room, a well-turned-out older couple had recognized Melanie. They'd found their cell phone and were in the process of sharing their Hollywood moment with somebody more distant and thus less fortunate than themselves.

Her eyes found his. "You're not going to ask me, are you?"

"If you want to tell me, you will."

He watched in silence as she had a conversation with herself. She gave him a wan smile and pushed back her chair. "You're right," was all she said.

She tried again and managed a better smile the second time around. "This was lovely. Thanks for sharing it with me."

"Thanks for the rescue."

"My pleasure," she assured him.

He looked around for the waiter.

"I already took care of the check," she said.

"Other people's money again."

"Is there any other kind?"

He reached for her elbow. She let him take it as they wound their way back to the restaurant entrance and out into the elegant lobby.

"You must be bushed," she said.

"It's been an interesting few days," Corso hedged.

They stammered their good-byes and plans to meet for breakfast in the morning with all the smooth assurance of backward seventh graders.

She could feel his eyes on her all the way down the hall to her room. Before stepping inside, she snuck a peek. He made no attempt to hide his gaze. She gave him a little "toodles" wave goodbye with her fingers. He smiled, then turned and walked out of sight.

31

She'd been talking for two hours. Her life story. Pretty much from birth to the present, but not necessarily in that order. Heidi was not what you'd call a linear thinker. She tended to go off on tangents so long and complicated as to make the listener altogether forget what the original story line had been. The minute she'd started, Harry had pulled his jacket around his ears and scrunched down in the seat. Kehoe had lasted a half hour before leaning his head against the window and eventually beginning to snore.

"So anyway, when I first met Harry it was down at the bowling alley. Sharps Lanes they call it. Anyway, I used to bowl on Thursday afternoons with the girls from my church group. Harry had him a job there behind the counter. I mean it wasn't like love at first sight or nothing. Heck . . . I didn't think much of him at all when I first met him. I thought he was all stuck-up on himself. The way he stood back there passin' out shoes and flirtin' with all the girls. But then later on I come to see how he had a pure heart and I could see through that silly James Dean thing he had going on about himself. And then he bought me that box of chocolates. You know the kind in the gold box where they got all the names of the candies listed on the inside of the cover so's you'll know what it is you're getting ahead of time and won't taste somethin' you don't like."

"Give 'em a break, darlin'," Harry growled from the backseat.

"It wasn't like we had anything to do or anyplace to go. I mean I was livin' with my daddy and Harry was livin' with his aunt. We didn't have nothin' to do but hang around town. Maybe go over to Redlands to the movies once in a while whenever we could scrounge up a ride. So anyway, that's when we decided to make us a place of our own. Harry knew this little patch of woods between the highway and the railroad grade. Said he used to play there as a kid and that nobody ever went there so's we could be pretty sure of being left alone. Harry built us this little tree house. You know, up off the ground so's we could keep away from the bugs and the critters . . . someplace we could, you know, like be alone." She swallowed and took a deep breath. "I don't want you thinkin' bad about me, mister. I'm not a bad girl or nothing. Harry was my first . . . you know, boy my age." She hesitated. "I mean, you know, I let Wesley Miles put his finger in it back in the seventh grade and I mean did we *ever* get in trouble for that. You'da thought the world come to an end the way everybody carried on." She shook her head. "Never for the life of me could figure out why Wesley would tell his mama about a thing like that.

"Anyway, after Harry got promoted to assistant manager, he figured it was time to ask my daddy about getting married." She made a clucking noise. "Isn't like I didn't know what was gonna happen. I told Harry straight off my daddy wasn't gonna to be listenin' to anything like that. I mean . . . who was gonna take care of him if I was gone? Who was gonna do the cookin' and the cleanin'? Who was gonna . . ."

A wavy red line appeared on the near horizon.

"What in hell is that?" Driver asked.

Heidi closed her mouth with a snap.

Kehoe used the power lever on the seat to push himself upright. "A wreck maybe," Kehoe said after rubbing his eyes. He pointed up toward the blanket of clouds overhead. In the distance, just over the rise, pulsing lights could be seen bouncing off the dark clouds. Light bar lights. Red and blue and yellow.

Another quarter mile and they found themselves queued up behind a battered red Toyota Corolla, sporting a peeling Bush/Cheney sticker. Maybe ten cars separated them from seeing what was going on over the crest of the hill.

"I don't like it," Driver said.

Kehoe reached beneath the passenger seat and pulled out a tattered Rand McNally atlas they'd found earlier in the day. Kehoe snapped on the overhead light and found the page he was looking for. "We're comin up on the junction of eighty-three where we was gonna head north again," he said. "Ain't nothin' else around here, Captainman, less we wanna get out on one of these secondary roads." He used his fingernail to trace on the page. The cars in front moved up. Driver followed suit.

A pair of headlights bobbed over the rise and began coming their way. Driver pushed open the door and stepped out into the oncoming lane of traffic. The approaching pickup slowed and then, when it became obvious Driver wasn't going to step aside, braked to a stop.

Driver walked over to the window. "What's going on up there?" he asked. The driver leaned out the truck window wearing a green John Deere baseball cap.

"State cops got them a roadblock up there at the junction of eighty-three," the guy said. "Looking for a bunch of escaped convicts."

"No kidding," Driver said.

"No need to get yourself in a lather. They'll get you through pretty quick."

Driver took the hint and stepped out of the way. "Thanks," he said.

"Don't mention it."

Driver got back into the Mercedes and buckled himself in. Harry was alert now, sitting up and patting at his hair.

"What did he say?" Kehoe asked.

"It's a roadblock. Looking for us."

Another truck passed, going in the opposite direction, this one full of bales of hay. The line of cars in front of the Mercedes had moved up three or four car lengths. The driver behind them tooted his horn. Kehoe growled at the sound.

Driver spun the steering wheel to the left, going as far as he could without running into the ditch, then backed up and spun the wheel a second time, completing the one-eighty with only inches to spare.

"Somebody sure as hell gonna tell the heat we pulled a uey." Kehoe offered. "They gonna send somebody out to find out why."

"Nothing we can do about that," Driver said. "Check that map of yours and see how soon we can get off this road."

Driver took it easy for as long as they were in sight, then put the pedal to the metal, sending the big car careening down the two-lane road at nearly eighty. They passed the truck with the hay within the first mile or so. The other truck had disappeared. Probably turned up one of the many driveways and farm access roads they were passing at warp speed. " 'Nother mile or so," Kehoe said. "On your left. Provisionary road two twenty-nine. Looks like it winds through the mountains and runs into a pretty good-sized little town namea Drake about twenty miles north of here. Looks like maybe it ain't paved all the way."

"We'll have to take our chances," Driver said.

Kehoe pointed. "There," he said.

Driver gave the brakes all he had. Miraculously, they didn't lock up and skid. He fishtailed the Mercedes ninety degrees to the left, then used the accelerator to straighten the car out. First thing he did after regaining control was to turn off the lights.

They were tearing up a one-lane road toward a pair of jagged buttes looming in the near distance. "Got cop lights on the highway," Kehoe announced.

Driver kept his eyes on the road. "Let me know if they come this way."

Kehoe unsnapped his seat belt and turned partway in the seat. "Comin' up on the turn," he said. "Comin' . . . comin' . . . he's past. He thinks we went the other way."

Driver slowed the car but left the lights off. "Sooner or later he's gonna figure it out," he said. "We need to make it to the highway before it gets light."

The road narrowed as it began to ascend a series of low hills. Every half mile or so little graveled turnouts allowed drivers just enough room to pass. The high desert of the valley gave way to the layered sediment of an ancient seabed. The road seemed to sink beneath the layers of shale and limestone until they were driving along a series of boulder-strewn switchbacks, winding back and forth across the face of the steep butte; finally, after negotiating a particularly steep section of road, they crested the valley, very nearly becoming airborne as the car slammed back to earth just in time to take the sharp left necessary to prevent crashing into the canyon wall.

And then they were headed down again, knifing back and forth across the face of the canyon, braking for corners so narrow and steep, the car had nearly to be brought to a halt at the apex of each turn. Driver accelerated and snapped on the lights.

Mule deer. Three of them standing rigid in the road. Mesmerized by the furious glow of the headlights. Never so much as twitching as the Mercedes plowed into them.

The steering wheel jerked violently to the left. Driver hung on, trying to maintain control. The right side of the windshield shattered in the same instant the driver's airbag blew out of the steering column, pushing Driver back in the seat and preventing him from seeing the road.

Driver forearmed the airbag flat just in time to see the car throw its right headlight into the canyon wall. The impact shook loose everything in the car. Harry saw it coming, got his arms up in front of his face and let the seat belt do its job.

Heidi, however, wasn't strapped in. The impact sent her catapulting forward, crashing into the back of the driver's seat with sufficient force to partially separate her right shoulder. She came to rest on the floor behind the driver's seat, curled up in a ball, moaning as she checked herself for blood.

Driver's eyes rolled across the wrinkled hood and the dead doe, then came to rest on a bulge in the passenger-side windshield. About the size of a dinner plate, all cracked and looking like somebody tried to force something hard and round through the safety glass from the inside. Something with blood.

And then he knew. As he moved his eyes farther right, he wasn't surprised by what he saw. Kehoe was slumped in a heap. His body collapsed on the seat with his legs folded beneath him, his shoulders twitching, his mouth agape and full of blood. Although it was hard to tell in the near darkness, the silhouette of his head seemed, at one point, to lose its arc, as if perhaps it had been pushed in.

Driver turned the key. The grind of the starter announced that the Mercedes was still running. He threw it into reverse and gave it some gas. The twisted sheet metal popped and groaned as it came away from the boulder. He pulled left as far as he could go, jammed the lever into park and got out of the car, leaving the door hanging open.

One headlight had been completely destroyed, the other pointed up into the sky as if searching for satellites or something. The passenger door had been warped by the crash. It took two hands and every bit of strength Driver could muster to pull it open. If he hadn't been there to get his arms under him in time, Kehoe would have fallen out onto the ground.

Carefully, he took Kehoe beneath the arms and pulled him out onto the road. The sheer volume of blood made it impossible to tell exactly how bad the damage was. He carefully set Kehoe's head down and started to rise. Kehoe grabbed onto his forearm with a surprisingly powerful grip. He opened his good eye and Driver could tell he was conscious and knew what was going on. He wanted to know. Driver could tell.

"Bad," Driver said. "It's real bad." He removed Kehoe's hand from his forearm. "Don't move," Driver told him. "I'll be right back."

He moved quickly. Retracing his steps back around the front of the car, pulling the keys from the ignition, then continuing on to the trunk, where he gathered a handful of towels together and started back toward Kehoe.

Harry was out of the car by then, standing on the far side of Kehoe with his hands behind his back. "Help your girlfriend," Driver told Harry. Driver knelt at Kehoe's side, slipping a folded towel beneath his head. Harry still hadn't moved.

Driver picked up a clean towel and began to daub at the blood, trying to wipe away enough to be able to see the wound. He didn't get far before Harry's voice hijacked his attention. "Get up," Harry said.

Driver looked up to find Harry pointing Kehoe's shiny Colt revolver at his head. Kehoe grabbed his arm again. Stronger this time. Driver looked down into his eye expecting to see a man using the last of his strength in a death grip. Instead, in that single blue eye, he saw Cutter Kehoe in all of his murderous rage. Felt Kehoe release his arm. Saw the look in his eye. Watched Kehoe slip his hand down into his pocket and, in that instant, he knew exactly what to do.

Driver got to his feet and began to mosey backward, away from Kehoe and Harry. It worked. Harry followed along, stepping over Kehoe. Must not have had much faith in his marksmanship. Wanted to shoot at point-blank range.

Heidi was out of the car now, holding one arm across her chest. She looked from Harry to Driver and back. "Honey . . . you sure you wanna—"

"Shut up," he said and pulled back the hammer. A smile crossed his full lips. He aimed down the barrel at Driver. "*Adios,* motherfucker," he said.

And then Kehoe reached up and did what he did best, he cut him, hard and deep across the back of the leg with that awful boning knife of his, severing the artery and the tendon both, dropping him to one knee in the road like a puppet with a broken string.

Harry emitted a high-pitched squeal as he pivoted on his knee, pointed the revolver and shot Kehoe in the face. And then again and a third time, before toppling over on his side in the road, rocking back and forth in pain.

Driver stepped around the back of the car, keeping the trunk between him and Harry. He watched as Heidi ran around the front and knelt at Harry's side. The river of blood pouring out of Harry's leg told her all she needed to know. "Oh baby," she said. "You're hurt bad. We gotta stop the blood . . . oh baby . . ."

She lifted his head and put it in her lap. Driver followed her footsteps around the front of the car, She was stroking Harry's hair when Driver reached down and plucked the gun from his fingers. He weighed it in his hand for a moment, then heaved it as far out into the barren field as he was able. When he looked down at the ground, Harry was a whiter shade of pale, looking into Heidi's big blue eyes and mouthing silent words.

"You're bleeding out, kid. You got something to say to your girl, now's the time for it," Driver said.

Overhead, the clouds were on the march; shaded and scattered, they moved westward across the night sky like circus elephants joined trunk to tail. To the north, the lights of a town twinkled from the valley floor below.

Harry died without a final word. His lower lip trembled as he sought to speak, then he was gone, lying there in the road with his hair all nice and neat in Heidi's opulent lap.

"Never said a word," Heidi said, her face darkening. "After all we been through that son of a bitch never said a word to me. I can't believe it. Not a single word."

"I'm guessing most people die without saying anything," Driver said. "I've always figured that 'famous last words' stuff was made up by other people afterward. Something to make the whole thing seem more momentous than it really was."

She pulled herself away, letting Harry's head drop to the road with a *thunk* not unlike the sound of a melon on a concrete floor. She scrambled to her feet, dusted off her hands and looked down at Kehoe.

"Sorry about your friend," she said.

Driver shrugged. "The Cutter went out like he would have wanted to," he said.

"Harry always said he was gonna die in bed with his boots on."

Driver looked down at Harry's twisted body. "I guess he was half-right anyway."

Driver wrapped the remains of Kehoe's head in a clean towel, tied the ends in knots so it would stay in place, then picked the body up in his arms, maneuvering it into the backseat of the Mercedes, where he laid him out with great care, before straightening up and returning the back of the passenger seat to the upright position.

"What about him," she said, pointing down at Harry's remains.

Driver reached down and put a finger through one of Harry's belt loops. He lifted hard, turning him over, setting the body to rolling down the incline into the overgrown ditch, where he slipped among the thick weeds and disappeared from view.

When she looked up again, Driver had the black automatic in his right hand.

"Oh please, mister," she stammered. "I can . . . oh God I . . ."

"Looks like your time isn't here yet. Like maybe you get to be more than just protein. Like maybe some of you goes on from here."

"You can just leave me here . . . uh . . . you know, I don't even know your name."

He pointed the gun at her head. She wet her pants, then her shoes, then the road.

He snapped the safety on and returned the gun to his waistband. "You can stay here or you can come along. It doesn't matter to me," he said. "It's not my place to interfere with the river."

She was already in the car with the door closed by the time Driver dropped the transmission into drive and started down the hill. They moved slowly, running with the lights out and the radio off. Took fifteen minutes before the road leveled out a bit. All the way down to where they could make out a pair of church steeples at the far end of the town.

Driver braked the car to a stop. He pointed out over the damaged right fender.

"You see that gate there? " he asked.

"Yeah," she said.

"Open it up," he said.

Took her two tries to shoulder open the door enough for her to squeeze out. As soon as he moved the pole-and-barbed-wire gate aside, Driver rolled the Mercedes through. She watched as he headed across the field toward the pond on the far side.

One of those man-made farmer's ponds. A good week's work with a bulldozer. Probably full of bass. The near end had a little wooden dock, with a two-by-four ladder running down into the water. Something maybe you could dive off in the summertime. Up at the far end, a thinning grove of willows leaned over the water like supplicants.

Driver parked the car thirty yards uphill from the center of the pond. He lowered the windows to half-mast, turned off the engine and set the emergency brake. From the trunk he retrieved the pair of Nike bags and set them on the ground behind the car, before returning to the driver's side, releasing the emergency brake and closing the door, as the car began to move forward, slowly at first, then gaining momentum as gravity pulled it toward sea level.

The Mercedes hit the water with a splash. Moving easily as the water covered the hood and started rushing through the windows. Then it stopped. Three-quarters of the way into the pond. Hung up on some subterranean obstruction with its ass sticking up in the air. Driver cursed. He walked uphill and picked up the bags. As he began to walk off, the big car shivered and seemed to lower its head as it began to move again, more slowly now, as if it wanted to enjoy the view for as long as possible, until, finally, after what seemed like an eternity, it slipped beneath the brackish water and vanished.

"What now?" she asked as she latched the gate back into place.

"Now we walk," he said.

32

"You want to do the honors, this morning?" Rosen asked.

Special Agent Westerman blanched. "Me?"

"No time like the present," he said with a smile.

"I haven't been briefed."

"You don't need to be briefed. We're not telling them anything."

She laughed and flicked a glance in Rosen's direction. Half to see if he was kidding, half to get another feel for where he was coming from. For the past couple of days, she'd had an inkling that Rosen was working his way up to hitting on her, then she'd had second thoughts, wondering if perhaps her misgivings were nothing more than a girlish interpretation of an otherwise purely professional situation. As one of her favorite adages was "when in doubt, trust your instincts," she figured she'd go with the inklings.

The offer to let her do the press conference added another straw to her burgeoning suspicions. Agents went entire careers without ever getting their faces on TV, let alone briefing the press on anything as lurid as escaped convicts and multiple police officer murders. Even better, these weren't the type of fugitives who were going to lose themselves in the south of France. Yahoos like these got caught or killed in fairly short order, making this the kind of case where her face and name would be associated with a positive outcome. No doubt about it, opportunity was rapping its knuckles on her door. As decisions went, this was strictly a no-brainer.

"What are we telling them?" she asked.

From the corner of her eye, she saw a come-and-go smile cross his lips.

Rosen removed a single sheet of folded paper from the inside pocket of his suit jacket. He handed it to Westerman, then stood with his arms folded across his chest for the ten seconds it took her to read the three short paragraphs.

"That's it?" she said.

Rosen stepped over and looked at the paper in her hand. He pointed at the first paragraph. "Introduce yourself, and then just run over the facts for them. Two officers down at Utah rest area. They were transporting Harry Gibbs and Heidi Anne Spearbeck. Yadda yadda. Kehoe's fingerprints at the scene. We're assuming they're together, but probably not for long. The officers' names are being withheld pending notification of next of kin. Subjects are considered to be armed and extremely dangerous."

He leaned in closer, pointing to the second paragraph, brushing his shoulder against hers. "We're here in Salt Lake City working with the Utah State Police, in conjunction with the local Bureau office." He rolled his wrist over the top of itself as if to say "and so forth." "Nationwide manhunt. Judging from the direction they've been moving thus far and the capital crimes they've committed along the way, we're assuming they're trying to make for the Canadian border, as Canada has a long history of refusing to return anyone facing the death penalty."

"Is that what we believe?"

"Not necessarily."

"You think Driver's headed for his mother."

"Yes," he said. "I'm sure of it."

"Why?"

"Because I saw her during his trial. I was Bureau liaison to King County." He anticipated her question. "Driver was a federal employee, so the situation required a federal presence. By the time it was over she'd been cited for contempt, carried out of the building several times and eventually was no longer allowed in the courtroom at all. She took a swing at a witness. She spit on reporters." He leaned in even closer. "Blood may be thicker than water, but that lady's support of her son was way over the top." He shook his head. "Maybe it's got something to do with the father walking out on them or something, but there's a bond between those two that's positively . . ." He searched for a word. ". . . positively unhealthy," he said finally.

"You mean like . . . ?"

"Let's leave it at that," he said.

She was relieved. Others would have taken the opportunity to delve into the subject. His refusal gave her pause to wonder about her earlier suspicions.

"What about Corso?" he wanted to know.

"He left the Phoenix office in a motor home with Melanie Harris . . . you know, the host of that TV show *American Manhunt.*"

He nodded that he knew.

"We've located the motor home in Scottsdale. They're both registered at the Phoenician Resort. I should have word within the next half hour or so."

He raised his eyebrows. "A tryst?"

"Separate rooms. In which they slept separately."

He seemed disappointed. "Let's do it," he said.

● ● ●

"What happened to your hand?"

"And you'd been doing so well," Corso said. "Just chatting along. Not running your reporter number on me at all."

"It's in the blood," Melanie said with a laugh.

"What say you keep it up."

"But I've got the number one interview in America sitting right across from me slurping coffee. How could I resist?"

"Do us both a favor. Resist."

As she laughed again, the warm desert breeze lifted her hair, illuminating the highlights. The double French doors, separating the private balcony from the main dining room, eased open, allowing the buzz of muted conversations to wash outside. Corso stifled a frown. One of the joys of places like the Phoenician was that the staff generally had impeccable timing, arriving when they were needed but otherwise fading into the background. The waiter had peeked out five minutes ago. Again now was too much.

Wasn't the waiter though. It was Oscar, the concierge. Oscar was Swiss and had mastered the art of patrician disinterest. Today, however, he looked a bit nonplussed. He nodded politely at each of them, then closed the doors behind him.

"You have . . . er . . . some guests, Mr. Corso."

"Guests?"

"Official guests."

"Official as in badges?"

"Exactly, sir." Before Corso could ask, he said. "FBI, sir."

"How many?"

"Eight, ten, a dozen. Perhaps more. They're blighting the lobby in those dreadful suits. They're waiting in your rooms for both of you. They've also let themselves into Ms. Harris's recreational vehicle." His tone implied disapproval of such recreation even more than FBI tailors.

Corso thought it over. "As a citizen and a taxpayer I believe a person should assist our law enforcement agencies in any way possible, don't you, Oscar?"

"Certainly, sir."

"To the extent that your research among the staff has revealed that I left early this morning."

"Yes sir."

"Asking that you forward my meager belongings to the usual Seattle address."

"And the young lady?" Oscar inquired.

"Hopefully, Oscar, the young lady is going to do what she does best."

"Very good, sir," he said with a short bow. "Uh . . . by the by, sir, it might be best if you exited via the kitchen. I'll inform Fritz. There will be no problem."

"Thank you, Oscar. As usual, my visit here has been a pleasure."

"I will inform the manager, sir."

Corso waited for the soft sound of the doors latching.

"You want that interview?" Corso asked. When she didn't answer immediately, he went on. "The interview all America has been waiting for. The man on the inside of the prison break. The perfect closer for this Arizona sojourn you've been on."

"Why do I get the feeling this isn't going to be free."

"Nothing's free."

"What do you want?"

"I want you to get me out of here."

She looked at him as if he'd lost his mind. "You heard the man. They're waiting in my trailer."

"So, go to the trailer. Tell them we had dinner last night, then said good-bye. You've got no idea where I am right now and what are they doing in your trailer without a warrant anyway. Get huffy with them. They'll leave in a heartbeat."

"And then?"

"Leave the door unlocked. They'll have to consult. I'll get in while they're figuring out what to do next."

"What if they see you sneaking in?"

"Then I get a ride downtown. And you go on your way."

"Why don't you just see what it is they want?"

"They had me in custody all day yesterday. This is something new. With this kind of manpower expenditure, whatever it is can't be good."

"They'll follow us."

"Yes, they will," Corso said. "For a while." He paused. "About the time you get on the freeway and start following the signs to L.A., they're gonna lose interest in a big hurry. Six hours of desert isn't what they've got in mind."

"And then what?"

"And then you have me all to yourself, all the way to L.A."

"And you'll answer my questions? Not give me that snotty stuff you usually throw at the press."

He held up two fingers. "Scout's honor."

She grabbed his fingers. "You're the least likely Boy Scout on the planet."

He shrugged. Left his fingers locked in hers. "What do you say?"

She didn't hesitate. "It's a deal," she said, letting go of his hand.

Corso got to his feet. "I'll meet you outside."

Melanie took a last sip of her coffee and stood up. "At some point, I'm going to need to get some video."

"When we get to L.A. I promise."

"Ooooh," she mocked. "I can't believe it. That elusive heart-throb, Frank Corso, baring his soul on *American Manhunt*. We'll pull a twenty share."

"You don't know how disappointing it is to hear my charms reduced to mere numbers."

She laughed again. "Somehow, Mr. Corso, I think you'll get over it."

Corso threw twenty bucks on the table for the waiter and opened door on the right.

Melanie passed by close enough for him to smell her scent. Some version of Chanel. He was sure of it. Coco maybe.

She never looked back as she sashayed across the dining room, turning heads all the way, and disappeared from view.

Corso turned left and walked quickly through the door to the kitchen. A pink-cheeked specimen in a spotless white uniform nodded politely and pointed the way. Corso returned the nod and followed the finger through the bustling kitchen, out past the freezers to the loading dock and finally to the staff parking lot behind the main building.

By the time he made his way to where they'd parked the trailer, the fireworks were mostly over. Melanie was standing in the doorway hands on hips. Corso couldn't hear what was being said, but the body language told him the FBI agents were in full apology mode. Corso watched from behind a palm tree, forty yards away as they made their way around the back of the RV and disappeared.

He didn't hesitate. The minute they were out of view, he went skipping through the shrubbery and tropical flowers, moving quickly from tree to tree. Melanie saw him coming and stepped aside. He jumped up and stayed low, duck-walking beneath the windows all the way to the back. She closed the door and locked it. They waited.

Corso sat on the floor with his back against the bathroom door. Melanie bent over and peered out the side window. "They're sitting in a burgundy Ford about four rows down," she announced. "One of them's talking into his collar."

"Let's go," Corso said.

Melanie walked up front and belted herself into the driver's seat.

"L.A., here we come," she said.

33

On the TV a man in a white apron was showing folks how to stick a turkey into some kinda little oven that collected the grease in the bottom as it turned the bird round and round. "Just set it and forget it," he kept saying every time he stuffed something else into the contraption. Got the audience to shout it along with him too. Never seen anybody so damn happy about cookin' something. Guy had a grin on him, you'd think he won the damn lottery or something.

Heidi wished she could change the channel, maybe find some cartoons, except she couldn't be sure whether what'shisname was watching or not. He was sure enough staring at the screen, but with this guy that didn't necessarily mean he was taking any of it in. Whatever his name was had his own inner TV set he looked at most of the time. Rolled his eyes back into his head and went off to wherever the hell it was he went to. All he did was sit there and play with his guns. Taking them apart and putting them together over and over. Didn't have to look at them neither. He could do it from memory and the feel in his hands. Scary.

She'd tried her best to get his attention. Washed out her pissy undies and dress in the sink, then threw 'em on the radiator to dry.

She'd spent the past four hours parading around the motel room in a towel not much bigger than a washcloth and he never so much as twitched an eyeball in her direction. First man she ever met wasn't the least bit interested in seeing her naked. If he hadn't been so damned crazy it would have hurt her feelings for sure.

She was trying to decide whether to discard the towel altogether, change the channel, or more likely, both, when the channel up and changed itself to a public service bulletin. Blond-haired woman standing behind one of those wooden speech-making things. Half a dozen men in suits stood behind her on the platform. The graphic read FBI SPECIAL AGENT LINDA WESTERMAN.

She was goin' on about how the various cops were all cooperating together like one big happy family when the pictures appeared at the bottom of the screen. Harry and her and Kehoe and Captainman, right there on the TV screen big as life. She hated her picture. Made her look like she had no upper lip. His picture didn't look much like him neither, but if you used a little imagination, you could see him in it. The label said his name was Timothy Driver. Used to be some kinda Trident submarine captain. Said he was sentenced to double forever for offing his wife and her lover nine years ago. Said he was armed and dangerous. She almost laughed out loud. Armed and dangerous? Hell . . . they didn't know the half of it.

Driver set the shotgun on the bed, felt around and came up with the remote control and turned up the volume. The Westerman woman said they figured the fugitives . . . that's what she called them, fugitives . . . were headed for Canada 'cause Canada wouldn't send nobody back to the U.S. to be executed. Asked everybody to be on the lookout and to call the number at the bottom of the screen if they had anything to report. And that was that. Next thing you know she's legging it off the stage and they're back with that grinning yahoo stuffing a pork roast into that same dumb-ass machine.

"When it gets dark, I'll be leaving," he said.

The words felt like somebody dragged a rusty nail down her spine. She made like she didn't understand. "You mean like us . . . right?"

"I have to go alone. It's my calling."

"Oh please," she said quickly. "Don't leave me alone. I'm not good about being left alone. I've got issues."

"We're born alone. We die alone," he said solemnly.

"But not here . . . not now," she said. "Right?"

When he didn't answer, she leaned closer to him, allowing the top of the towel to fall into her lap. For the first time, he dropped his gaze from her face and looked at her breasts. She watched his Adam's apple bob up and down . . . suppressed a smile. "My mama left us when I was five. Her name was Rose and she was very beautiful. School sent me to counseling over it. Everybody said it wasn't my fault. Said it was between her and my daddy. Wasn't nothing I coulda done about it." She shrugged. "It's probably true," she said. "For somebody somewhere's else." She paused and looked him in the eye for the first time. His eyes were black and cold as a pair of rivets. "For me though . . . I still figure it musta been something I done . . . or something I shoulda done and that maybe . . . if one little thing had been different . . . if maybe we hadn't found just one thing we coulda done to make her life a little better . . . then you know maybe she woulda stayed."

His steel gaze seemed to bore a hole right through her skull. Almost against her will, she began talking. "You know . . . like a short story I read back in high school, where they had like a time machine. And about these white hunter guys who paid a lot of money to go on a safari back to dinosaur times. Except they had to be careful not to touch anything while they were back in the past lest . . . you know . . . they screw things up or something." She became more animated, waving her hands around as she spoke. "And like somebody, by mistake, steps on a butterfly . . . just like one tiny butterfly . . . and when they get back everything is different . . . different government . . . different everything . . . all because of just one little butterfly that got stepped on way back when."

He was looking at her now. His gaze was empty and pitiless.

"You know what I'm talking about?" she asked. "I'm talking about abandonment issues here."

"You can't mess with the river," he said in a low voice. "The river goes on with you or without you. It doesn't care. It just goes on being a river."

"Not rivers, man . . . butterflies."

"It's the same," he said. "Everything's on its way back to where it came from. Some of it makes it all the way to the ocean. Some of it falls along the way."

She jumped to her feet and stamped a foot. The violent movement sent the towel to the floor. She felt a rush of blood in her cheeks. Then watched the ghost of desire wash across his face. She squared her shoulders and took a step forward, nearly putting her pubis in his face. "You can't just leave me here," she whined in her best little girl voice. "I don't even know where we are." She edged even closer. "I could make things good for you," she whispered. "Really I . . ." For a moment, it seemed as if he was reaching for her. As if he might plant a kiss right in the middle of her thatch. She shivered at the thought. Instead, he picked the towel from the floor.

"Cover yourself," he said.

34

Melanie Harris checked the side mirror again and smiled. The burgundy Ford Taurus had been hanging three or four cars back ever since they'd left Scottsdale half an hour before. Now, the turn signal was on. She watched in the mirror as they motored up the exit ramp, made a couple of left turns and headed back the way they'd come.

"Looks like you were right," she said. "Our federal friends seem to have had enough of our company."

Corso was sitting on the floor at the rear of the coach. He'd removed his black leather jacket and was leaning back against the bathroom door, one long leg up, the other stretched out along the floor. She watched as he got to his feet, flicking her attention back and forth between the mirror and the road ahead as he made his way to the passenger seat, pushed it all the way back to accommodate his long legs and strapped himself in. "Six-hour jaunts across the desert aren't in the federal job description," he said.

"They're not generally part of mine either. I always fly back home when we do a remote."

"But for a good story . . ." He let it hang.

"Neither rain nor snow nor dead of night . . ."

Yesterday's clouds had scattered, leaving the sky a shade of azure blue only seen in *Arizona Highways* magazine.

"You want anything?" she asked.

He gave her a shy smile. "Like what?"

"Like water or pop."

"I'm good."

She returned the smile. "If you change your mind, feel free to help yourself from the fridge."

"Thanks," he said.

"So tell me about this guy Timothy Driver."

"Which one? The one I wrote the book about or the one they're chasing all over the place right now?"

She thought it over. "The one you wrote the book about."

Corso laid it out for her. Took him fifteen minutes to come up with everything he could remember about Driver's past. Finally, he took a deep breath, and said, "*That* Tim Driver was a good man who found himself in a bad situation. After twenty years of self-discipline and single-minded service to his country, he came home one day and found himself confronted with something completely outside his realm. Something there was no manual for. The idea that somebody could break their word to him like that. That somebody he loved could be mixing it up with somebody else in his own bed . . . it just wasn't something he was prepared to deal with."

"Lotta people catch their spouses flying united and don't kill anybody."

"Most of them don't live by the same code of honor he did. We're talking about a guy who had a couple of dozen nuclear weapons at his disposal. For him it was just the worst kind of betrayal imaginable. I think maybe it's somehow tied in to the fact that his father deserted the family when he was a little kid. Like maybe the whole thing with his wife was just one straw too many for his psyche."

She checked the mirror and moved over one lane to the left, wheeling the RV around a lumbering flatbed truck awash in rusty machine parts.

"What did he want with you?"

Corso laughed. "Believe it or not, I'm still not real clear about that. I think he wanted me to be his Boswell or something. I think he wanted me on hand to document whatever he had in mind for a grand finale." He shrugged off her disbelief. "When he's talking like that he doesn't make a lot of sense to anybody but himself. I think it's what he thought about the whole time he was isolation. I think he tried to keep from going nuts and failed."

"So you think they drove him crazy."

"Either that or he's got some progressive brain disease. Something that overcame him during this last phase of incarceration."

"Or he's got bad genes. The father walked out. You said yourself that his mother was pretty far out there. Maybe he's just the next generation of loony."

"Could be."

"But you don't think so."

"No."

"You blame the state."

"It's not the state. It's the Randall Corporation."

"And you don't approve?"

"It's like you have badly behaved kids, so you give them to the neighbors and move out of town. It's just not right. Privatizing changes everything. Prisoners are suddenly part of the 'profit motive' equation. They lose their rights and become numbers on a board . . . a board with the only number that matters on a line at the bottom."

She threw him a quick look. "Anybody ever suggest you had a self-righteous streak about a yard wide?"

"Just about everybody."

The air inside the camper began to rumble as a herd of

Harley-Davidsons passed them on the left. Fringed and fitted out. Stripped down. In singles and in doubles, they roared past, twenty-five maybe, all decked out in the latest biker gear. Twenty years ago, they would surely have been a band of speed freak commandos, armed and dangerous and ready to rumble. Nowadays they might all be urologists.

"You think they're going let themselves be captured?"

"No way. Not Driver. Not Kehoe. They're not coming in alive."

"Any idea where they're headed?"

"Kehoe's looking to get across the Canadian border. Just in case he gets caught, he figures that's the only way he's going to avoid the death chamber."

"And Driver?"

"Sooner or later, Driver's headed for his mother. I think that's what he means when he's always talking about getting back to where he started."

"The feds can't find his mother," Melanie said. "Turns out she doesn't live where they thought she did."

A minute passed. When she looked over at Corso she found him deep in thought.

"You know that for sure?" he asked finally.

"It's in the info Marty bought from somebody in the prison hierarchy. Her letters had been postmarked from the same little town in Oregon for as long as he's been in Meza Azul. Turns out she doesn't live there though."

"Oregon?"

"Pineville . . . something like that."

"Prineville," he corrected. He chuckled. "Well I'll be damned."

"What am I missing here?"

"At least now I know why the feds were looking so hard for me back in Scottsdale."

"Why's that?"

"They want to know where Driver's mother lives."

Her foot came off the accelerator. The big RV began to slow. "Are you serious?"

He nodded, sat back in the seat and folded his arms across his chest.

Melanie Harris used her turn signal and slid the motor home off the highway and onto the shoulder. She set the parking brake and turned toward Corso.

"They think you know where she is?"

Again he nodded silently. Something in his facial expression alerted her.

"Do you?"

His eyes got all-of-a-sudden cagey. "Do I what?"

"Don't start with me, Corso. You know what I mean. Do you or don't you know where his mother lives?"

"Yeah," he said after a minute.

"How come you know what nobody else knows?"

He shrugged and looked out the side window. "After he got sent to Meza Azul . . . Doris—that's his mother's name, Doris— the press were driving her crazy. She asked me if I knew anybody who could help her disappear for a little while. I turned her on to a guy I know specializes in helping people get lost. He snuck her out of Seattle. Set her up with a new address and a phony ID. Put together a mail drop for her so nobody could find her that way either."

"How long ago was that?"

"Almost seven years."

"And you think she's still where your friend put her?"

"She's still using the mail drop."

"I want to go there," she said instantly.

He raised a hand, waving the idea off. "No way," he said. "She's a very private woman." He sat there shaking his head.

"You promised."

"I didn't promise to go anywhere other than L.A."

"You promised to do everything you could to help me wind up this story." Corso opened his mouth to protest but changed his mind and shut it again. Cars zipped by on the highway. An eighteen-wheeler ripped the air.

"I'm gonna need a map," he said.

"Where are we going?"

He told her.

"Where's that."

"Up in the mountains."

"How far?"

He checked his watch. "We should get there before dark."

35

Special Agent Westerman closed her cell phone with a snap. "I'll be damned," she said with a wry grin. "You were right."

Rosen smiled. "Tell me."

"As soon as the first unit dropped off their tail, lo and behold if Mr. Corso didn't suddenly appear in the passenger seat. They drove another fifty miles down the road, then pulled over. They bought gas and a map of California. One-twelve fifty-nine, on her *American Manhunt* credit card. Harris called her producer in L.A." She sensed his next question. "She wasn't on long enough for us to pick up on the call."

"Pity."

"Then an hour or so and about eighty miles later they get off they freeway at exit one-fifteen, the Mountainview Highway exit, heading up into the Sierras. I don't know where they're headed. but it's sure as heck not L.A."

"Good."

"We've got an electronic transponder on the RV and two units doing ground surveillance. We've also got a pair of units on her producer, who, as of an hour ago, was on his way to LAX."

"Too bad we don't have an ear inside the RV."

"She showed up before they could get it in place."

Rosen nodded his understanding. "Tell them to keep their distance. Make sure they don't get made. With the electronics in place on the RV there's no sense crowding them."

She assured Rosen that she'd relay his message to the agents in the field.

"How'd you know?" she asked. "Is this one of those esoteric things an agent only learns to sense after thirty years in the Bureau?"

He laughed and waved the idea away. "I didn't know," he said. "It was a shot in the dark. Sometimes they pan out, sometimes they don't." He showed his palms. "Better to be lucky than good."

"What now?"

"We wait."

"Be still my heart."

She began to walk around the carpet in tight circles.

"You had lunch?" he asked.

She said she hadn't and kept on walking.

Next time she walked by, he caught her elbow in his hand. "Come on," he said. "We'll spend a little of the Bureau's money."

She stopped her pacing and fixed him with her gaze. She opened her mouth, closed it, and then seemed to have a short discussion with herself before speaking again.

"Agent Rosen," she began.

"Ron," he corrected.

"This may not be politic or even polite, but it's going to be in the way until I get it said."

"In the way of what?" he wanted to know.

"For the past week or so . . . ever since we've been out of town on this Meza Azul business . . . I've had the feeling." She hesitated. Made eye contact. "I've had the feeling that you've been hitting on me." She started to pace but stopped herself. "Maybe I'm making it up. Maybe I'm misinterpreting. If that's the case, then I apologize." She threw her hands in the air. "But I'm not going to feel comfortable until you and I talk about this."

He thrust his hands deep into his pants pockets. She watched as he knit his eyebrows and considered his response.

After a while, he said, "I'd like to tell you the whole thing was a figment of your girlish imagination, Agent Westerman," he began. "I'd like to tell you that . . ." He paused for effect. ". . . but it wouldn't be true." He captured her eyes. "I guess I *have* been hitting on you, in some small childish way," he added. "I want you to understand it wasn't like I expected anything to come of the matter. We both know that's impossible."

She nodded her understanding.

He pulled his hands from his pockets. "I know it sounds foolish," he said. "I think maybe I just wanted to know whether I was still attractive. Whether I could capture the attention of a young woman such as yourself. I hope you'll forgive me for . . ." He searched for a word. ". . . for any indiscretions. . . ."

"There were no indiscretions," she assured him.

"I like to tell myself I survived my recent divorce unscathed." He made a wry face. "I may have to reexamine that particular supposition."

She started to speak, but he cut her off. "I wouldn't blame you one bit for reporting me to my superior. My actions were—"

This time, she interrupted him. "For what? You've never been anything but professional and a gentleman. There's nothing to report. I just didn't want this feeling I had to come between us, either personally or professionally."

Again, he paused to consider.

"Thanks," he said, studying the floor

"That offer of lunch still hold?"

He looked up. Smiled. "You bet."

• • •

"Turn on the interior lights will you?"

Melanie Harris fumbled around on the dash, then the steering column without finding the proper switch. The road ahead was dark, two narrow lanes in each direction, lined with fir and pine trees whose stout alpine limbs had been picked clean by the fierce mountain winds. The road shoulders were marked by long poles, painted orange at the tops, designed to define the edges of the driving surface when everything for miles around was covered with six feet of snow.

"I better watch where I'm going," Melanie said. "Lest we end up in the ditch." She was paying attention, driving with two hands. Giving it all she had.

Corso dropped the map in his lap and began to scan the area above his head. Took him half a minute to find the little sliding rheostat switch that controlled the overhead lights in the cockpit. He pushed it to high and brought the map up close to his face. "What was the last town we went through?" he asked.

"Winthrop . . . if you call that bump in the road a town."

"Yeah . . . well hang onto your hat because Elk Creek is even smaller. Last time I was here, it was a one-building town. Store, gas station and post office all in the same building."

"When were you here?"

"Right before the book came out. I was writing the foreword for it and thought maybe his mother might have something she wanted to add."

"Did she?"

"All she wanted was for me to get the hell off her front porch." He pointed out into the darkness. "There," he said. "See the sign?"

Blue-and-white road sign. Arrow to the left. Elk Creek three miles.

Melanie wheeled the RV around the corner. Two lanes now, one east, one west. Trees folding over the roadway like a cathedral. Through narrow gaps in the greenery, wild snow-covered peaks could be seen in the distance.

Melanie was leaning forward trying to get a better view of the road. She snapped on the high beams, which merely made the trees seem thicker, then snapped them off.

They rode in silence until a dim halo of light appeared in the distance. A minute later they could make out a pair of gas pumps and a red-and-white sign that read CASCADE CAFÉ. Tree limbs brushed the top of the vehicle, as Melanie eased the RV to a stop between the store and the gas pumps. Neon COORS LITE sign in the store window. The simple wood sign above the door read ELK CREEK STORE.

"Seems like they've added a building since I was here," Corso said.

"The march of progress," Melanie offered.

The RV's headlights illuminated a red Chevy Blazer backed into the bushes next to a silver propane tank. Parked along the back edge of the lot was a black Ford pickup truck with tires so big you'd have to be airlifted into the driver's seat. Before Melanie could shut down, a short guy with a thick mane of white hair was out the car door and hustling their way.

"There's Marty," Melanie said, turning to Corso. "We might as well fill up while we're here."

Corso jumped out and set the pump to working. He stepped over the hose and walked around the front of the RV to the driver's side, where Marty had just arrived. "Where's the crew?" Melanie asked.

"You're looking at him," Marty answered. "No way I could call the regulars back. We were already way past their weekly limits. Between the overtime and what it cost me to fly up here, we're big-time in the hole. I brought the handheld. We'll give it that

Blair Witch Project look." He held up a restraining hand. "That's the bad news. You want the good news?"

"I'll bite . . . what's the good news?"

"It's going to make the network news. The network's interrupting the national news for a special report."

She noticed Frank leaning against the front of the vehicle. "Marty," she said. "I'm sure you remember Frank Corso."

Marty turned and stuck out his hand. "Certainly," he said.

Melanie watched as Marty and Corso traded pleasantries. She heard the *clank* of the gas nozzle shutting itself off. She sighed and leaned against the door.

Two minutes later Marty was headed for the rental car and Corso was headed inside to pay. Behind the counter, a seriously tall lanky kid wearing a purple Lakers baseball cap sat on a metal stool. On a small TV mounted up near the ceiling Oprah Winfrey was nestled up close to Tom Cruise. Tom seemed mildly amused.

"That your truck outside?" Corso asked.

"Sure is," the kid said.

"I thought only short guys owned those big tall trucks."

The kid laughed. "I bought it from a guy named Tom Payton. He claims to be five-eight but ain't nowhere near."

"See." They laughed together.

"It's got a lot of headroom and runs great in the snow."

"How tall are you?"

"Six-eight. You?"

"Six-six," Corso answered.

"World ain't made for guys as tall as us," the kid complained.

"No it's not," Corso agreed. "You got a map of the local area?"

The kid rummaged under the counter and came out with a map. "One of our local arteests drew this up for the tourists. It mostly shows the hiking trails and picnic spots."

Corso took it from his hand. "With the gas, that's fifty-seven fifty-six," the kid said. "The RV yours?" the kid asked.

"Belongs to a friend."

"Pass anything on the road but a gas station," the kid said.

Corso passed him a credit card. The kid swiped it, waited a second and handed it back. "Thanks for the map," Corso said. The kid told him not to mention it.

The sky above was somewhere between blue and black, its uniform density threatened here and there by the suggestion of stars.

The woods were, like the guy said, "dark and deep."

She dreamed of elevators. The kind with an operator. Those old-fashioned, brass-festooned carriages of a bygone century. She watched as the bronze dial over the door aimed its arrow upward, then felt the weight of stopping in the seconds before she heard that lovely *bong*, announcing their arrival at some new world of wonder. *Bong. Bong. Bong.*

She sat up in bed and, for the briefest time, had an inkling as to why she'd chosen that particular sound as the ring for her cell phone. The epiphany, however, was short-lived.

She checked the bedside clock. Six-forty-three. She'd lain down after lunch, hoping for a short nap before being called to action. The dim light filtering in through the curtains told her she'd slept all afternoon. She sat up and grabbed the phone.

"Westerman," she said.

"We lost 'em," the voice said.

Her body stiffened. She ran a hand through her tangled hair.

"How could you lose them? You've got a transponder on the—"

"The mountains are huge. They're getting in the way."

"Where are you now?"

"Place called Sierra Summit."

"Retrace your route."

"Huh?"

"What's the next town back?"

She could hear the crackle of the map as he looked at it.

"Winthrop," he said.

"How far?"

"Twenty miles."

"Go back that far. If you don't pick them up, stay there. If you do pick them up, call me on this number."

She didn't wait for his reply. She broke the cellular connection and reached for the landline. The hotel operator came on the line. "Please connect me to Ronald Rosen," Westerman said.

36

"There," Corso said, folding the map. "That's the driveway right there." He pointed to an unmarked track running at a westerly diagonal from the road.

Melanie nosed the RV into the first fifty feet of gravel and stopped. She killed the lights and swiveled her seat in a half circle. "We ready?" she asked.

"Not quite," Marty said. He sat at the table putting together the plastic harness that attached the camera to the operator. "These kinda ambush interviews . . . we gotta be a hundred percent ready when we hit the bricks. Got no room for do-overs here. It's strictly wham-bam-thank-you ma'am." He pointed up at Melanie. "You want to powder your nose or anything . . . now's the time."

Melanie took her cue, pulling a red-and-white-striped makeup kit from the glove compartment and opening it in her lap. "Here's how we do this," Marty said. "We've got to get her to come outside of the house. We do this on her front porch and she's just gonna slam the door in our faces and disappear."

Melanie said she understood.

"The secret is to be patient," Marty went on. "Just stay put until she gets curious. Somebody pulls into your driveway, you look out the window first. Maybe poke your head out the door after that. Takes a while before you slip out on a jacket and go outside to see what's going on."

"What if she refuses to talk to us?" Melanie asked.

"Then we've got her on tape refusing to talk to us."

"And if she goes ballistic?"

"Same deal. Except it's *us* does the leaving."

Marty set the camera on the table and got to his feet, moving quickly forward to a control panel built into the wall just behind the driver's seat. As he opened the cover and began to push buttons, a collection of red and green lights appeared. He kept at it until everything turned green. "Satellite system loves it up here at the top of the world," he announced. "We could broadcast all the way to New York from here." He threw a quick look Melanie's way. "Nice to see we're finally getting some use out of this thing," he said, in a tone implying he was only half-kidding.

Melanie laughed as she returned the makeup kit to the glove compartment. She looked over at Corso. "How do I look?" she asked.

"Beautiful," he said. "You'll be the belle of the airwaves."

"Do tell, Mr. Corso. Do tell," she drawled.

The genuine playfulness of her tone caught Marty's attention. "Cut it out, you two," he admonished. "This is no time to be fooling around. Network's got a whole studio crew waiting for us at the other end. We're spending money like drunken sailors here."

He slipped his shoulders into the camera harness. The lens rested at the level of his solar plexus. He switched on the camera and looked down onto a small screen just beneath his chin. Next he pulled several metal pieces from one of the camera cases and efficiently assembled the hodgepodge into a tripod, which he collapsed before attaching it to the bottom of the camera. Satisfied, he walked to the control panel again. He pointed to an insistent orange light now blinking in the center of the control panel.

"They're ready for us," he said. "Let's go."

Melanie took a deep breath and snapped on the RV's lights. Tree branches scraped the roof as they moved forward up the driveway. One gentle right-hand curve and the house came into view. One of those woodsy cedar homes they sell beside the highways out West, set in a two-acre clearing atop a south-facing rise. Nice spot.

Melanie turned the engine off and set the parking brake. Up at the house, the porch light went on. Marty handed Melanie a microphone. She clicked the switch and said, "American Manhunt *here*." Marty checked the dials on the top of the camera and bent his fingers into the okay sign.

A minute passed, then the front door swung open. A woman stepped out onto the porch, hugging herself against the night air. Wasn't until she was all the way down the stairs and caught by the headlights that Corso could make her out.

It was Doris Green all right. A little leaner perhaps, and he'd never seen her with her hair down before, but there was no doubt. It was her.

"That's her," Corso said.

"Wait," Marty whispered.

Unable to see through the RV's tinted windows, Doris Green passed through the cone of lights and made her way toward the driver's door.

"Now," Marty whispered.

Melanie hopped out one side; Marty hopped out the other. Melanie kept the microphone close to her chest, so as not to frighten her quarry. "Mrs. Green," she began. "I'm Melanie Harris. We've been following your son's story. We were hoping . . ."

Doris Green's attention was diverted by Marty and the bright lights of the camera. She brought an arm up to protect her eyes from the glare.

"You think he's here? You think my son would be stupid enough to come here?"

"No, ma'am," Melanie assured her. "We just wanted . . ."

Doris pointed a long thin finger at Melanie. "I've seen you," she said. "I've seen you on the television."

"Yes ma'am," Melanie said.

She looked from Melanie to Marty and back again, as if her eyes were calibrating with her mind, making sure she wasn't making this whole thing up.

"You get out of here," she said. "You take that filthy camera and that trailer of yours and you go right back the way you came." She cut the air with her hand. "There's nothing here for you. You get out of here now."

Undaunted, Melanie took another step forward, proffering the microphone as she spoke. "Mrs. Green, we were hoping you could . . ."

Doris Green pushed the microphone back in Melanie's face. Then she began to shout. "A story. All any of you want is a story." She waved both arms. "I'll give you a story. I'll give you a story about a man with too much honor for this world. A man who did his duty. A man who served his country only to have some whore . . . some filthy whore . . ." Her face was red. Her lips flecked with foam. She rocked unsteadily on her feet and brought an arm up to wipe her mouth with her sleeve.

She got most of it. A single piece of spittle still clung to her upper lip when the first sign of distress appeared on her face. A quizzical look. Not so much of pain as of confusion, as if she'd forgotten what she intended to say next. She brought one hand to her breast, then the other, almost like she wanted to guard against something escaping her chest. And then, as if a giant had grabbed her by the shoulders and thrown her on her back, she went down in a heap, looking astonished in the seconds before she hiccuped once and froze in place with her eyes closed and her mouth wide open.

"Mrs. Green, Mrs. Green . . ." Melanie's voice was the only sound in the night air. She stepped forward and looked down at Doris Green for a second, as if trying to decide if this was really happening, then dropped to her knees. She looked up at Marty. "She's had a heart attack or something," Melanie shouted. "Oh God," she wailed. "I think she's dead." Tears began to run down her face. "Oh God. What do I do? What do I do?"

Corso hopped down onto the ground and loped around to where Doris Green lay stretched out on her back among the leaves and bracken. Her limbs were stiff; her face was ashen.

By that time Marty had left the camera whirling away on the tripod and was beginning the initial sixteen compressions of CPR. He looked up at Corso, without losing his compression rhythm. "There's a satellite phone in one of the camera cases. Call 911." Corso turned and sprinted for the phone.

37

Driver sat on the edge of the bed watching TV with the sound off. He was getting ready to leave. She could tell by the way he was breaking down those precious guns of his and wrapping the pieces in towels from the bathroom.

"Pleeeease," she whined. "Don't leave me here all alone."

He looked up at her with those hooded black eyes.

"Come here," he said.

She crossed the room and knelt at his feet like an apostle. She leaned hard against his leg, hoping the feel of her breast would kindle a flame in his loins. No such luck.

He looked down at her. "Anybody see you kill anybody?"

"What?"

"In your travels with Harry . . . did anybody see you kill anybody." He zipped the bag on his left.

"I never . . . ," she stammered.

He cut her off. "I don't give a damn whether you did or you didn't kill anybody, girl. I just want to know if anybody still alive saw you grease anybody, or even point a gun at anybody, anything could make you look like you were going along with the program of your own free will."

She thought it over, trying to decide whether he would prefer she'd killed somebody or not. "Only person I killed was that old woman in the drugstore. Only person there was her old man and Harry shot him a bunch of times."

"Well then," he said. "Here's what you do . . ." When he looked down, she was lost in her own thoughts. "You listening to me?" he asked.

"I'm listening," she said.

"Room's paid up through noon tomorrow," he said. "You get yourself a good night's sleep. In the morning you call up the desk and tell the lady there you need to see the cops. You tell her you've been kidnapped. Tell 'em I left sometime during the night. Soon as you saw I was gone you called the desk. Right?"

She batted her blue eyes and nodded.

"It's important that you make the call. You don't want to get caught by the cops. You gotta turn yourself in. You understand what I'm telling you here?"

She said she did and began to rub his leg with the flat of her hand.

"You tell that story and you stick to it. No matter what any-body says or what any lawyer says to you, you tell the same damn story. You were kidnapped from the beginning. Harry murdered your father and dragged you off kicking and screaming. He did all the killing. You were there against your will. After Harry was dead, it was Kehoe and me. We kept you captive after that. Tell 'em where to find Kehoe. Show 'em where Harry lies. Anything you can do like that will work to your advantage."

She stopped toying with his zipper for long enough to ask, "You think they're gonna believe that?" she asked.

"They're gonna hate the idea," he said. "There's a bunch of cops dead, so they're gonna want a fish to fry for sure." He held up a finger. "But . . . you tell that story long enough and loud enough and you're going to attract the attention of women's groups, of victims' rights groups, of groups neither you nor me ever heard of. Big-time attorneys are going to come out of the woodwork, fighting each other for the right to take your case. All you got to do is help the cops and stick to your story and you'll make it hard for Texas or anyplace else to convict you of anything."

By the time he'd finished talking, she'd eased his fly all the way down and had begun the somewhat contorted process of extricating his manhood from the confines of his briefs. Just as it seemed she might actually pull it off, his hand reached over and grabbed her wrist. He began to remove her hand from his crotch, when, all of a sudden, he seemed to lose interest, dropping her arm and grabbing the remote control from the bed.

Sensing an opening, she used both hands to free her quarry. As the TV volume began to rise . . . *"We've been following your son's story. We were hoping . . ."* she slipped him into her mouth. The TV got louder. *"I've seen you. I've seen you on the television,"* screamed the first voice. *"Yes ma'am,"* bellowed the second.

Within seconds, her efforts began to achieve the desired results. Even with his attention diverted by the television, the natural laws of anatomy and physics began to take over. Thus emboldened, she fell into a regular rhythm. *"You get out of here,"* the first voice cried. *"You take that filthy camera and that trailer of yours and you go right back the way you came. There's nothing here for you. You get out of here now."*

And then, a moment later, she sensed something had gone terribly wrong. The voice coming from the TV screamed of terror. *"Oh God,"* the second voice wailed. *"I think she's dead. Oh God. What do I do? What do I do?"* Despite her best efforts to maintain control, he shifted his hips and extricated himself from her mouth with a wet pop. Before she could regroup, she felt a cold oval of steel press against her lips, felt the front sight bang against her teeth as the barrel slid into her mouth. She looked up. Men liked it when you looked up. The expression on his face sent a wave of fear through her body. He was crying as he used his thumb to release the safety. She closed her eyes.

It took Melanie Harris three tries to dial the number. She brought the receiver to her ear with both hands. Brian answered on the third ring. His voice was husky with sleep. " 'Lo," he said.

She flicked her eyes at the bedside table. The digital alarm clock read three fifteen. Five-fifteen in Michigan.

"Brian," she said. "It's me."

"Hello," he said again.

"It's me."

The bumping and groaning at the other end told her he'd dropped the phone on the floor. She was waiting for him to get everything organized when she heard the woman's voice in the background . . . plain as day. Except it wasn't daytime.

"Who is it, Bri?" the sleepy voice asked.

She heard his breathing again as he righted the phone.

"Hello," he said.

Melanie used her thumb to break the connection and replaced the receiver. She drew several ragged breaths . . . rubbed her nose with her arm . . . thought she was going to cry . . . but the tears never came. Instead, she lay back on the bed and stared at the cheap light fixture on the motel ceiling. She brought her legs up onto the bedspread, closed her eyes and the events of the past eight or nine hours flashed across her mind's eye like a bad movie in fast forward.

It had taken an aid car just under an hour to reach Doris Green. The county police arrived five minutes later. Marty and Corso had traded off CPR for the whole time before being forced to give up the ghost. Even after her lips had become blue and cool to the touch, they'd maintained their faith they could breathe life back into her. It took the arriving EMTs to convince them there was nothing more to be done. By that time, Marty was so exhausted, he could barely raise his arms from his sides. When the time came to leave, Corso had to help him back to the RV.

Once the excitement was over and Doris Green had been carried down from her mountain, they'd backtracked seventy miles to a town called Jenner Peak, an alpine hamlet close enough to the Mountain West ski area to support half a dozen cheap motels, a pair of which stayed open year-round. Since ten-thirty, they'd been holed up in rooms three, four and seven of the Ski Chalet Motor Inn.

She'd been too cold and hollow to sleep. Spent the night pacing to the bathroom and back. Now . . . now she was something else. Something she hadn't felt in a long time. Not since Samantha's death. That feeling of disconnectedness, of being alone on the planet in the midst of all the hustle and bustle of people and things equally singular. She wondered how she'd come so far toward cynicism as to make her call to Brian insufficient cause for tears; and then, in the same instant, she knew the answer. It was because whatever it was they had to lose had been lost a long time ago, flung facedown in that frozen ditch in Grand Rapids, Michigan, with the rest of her hopes and dreams.

It was as if her life, from that moment on, had become little more than a holding action. Nothing more than a leaking boat and a mindless need to stay afloat.

Again she tried to cry and again she was unable.

38

Corso was wide-awake when the knock came. He'd nodded off a couple of times but had not been visited by anything resembling restfulness. Funny too, because the vagaries of life and death generally rolled off him rather easily. Too easily, he often thought in his more reflective moments, when he wondered if his capacity to move forward in the face of tragedy was not somehow an indictment of his inability to feel. When others found themselves numbed by the moment, and unable to do anything more than question the universe, Corso had always been able to take a deep breath and move on. In his more self-indulgent moments, he attributed his resilience to the horrors he'd witnessed as a reporter, but in his heart he knew better, knew that he'd been that way for as long as he could remember. Remembered way back when he was nine and watched his grandmother's funeral, standing amidst the wailing and the hand-wringing, clear-eyed and detached, wondering if he should join the chorus of sorrow and knowing, with certainty, that something in his makeup made such expressions impossible.

He levered himself from the bed and padded to the door in his bare feet.

"Yeah," he said through the door.

"It's Melanie," the voice said.

"Melanie who?"

"Stop it."

"Just a sec," he said.

Corso pulled his jeans from the back of the chair and slipped them on. His shirt was hanging in the closet at the far side of the room. Too far for four in the morning. He was still bare-chested when he walked back to the door and opened it.

Melanie Harris. Black cashmere overcoat, no shoes. She stood, holding her coat closed at the throat, shivering in the wind. Corso stepped aside and motioned her into the room.

"I saw your light," she said as they passed in the doorway.

"I haven't had much luck getting to sleep," he admitted.

She sat on the edge of the bed and looked around. "Looks familiar," she said.

Corso laughed. "Yeah . . . I'm thinking of booking this one for my next winter vacation." He lifted the plastic armchair from its nook beside the nightstand and set in on the floor next to the bed. Before sitting down, he crossed the room and slipped his shirt over his shoulders, without bothering with the buttons.

By the time he worked his way back around the foot of the bed, Melanie had stretched out a bit, putting her hands on the bed and leaning back on her arms.

"So . . . ," he said tentatively, "what can I do for you at this ungodly hour of the night."

"Actually, I think it's morning."

"At this hour of the morning," he amended with a smile.

She looked away, embarrassed. A silent moment passed before she said, "I didn't want to be alone. I kept seeing that old woman's face."

Corso nodded his understanding. He sat in the chair and ran his hands over his face. "She's going to be with me for a while too," he admitted.

"I can't help thinking we were responsible for her death."

Corso was shaking his head. "You give us too much credit," he said. "We may have had a part in it, but there's no way we were what I'd call responsible. The way I see things, each of us is responsible for himself. We each forge our own relationship with the universe and take our chances from there." He put his feet up on the bed. "There's a lot of luck involved. It's like something I heard Driver say while he was babbling about fish. Some are destined to make it all the way back to the spawning grounds, some are destined to fall victim to bears, some to eagles and others just don't have the juice to complete the journey. They just melt back into the water and feed the algae."

"I don't want to feed the algae," she said.

"Nobody does."

They were silent for a while. It was comfortable.

"You check out the tube?" Corso asked finally.

She shook her head. "I haven't had the stomach for it."

"We're everywhere," he said. "Live at six o'clock."

"Somehow it doesn't seem important right now."

"I've been thinking about it."

"And?"

"Might be one of those times we weren't careful enough about what we wished for."

She let herself slip down onto her back. "We weren't careful at all," she said. "We . . ." She waved the thought away, then used the hand to cover her eyes.

He heard a quick intake of breath and, before he could be certain, the noise of an eighteen-wheeler, low in its gears, laboring over the summit, overtook the sound in the room. When the roar had faded and nothing could be heard above the wind, the sounds of her crying became audible. Corso sat quietly, staring down at the cigarette burns on the wooden arms of the chair. Her measured tears came in fits and starts; angry and aggrieved, they escaped from her eyes like reluctant refugees.

Corso waited for a lull. "Anything I can do?" he asked.

At first she shook her head. And then, in a voice he'd never heard before, she said, "I think maybe I need a hug."

"Come here," he said.

A moment later they stood by the side of the bed wrapped in each other's arms. The solace gave Melanie Harris the strength to let it out. Her body shook with sobs; the tracks of her tears coursed down Corso's bare chest. Corso hung on and waited for the storm to subside. Seemed like she had a lot of tears stored somewhere inside her, so it took a while. More like she ran out of energy before she ran out of tears. By the time she stopped shaking, Corso reckoned he'd been hugging her for longer than he'd ever hugged anyone before. He whispered in her ear. "You know . . ."

"No," she said, disengaging slightly. And kissed him, full on the mouth, a kiss whose intent filled the air like a rising note. He pushed her back to arm's length. "You sure?" he asked. She kissed him again and they were both sure.

"I thought you were spoken for."

"It's algae food," she said, stepping closer, running her hands inside his shirt, caressing his back as she pulled him closer. "We've fallen by the wayside."

Before he could respond, her fingers had the overcoat half-unbuttoned. Corso saw it coming. The point of no return. He opened his mouth to speak, but it turned out the overcoat was the only thing she was wearing. The sight of her naked body froze the words in his throat. He felt the hot rush of blood and knew some things never changed.

Ray Lofton made this run every Saturday morning rain or shine. Being low man on the seniority totem pole just naturally got him the weekend work. On a good day he could be back at the office in three hours flat. When it got snowy he'd have to chain up. Took all damn day in the snow. This year, summer had lingered, sending the slanting rays of Indian Summer down onto the alpine meadows well into October, making Ray's life way easier. Company he worked for had the contract to pick up the trash on the west side of the divide. Once a week they had him take the ancient International Harvester garbage truck up to the summit and pick up everything on the way down.

Mary the dispatcher told him to do it that way . . . from the top down, when he first started on the route, but Ray, never being one to follow orders, figured as long as he was driving by he might as well pick up whatever was there. What he discovered was that the old truck wouldn't pull the grade unless it was empty. He'd had to go down, dump out, then go back up to the summit. Didn't get back till dark and don't think he hadn't taken a ration of shit from every damn person in the company.

The grade was always steeper than it looked. Ray Lofton shifted down into third gear. The old truck roared its disapproval; the windshield shook until it made a noise like a tambourine. The guy in the passenger seat reached out and put one hand on the dashboard like he was trying to prevent the rig from shaking itself to pieces .

"Don't worry," Ray shouted over the rising din. "She'll make it. She always does."

The guy shot him an uncertain smile and braced himself harder. Ray Lofton liked to talk, which was why he picked up hitchhikers whenever he got the chance. Just to have somebody to talk to. But this guy . . . this guy spent words the way other people spent money. He'd known that an hour ago, he wouldn't have picked him up.

He'd felt bad for the guy, standing out there in the wind trying to thumb a ride in the middle of the night on a road nobody drove this time of year, so he'd picked him up. Guy hadn't even told him his name. Just threw his gym bags down on the floor at his feet and thanked Ray for the ride. Hadn't uttered a peep since. Just sat there staring out the front window.

So . . . it was no great sorrow for Ray when, halfway to the summit, the guy suddenly threw himself forward in the seat, scanned the roadside like it was full of naked cheerleaders, and said, "Stop."

Ray, who likewise had been lost in his own thoughts, didn't react right away.

"What?"

"Stop," the guy said again.

Ray eased the rig off the road and into the deserted parking lot of the Sierra Motor Inn. Maybe two dozen detached cabins spread out among a little grove of pine trees. Place was closed for the winter.

Ray kept his foot jammed on the brake and turned to the guy. "You never did say exactly where you was going. I never figured you was . . . you know . . . Jenner Peak."

But by then it was too late. The guy was already out of the seat and down onto the ground, bags and all. "Thanks," he said again and closed the door.

Ray watched him in the mirror as he crossed the highway with a black Nike bag in each hand and made his way over to the Ski Chalet motel across the street. When the guy disappeared behind a big old motor home parked along the edge of their lot, Ray lost interest. He took his foot off the brake, checked in both directions and gave the old girl all the gas he dared. Sounded like maracas.

39

The knocking was tentative at first . . . one knuckle. Corso groaned and rolled over. It went away. Corso kept his eyes closed, trying to convince himself the noise was part of his dream. Then it returned. Louder this time. The flat of a hand smacking against the door. He opened an eye. The noise had also awakened Melanie Harris. She was naked, wound around him like a vine, half-in, half-out of the bedclothes, propped up now bleary-eyed on one elbow.

"Don't answer it," she whispered.

Corso rolled onto his back and closed his eyes. The knocking started again, more insistent this time. "Yeah," Corso yelled.

"It's Marty," the voice came through the door.

Corso rolled over and threw his arms around Melanie. He drew her close. She kissed him on the ear. "We can't just leave him out there," she whispered.

"Just a minute," Corso yelled over his shoulder. He kissed her between the eyes, then on the mouth. "You want me to let him in?"

"You got a better idea?"

"You want to hide in the bathroom or something?"

She considered the matter. "Seems a bit Gothic," she said. "Besides . . . Marty's nobody to talk."

Corso smiled. He got to his feet, rummaged through the pile of covers at the foot of the bed, found his shirt and jeans and put them on.

Corso opened the door a crack. Martin Wells looked like the wrath of God. His smooth brown Hollywood face had recovered every year his plastic surgeon had so carefully removed. He had lines in his face deep enough to hide a quarter. He wore the same striped dress shirt he's worn the night before. The front of the shirt was stained with dirt and spittle, and somewhere along the way he'd lost the second button.

"What's up?" Corso asked.

"I can't find Melanie. I tried the . . ."

"She's okay," Corso assured him.

From behind Corso came Melanie's voice. "Let him in."

Corso stepped aside. Marty hesitated for a moment, then crossed the threshold. He sent an amused glance bouncing from Melanie to Corso and back again. "So . . . ," he said with a smile, ". . . what do we have here?"

Melanie looked embarrassed. "Don't start, Marty. You're nobody to talk." She turned her head toward Corso. "Marty here even cheats on his mistress," she said.

Marty looked hurt. "A man in my position needs his comforts."

Corso looked the little guy over. "You've got *two* mistresses?"

"Stephanie . . . that's my wife . . . she found out about Janice." He shrugged. "Took all the fun out of it." He looked them over again. "So?"

Melanie changed the subject. "So what happened with last night's feed?"

Marty's turn to wince. "A bit more than we had in mind eh?"

"Frank said it was all over."

"Apparently so was Frank."

"Stop it!" She tried to sound angry but didn't manage.

"A hundred fifty-five channels domestically. We're getting a lot of calls and e-mails. They're running about two to one outraged."

"What's the network saying?"

"Publicly, they're distancing themselves from us. Behind closed doors they're gloating over the ratings."

"At least they're predictable."

"I've got a budget meeting with Larry at six tonight," Marty said. "You gonna be able to get the trailer home?"

"It's an RV, Marty . . . an RV."

"You gonna be able to get it home? I could send—"

"I got it this far," she interrupted. "I'll get it back to the lot."

"Okay then," Marty said. "I'm going to jump in the shower and head back home. You need anything, you give me a jingle." He pointed over at Melanie. "You know, dearie, you got a certain blush this morning . . ."

"Shut up, Marty," she said. "Go take your shower."

Martin Wells laughed, said his good-byes and disappeared.

"Howsabout breakfast?" Corso asked. "The café across the street must be open by now."

Melanie sat up and surveyed herself in the mirror. She made a disgusted face. "Long as you don't mind waiting for an hour or so."

"Howsabout I go get it and bring it back."

She gave him a wicked look. "Thus fortified . . . do you suppose we might . . . ?"

"I do indeed," he said. "What do you want?"

"For breakfast?"

"Let's start there."

She told him.

He found his shoes and jacket, stuffed a room key into his pocket and headed out.

The Timberman's Café was a quarter mile downhill on the other side of the highway. The clock over the counter read eight-ten when he settled onto the stool.

"Be right with ya," a voice called from the back.

Corso looked around. Standard-issue rural café. Half a dozen tables replete with brightly patterned table covers, ten stools along the counter, restrooms on the uphill end, cute little sign Scotch-taped to the back of the cash register: PRICES WERE BORN HERE AND RAISED ELSEWHERE.

A guy in his early sixties slipped his shoulders out through the double swinging doors. He was as pale and skinny as the tooth-pick hanging out the side of his mouth. "What can I get for you?" he wanted to know.

Corso told him. He wrote it down.

"Gonna take a little longer than usual," the guy said. "My weekend waitress called in with the flu." He made a disgusted face. "Something about Friday nights seems to do that to her."

"Someplace I can get a newspaper around here?" Corso asked.

"Not this time of year," the guy shouted.

Corso spent the next five minutes ruminating on the joys of women. How his hand hadn't bothered him a bit last night. About how he liked to think of himself as a thoughtful, profes-sional person who generally approached things in an organized manner . . . and how all of that went completely out the window whenever he found himself confronted with a naked woman. How countless generations of social and religious admonitions fell by the wayside in an instant, as, all these centuries later, the primal need to spread one's genes upon the waters still ran ram-pant in the blood, leaving him little more than a gussied-up and shaved version of his feral forbearers.

He'd worked up a smile when the little bell over the door tin-kled. Before he could turn and appraise his fellow diners, a famil-iar voice pulled his attention back to the here and now.

"You're a long way from the Phoenician, Mr. Corso. Might have been better for all concerned if you'd stayed there."

Corso knew the voice, but peeked back over his shoulder just to be sure. Special Agent Rosen with Westerman in tow, the pair of them just as neat and unwrinkled as could be. Corso turned away, focusing instead on the promising smells of toasting bread and frying bacon.

They took the stools on either side of him. "Might have been better if you'd been straight with us," Rosen said.

"I *was* straight with you," Corso said.

"You knew where to find his mother."

"You didn't ask me that."

"You knew that's where Driver would be headed."

"So did you. You catch him yet?"

Their collective silence answered the question. "In retrospect, it seems like that little piece of information wasn't of much use, now was it?" Corso said

"No telling what might have happened if you and that Harris woman had kept out of it and let us do our jobs."

"She was just doing hers," Corso said.

"The public's right to know and all that," Westerman threw in.

"Don't you forget it," Corso snapped.

The cook backed into the room. His hands were filled with plastic bags jam-packed with an assortment of Styrofoam food containers. He set the bags on the counter in front of Corso and read through the order. "Two large coffees. One cream and sugar. One black," he said finally. Corso nodded his agreement.

"Sixteen dollars and twelve cents," the guy announced.

Corso dropped a twenty-dollar bill on the counter, picked up the bags and started for the door. Rosen and Westerman followed along in his wake.

"Sounds a lot like breakfast for two," Westerman commented.

Corso looked at Rosen. "Not much gets by her, does it?"

He went out the door backward, turning around in time to step over the molded concrete curb, stretching his long legs, making it difficult for anyone shorter than himself to keep pace.

Turned out the effort was wasted. Rosen and Westerman followed no farther than the dark blue Lincoln Town Car in the parking lot.

Corso had covered half the distance back to his room when the Lincoln came rolling by, headed west toward the top of the hill at a stately ten miles an hour. Perhaps because his attention was diverted by the car, he got all the way to the door to his room before noticing something was amiss. A "what's wrong with this picture?" kind of feeling in the pit of his stomach.

He looked around but couldn't quite place what was bothering him. Wasn't until his eyes swept over the downhill end of the parking lot for the second time that things began to click into place and his stomach took the elevator ride down to his shoe tops. He blinked twice, thinking he must be wrong, then looked uphill toward Marty's rental car and the motel office. No doubt about it. The RV was gone.

40

Ray Lofton stood on the front bumper and fanned the steaming radiator with his hat. On the ground behind him, a white plastic bucket held five gallons of water, a stash he kept in the back of the truck for just such an occasion, but, for the time being at least, the radiator was way too hot to take a chance on removing the cap.

He'd made that mistake once before. Lost his patience and tried to open her up with nothing but his shirttail between his hand and the radiator cap. Damn thing went off like Mount St. Helens, burned the living bejesus out of him. He'd spent the next month covered in salve. Folks at work took to calling him "greazy Ray." Assholes, all of 'em.

Problem today was the old girl lost her momentum when he stopped to let Silent Bob out back in Jenner Peak. The idea was to get her in third gear down on the flats and keep it there all the way to the top. Long as you kept her cruising along at about thirty in third, she was happy as a clam. This time, however, what with stopping right in the middle of the steepest part of the grade, he wasn't able to muster enough revs to get out of second gear and so had spent the past half hour doing maybe twenty miles an hour and watching the temperature gauge inch its way toward the red zone, until it got so bad he'd had no choice but to pull into a turn out and shut her down.

Ray climbed down off the bumper and stuck the hat back on his head. He felt a curse coming on. It was going to be at least and hour before he could fire her up and get on his way. Not only that but he had to make a stop way the hell out at the Lodge at White Lake. They'd hosted wedding receptions the past two weekends and needed a trash run. By itself, the Lodge was an extra hour each way. By the time he got back to the yard, the shank of the day was going to be history. He kicked a piece of loose gravel and watched as it rolled under the guardrail and over the edge of the embankment. The vista beyond stopped him in his tracks.

The easterly wind had prevented L.A.'s airborne sludge from working its way up the canyons today. The air was crisp and clean. From where he stood he could see the southern edge of the Sierra Nevada, the knobby spine that ran damn near the whole length of the state. From there, it wasn't hard to imagine the North American and Pacific Plates grinding on each other, shoving the Pacific Plate down into the bowels of the earth, down into the ocean of molten magma that covers the sphere, uplifting the North American Plate and tilting it westward. Ray smiled and sat down on the guardrail. "Who could get mad on a day like this?" he asked himself.

Corso set the breakfast bags on the concrete sidewalk to the right of the door. The smell of fresh coffee called to his nostrils as he reached into his pocket. His hand trembled as he fished out the room key and fit it into the opening. He stood to one side as he swung the door open and peeked into the room.

From that vantage point everything looked more or less like he'd left it. Except that Melanie was gone. He came into the room slowly, looking for any sign of haste or desperation. The air inside the room smelled of her. Of perfume and body lotion and whatever other oils and unguents she used. Her coat lay on the floor, so wherever she'd gone to, she'd gone naked. He pushed open the bathroom door. Empty. He couldn't decide whether to be relieved or terrified.

And then he suddenly felt foolish and melodramatic. Standing there like a bird dog on point. Maybe . . . there'd been a . . . maybe she'd . . . but, no matter how he tried, he couldn't finish the sentence. The tingle of fear began to inch up again.

He strode quickly out of the room, turned right and began to hurry toward Marty's room and the motel office. The door to unit seven was ajar. Corso could hear the shower running. He stepped inside and called Marty's name, then again, louder this time.

Corso hustled to the back of the room and pushed open the bathroom door. The shower was going full blast, but the stall was empty. Corso reached in and turned off the water. The floor was awash in soapy water.

He moved quickly now. Back across the room, toward the door. A quick glance to his left sent another shiver down his spine. The little table next to the window held Marty's cell phone, a handful of pocket change, the room key and the keys to the rental car. Marty's jacket was thrown over the seat of the chair because the chair back was already holding his shirt and trousers. Corso's head was spinning, trying desperately to come up with a scenario to fit the situation and failing miserably. He walked over and picked up the cell phone and the car keys. He stashed them in his jacket pockets and began to pat himself down, looking for the business card he'd stuck in one of his pockets the day before.

He found it in the back pocket of his jeans, pulled out the cell phone and began to dial the number. Nothing. No bars. No service. He cursed and scooped the change from the tabletop. He jogged to the phone booth, braced the receiver between his shoulder and his ear and dialed the number. An electronic voice informed him the call would cost a dollar ninety-five for three minutes. He dumped the handful of coins on the burnished metal shelf beneath the phone and used his forefinger to sort out two bucks' worth of quarters.

As he lifted the first coin toward the slot a flash of white among the weeds caught his attention. He palmed the coin and hung up the receiver. His body tingled, his legs were heavy and sluggish as he covered the twenty feet.

He stood looking down for a moment and then dropped to one knee. Towels. Two of them. White unmarked towels, nappy and rough like you get back from a commercial laundry. He picked one up. Brought it to his face and sniffed. He winced. No doubt about it. They smelled of sweat . . . sweat and gun oil.

He grabbed the other towel and got to his feet. Ten seconds later, he was dropping quarters into the slot as fast as he was able.

41

Martin Wells wore nothing but his shoes. He sat with his back to the bathroom door, with his legs curled tightly against his chest. He kept his mouth shut and face buried in his kneecaps, hoping to avoid another swipe of the gun butt, a casual motion of the arms, which had lifted a bloody flap of skin from his scalp and reduced his will to resist to slightly less than zero.

Nakedness was a state unlike any other. More honest. More to the point. A state in which one had to come to grips with oneself. Had to swim down into the waters of self-esteem as it were, hoping like hell what you had always imagined as a River of Resolve was not, in reality, a Sump of Self-Doubt.

As he cowered there in the back of the RV, Marty realized he was more concerned about being seen in the nude than he was about being killed. Sixty-three-year-old TV producers were never intended to be seen naked in public. That he went to the gym three times a week and was probably in better shape than the majority of his peers held no solace whatsoever. The experience of having had a shotgun jammed in his face and subsequently being clubbed to his knees had sent his privates squealing for sanctuary. Shriveled his dick up like a roll of dimes, as it were.

The blood from his head wound dripped steadily onto his thigh. The frothy smell of soap mixed uneasily with the acrid odor of adrenaline, creating the incongruous atmosphere of fresh-scrubbed fear.

In the best of times, Marty was modest. At his club, he always kept his towel in place, telling himself it was a matter of class and taste, rather than any misgivings he might have possessed regarding his own shortcomings. Guys like Barry Levin . . . always parading around . . . swinging it in everybody's face . . . they disgusted him.

Martin Wells shivered in the cold. He peeked between his knees but could not see his tormenter. Only Melanie's bare back, her muscles rippling slightly as she worked the steering wheel.

42

Special Agent Ronald Rosen held the towels at arm's length, as if he'd unexpectedly been handed a turd.

"Let me see if I've got this straight," he began. "You're trying to tell me that these towels are proof positive that Timothy Driver has arrived here and has kidnapped your girlfriend and her producer and is now holding them hostage somewhere locally." He waited a beat. "Is that it?"

"Yeah," Corso said. "That's about it."

Rosen thrust the towels back in Corso's face. "What the hell is the matter with you? " He didn't wait for an answer. "You're out of your mind. You know that? You called us back here over this? You told me Driver was here."

"I told you he'd *been* here."

"According to who?"

"The RV's gone."

Rosen and Westerman laughed together. "Maybe your charms weren't all you thought they were, Lothario," Westerman said with a smirk. "Maybe they just dumped your ass and headed back to La La land. You ever think of that?"

"Naked?"

"I'm betting they had fresh clothes in the motor home. The stuff he left behind in the room was a mess."

"He left his cell phone and the rental car."

Rosen shrugged. "In a hurry. Trying to get lost before you got back. Nothing there that can't be paid for or replaced."

"Driver's here. I'm telling you."

Rosen made a rude noise with his lips. "Bullshit," he spit. "What you need to do, Mr. Corso, is to go back to wherever you came from and get to doing whatever it is you do. That way you can leave Mr. Driver and his friends to us and stop making an ass of yourself."

He turned on his heel and walked away. Westerman lingered for a moment.

"What he said," she offered before turning and following in his footsteps.

Corso stood and watched them leave. He took deep breaths, trying to control his temper. He watched as Rosen got into the passenger seat and Westerman slid behind the wheel. Equal opportunity. All very PC these days.

Inside the car, Rosen buckled himself in and turned to Westerman. "Check with the units at either end of the highway," he said. "Tell them to let us know when that RV comes by."

"If they're headed for L.A., they must be driving west."

Rosen checked his watch. "It's forty-five minutes from here to the bottom of the western slope. Unless they stopped for something, they ought to be rolling by there sometime in the next fifteen minutes. Tell them I want to hear about it."

Westerman reached for her phone. "Get the unit with the transponder," Rosen went on. "Send them down the western slope. See if they don't pick up the signal from the RV. Once they get out of the mountains, they ought to come through loud and clear. I want a location on that damn thing. Yesterday."

A moment later, the driver's door opened and Westerman

stepped out. She wandered about, removing the cell phone from her ear now and then, moving in one direction and then another, looking for service like a dog looks for a place to pee. She eventually settled on a spot in front of the right headlight, whence she made three rather animated phone calls.

Corso waited until she got back in the car and started the engine. As soon as the Lincoln began to roll, Corso started walking back toward the rooms, bypassing Melanie's, then his own. Continuing all the way up to Marty's, where he grabbed the rental car keys from the table, turned off the lights and made sure the door was locked on his way out.

Wasn't until he was about to drive out onto the highway that all of a sudden he had a spasm of lucidity . . . a moment of clarity so powerful it brought him to a standstill.

In that dark insular moment, Corso realized he had absolutely no idea where he was going or what it was he should do next.

Ray Lofton had been to the promised land. He'd been to the mountain. All the way to the summit, where he'd picked up the trash and started back down. The old truck had barely made it to the top. The temperature needle had just crept into the red zone when he'd pulled into the summit. From here on it was all downhill.

He shook the Elk Creek Dumpster one last time and eased the lever back, setting it gently on the ground, before rolling it back into its little alcove in the blackberry bushes. On his way past the truck he reached in and turned off the engine. Might as well shoot the breeze with Kenny for a while, he figured . . . What with the trip all the way up to White Lake, hell, the morning was gone anyway. So he slammed the door and headed into the store.

"Hey, big fella," Ray shouted as he came through the door.

"Ray Ray . . . I thought I heard you grindin' away out there."

Before Ray could open his mouth, Kenny asked. "You seen this on the TV?"

Ray walked around the end of the counter. A Stay-Fresh Maxi Pad commercial was on the tube. "You seen anything about those cops killers runnin' all over Nevada?"

"Yeah . . . yeah . . . ," Ray chanted. "Ones where one bunch rescued the other from the cops."

"That's it, bro." He waggled a hand at the TV. "They just busted into the program for like this bulletin about them and like they had this picture of this guy who was like kidnapped by them a few days ago but got away . . ."

"Yeah?"

"That guy came in the store here last night."

"No shit."

Kenny crossed his heart with a long finger. "Swear to God," he said. "He stood right there on the other side of the counter. We talked about being tall and all."

"What'd he want?"

"Gas and a map." Kenny pointed up at the TV. "Here . . . here . . . here . . . It's coming back on," he said.

Across the bottom of the screen . . . photos of Driver, Kehoe, Harry and Heidi. The voice-over was doing the usual armed and dangerous routine. Then a picture of Corso.

"Him," Kenny said. "That's the guy right there. He don't have the ponytail anymore, but that's him for sure."

Ray Lofton's face was the picture of stupefaction. He pointed up at the TV.

"Wait," he said. "Bring it back."

"It's regular TV, man. I can't roll it back."

"The first guy."

"What about him."

The TV returned to its regular programming. Montel.

Ray rubbed the corners of his mouth with his thumb and forefinger. "Swear to God I saw that first guy."

"Give it a break man," Kenny scoffed.

"No . . . swear to God." He pointed at the screen again. "He shaved his head and grew a little beard, but I swear that's the same guy I gave a ride to this morning on the way up." Before Kenny could respond, Ray went on. "Crazy bastard. Just sat there mumbling to himself the whole way up the damn hill."

Kenny waved him off. "You're jamming with me, man. You can't stand it . . . I seen something and you didn't."

"No, man . . . I'm telling you . . . this is for real here . . ."

"You was always like that, Ray Ray. Somebody's family had a baboon, yours had one too."

"That's cold, man."

The door opened. Kenny leaned down to greet the customer.

Corso walked into the store. Kenny's face lit up like it was Christmas.

"Man . . . you won't believe what this retread's been trying to tell me," Kenny said. "He's been . . ."

43

Melanie Harris sat straight and rigid in the driver's seat, hoping some passing truck driver might notice her nakedness and call the authorities. Then, of course, there was the matter of how she looked in the nude. Bad enough to be kidnapped naked, let alone slouching and allowing one's attributes to tumble and sag into an amorphous bag of flesh. No way that was going to happen. Bad enough her Brazilian was partially grown out, leaving her mound with the look of a sugarcane field after a typhoon. She had an appointment for a waxing next Thursday. Sometime in the morning. The exact hour escaped her at the moment. She wondered if she'd be charged for the appointment even if she was dead.

Brian had liked the Brazilian at first. Later he came to see the procedure as a California affectation and heaped upon it the same degree of scorn he used for anything overtly Hollywood.

Started out, she'd done it as a lark. It was a couple of weeks after she'd had her eyeliner tattooed on. Melanie figured, "What the hell. It's a week before Valentine's Day; it'll make a nice surprise."

Go figure. She'd discovered she liked it. It made her feel not only cleaner, but in some odd way allowed her access to the vestal maiden she'd left so far behind so many years before. Allowed her to feel like a girl again, as it were.

She threw a quick glance over at Driver. He was reading the map Corso had bought at that little store last night. The barrel of the shotgun was pointed directly at her right breast. She felt the blood rise in her cheeks. There she was . . . sitting stark naked, no more than five feet from him and he wasn't paying the slightest attention to her. She again gave thanks to God. No matter what might transpire here, at least she wasn't going to be raped. Even if he killed them both, at least she wouldn't have to bear that frightful indignity. She returned her eyes to the road and resumed her prayers.

44

"See," Kenny said. "This is the dude right here."

"Hey, man, I just saw you on the tube, 'cept you had long hair in the picture they was showin'," said Ray. "You was like captured by those guys the heat are lookin' all over for, huh. That musta been a trip."

Corso allowed as how the experience had indeed been "a trip." "You got another one of those tourist maps?" he asked Kenny.

Kenny shook his head. "Sold you the last one the other night. Only one I got left is the one we use to order from." He pointed at Ray. "You know what Ray Ray here has been trying to tell me?"

"What's that?"

"Ray Ray been trying to tell me he give one of those guys a ride up the mountain this morning."

Corso stiffened. "Which one?" he asked as calmly as he was able.

"Big guy with a shaved head."

"Was he carrying anything?" Corso held his breath.

"Couple big gym bags. Black Nike bags. Had the little swoosh on the sides of them."

Corso's knees nearly buckled. He put a hand down on the counter to steady himself. "Oh Jesus," he whispered.

"You okay?" Ray asked.

"I been half-hoping I was wrong," Corso said. He took a deep breath, then pushed his way past Ray and out the door. He pulled Marty's cell phone from his pants pocket and waited impatiently for it to come alive. When the little tone told him the phone was ready, he dialed Rosen's number. *Beep, beep.* Busy. Hoping maybe he'd made a mistake in dialing, he tried again. Same, *beep, beep,* busy. "Shit," he screamed at the top of his lungs. He ran back into the store.

"You callin' the cops?" Ray asked.

"Where could you hide a motor home around here?" Corso asked.

"You mean here on the mountain?" Kenny asked.

"Why would anybody wanna do that?" Ray wanted to know.

Corso thought it over. "The RV is also a remote satellite rig. You can broadcast from it. I think maybe he wants to broadcast something . . . something where he gets to tell his story, then goes out in a blaze of glory." He slapped the side of his head. "I'm just guessing. His motivations are mostly lost on me, but that's as good a guess as any."

"Where'd he get a motor home? When I left him off, he was hoofin' it."

"He stole it from some friends of mine. Kidnapped them and I'm guessing at some point he's going to kill them."

"This the guy shot them guards?" Kenny asked.

"The very same. That's why we gotta find him. Right now. Yesterday."

"Best place to hide something that big would be"—Kenny waved a hand—"you know, other than in somebody's yard or something . . . the best place would hafta be somewhere on the old highway."

"Where's that?"

"Everywhere," said Ray. "It's old route 180. It winds around the mountain about six times before it gets to the top. Then winds back down."

"Crosses the new highway . . . what . . . a dozen times or so on each side."

" 'Cept they try to keep it all blocked off, of course," Ray added.

"Who tries to keep it blocked off?" Corso asked.

Kenny shrugged. "You know . . . the Forest Service, the Road Department. It's like a game of cat and mouse. They lock 'em up. The locals bust 'em open. Mostly they're open, cause there's way more of us than there are of them," he said with a grin.

"He's got that map you sold me last night."

"Then you're just gonna have to check all the gates . . . see if you can't find where they went through."

"That's presuming they're still up on the mountain," Kenny said.

Corso shook his head. "If they'd gone down either side, the FBI would have had them by now. And if the feds had them, it would be all over the tube." He pointed up at the TV where Montel Williams was massaging the forearm of an enormously overweight woman in a wildflower print dress. "The feds never miss a chance to look good," Corso said. "Never."

"Everybody around here knows about the old highway. It's where most of them hunt during deer and elk seasons."

"It's where most of us used to take girls back in high school," Kenny said.

"Two things everybody up here owns are a snowmobile and an ATV," Ray said. "Both of which work just fine all over the old highway."

"Thanks for the info," Corso said, reaching for the door handle.

"You ain't gonna find 'em all on your own," Kenny said.

A glum silence settled over the room.

"I'd show you where to look, but I gotta finish my route. I don't finish . . . my ass is grass and the company's the lawn mower," Ray said.

"He's going to kill them. Just as sure as God made little green apples, he's going to kill them."

With that, Corso yanked open the door and strode outside. He had the rental car open and one foot inside when Kenny appeared. "I'll show you where," he said. "Gimme a minute to close up." He inclined his head toward the truck. "We probably better take my rig."

Corso slammed the door and pulled out his phone. *Beep, beep,* busy.

Rosen's ear was beginning to sweat. "Okay . . . okay . . . thanks," he said before breaking the connection. He ran both hands over his face. "Nothing," he said.

"Really?" Westerman was genuinely surprised. "Not a peep?"

Rosen first pursed his lips, then covered them with his rigid index finger.

This gesture was one of the few Rosenisms Westerman was yet to interpret reliably. Sometimes it meant "Be quiet; I'm thinking." Other times it meant she was supposed to come up with an alternative. At that moment, she was hoping like crazy it was the former rather than the latter, because the only thing she had to say was almost guaranteed to piss Rosen off to the nth degree.

It had bothered her for most of the past hour. Nothing in the facts. Mostly, it was just her read on Corso. Aside from his adolescent rebellious streak, she'd been quite impressed. Not only was he about as good-looking as guys got, but there was no denying this was one smart cookie. Ruthless . . . to be sure . . . even un-

caring . . . to a fault perhaps, but nonetheless, one sharp cookie.
What if Corso was right? What if Timothy Driver had indeed kidnapped a well-known TV personality and her producer, stolen
them right from beneath the FBI's nose . . . in a big old motor
home . . . one the Bureau had a bug on but now can't locate, because they never factored mountains into the surveillance equation? "Jumpin Jesus," she thought.

Mercifully, today the gesture meant "Be quiet; I'm thinking."

"Alright . . . ," Rosen began, ". . . let's start with the obvious.
The motor home and its occupants are, in all probability, still up
here in the mountains somewhere." He counted off on his fingers.
One "I've got units on either end of Route 196 as it crosses what's
generally known as Jenner Peak. The RV hasn't come past either
of them." Finger two. "Electronic surveillance is picking up nothing. Ground surveillance reports the RV is nowhere obvious."
Finger three. "Ms. Harris and Mr. Wells are not in contact with
their colleagues in Los Angeles, which I am led to believe is a most
unusual circumstance." He paused and snuck a glance her way.
He closed his mouth. The muscles along his jawline tensed. He
started to speak but stopped himself.

"So?" she said.

Rosen heaved a sigh. "So . . . perhaps we give a little consideration to the possibility . . ." He waved a hand. ". . . to the possibility that Mr. Corso was correct. To the possibility that Driver is
indeed here."

"How much consideration?" Westerman asked.

"To start with, let's get everyone we've got up here looking
for that motor home," he said. "Then get me the Forest Service on
the line."

45

"Get your TV camera out," Driver ordered.

Marty pulled his head from between his knees. "Me? You mean . . ."

"The camera . . . now," Driver growled.

When Marty failed to move, Driver started his way.

Melanie reached out and grabbed him by the arm. "Don't hurt him," she pleaded.

"He's lucky I need him," Driver said, pulling his arm from her grasp.

Marty was on his feet now and shuffling forward. Driver watched impatiently as Marty pulled the steel case from the closet and set it on the table.

"Open it," Driver said.

Marty fumbled with the snaps a bit but managed it. Driver pushed him aside, peered down into the case. He pulled out the satellite phone and handed it to Marty.

"You call that network of yours. You tell them we need a half hour of airtime." He looked up at the clock over the cockpit. "In an hour. Thirty minutes. Two to two-thirty."

Marty started to babble. "They can't just . . ."

Driver brought the gun butt crashing down on Marty's toes, sending Marty to the floor clutching his foot, his throat emitting a high, keening sound as he rolled around on his hip. Driver bent at the waist. "You listen to me, little man," he intoned. "You tell those friends of yours . . . we don't get our airtime, I'm going to off ONE OF YOU out there. On national television . . . big as life, for everybody to see." He kicked Marty in the side. "I get through with the first one and it's going to be the other. You hear me?"

Marty nodded and got to his knees. He dialed the phone and waited three rings for an answer. "Let me have Ellen Huls," he said. "Martin Wells," he said a question later. He quickly lost patience. "Phyllis," he croaked. "It's Marty. It's an emergency. Just put her on the goddamn phone."

A frozen moment later. "Ellen, it's Marty." His face was etched with exhaustion. His hand shook. "No . . . no . . . no," he said. "Just listen to me." He listened again. "I know, Ellen . . . he's standing right here, Ellen." Marty massaged his throat. "Yes . . . he's got Melanie and me. Right. Just listen. He says he's going to kill one of us if we don't put together a half hour of network airtime." He listened again. When he spoke again, his voice took on a pleading tone. "Call whoever you need to call, Ellen. He's not kidding. This is the same guy . . . yes . . . yes . . . Meza Azul, that's right."

Driver grabbed the phone away from Marty. "Listen to me, whoever you are. I want a call back on this line within thirty minutes guaranteeing me thirty minutes of airtime. If I don't get it, I'm going to start doing things to these people you won't believe. Do you hear me?" He didn't wait for an answer. He hung up, dropped the phone on the desk and lifted Marty from the floor by the hair.

"Get the satellite ready," he said.

Marty limped noticeably as he scrambled to obey. He opened

the dish's control panel and pulled the lever down. The whine of hydraulics sounded as the dish began to move into place.

H e watched her pocket her phone. "Something?" Rosen asked. She shrugged and made a pained face. "Nothing to help us here," she said sadly.

"So?"

"Local authorities in some place called Drake, Nevada, found a body in a ditch this morning. Prints came up Harry Delano Gibbs."

"They're sure?"

"We had the file flagged, so the minute they got the match, they called."

"What else?"

"Guess what they found in Doris Green's house."

"Tell me."

"Passports. Birth certificates, California driver's licenses, social security cards. Two or three each for Doris and Driver." She held up a finger. "Here's the thing," she said. "They're all real. Run them through the system and they come up valid. Where do you get something like that?"

"I'd bet it's the same person set up the mail drop for her."

"Mr. Corso knows some interesting people."

Rosen nodded. "How much time have we got?" he asked.

Westerman checked her watch. "About six minutes."

Rosen leaned back against the Lincoln's front fender and sighed. If the L.A. office was right and the local ABC affiliate had indeed been given an ultimatum by Driver himself . . . he closed his eyes and massaged the bridge of his nose with his thumb and forefinger.

"What's the holdup?" Westerman wanted to know. "All they've got to do is tell him he can have his half hour."

"The network took a lot of flack lately. Once for the footage in the Meza Azul control module and again for running the segment on the mother last night," Rosen said. "The FCC just hit them with a hundred-thousand-dollar fine for *each* of their twenty-three affiliates. That's a lot of money. They're gun-shy about what might happen this time. They're not doing anything without approval from the top."

Westerman's mouth hung open in disbelief. "This guy's going to kill somebody, and these people are waiting for approval."

"From the people who brought you Janet Jackson's breast."

"We've got to do something."

Rosen shook his head in disgust. "We're doing everything we can do, Agent Westerman. We've got forty agents poking into every driveway on this damn mountain and forty Forest Service rangers working the woods. If they're out there, we'll find them."

She felt her phone buzz, found it and brought it to her ear. Special Agent Timmons on the line. "We've got the motor home," he said.

"Where?"

He told her. Rosen had started back for the car. "They found it," stopped him cold.

"Tell me," he said.

She did. He listened in silence. "Get me the closest four units. Have them meet us at the highway entry point."

"Any help from the locals or the Forest Service?"

"No, we'll handle this one on our own."

46

Special Agent Rosen squatted in the bushes. Overhead, a jig-saw puzzle of blue and white rolled east like a fast train. An inconsistent wind tousled the treetops. Seventy yards away, on the far side of the clearing, a big brown-and-white motor home sat silent and dark. Special Agent Randy Timmons leaned close and whispered in his ear. "Property belongs to a couple name of Kelly. Dick and Donna Kelly. Neighbors say they've got plans to build a retirement house up here next summer. Say they spent most of this summer clearing the lot and getting utilities installed. Went back home to Orange County about two weeks ago. Neighbors say the Kellys stay at a motel when they come up here. Say they don't own a motor home."

Rosen thanked him for the info and made a gathering motion with his arms, pulling everyone in as close as he could get them. Counting Westerman and himself, there were ten of them. "Al-right . . . debriefing Mr. Corso tells us that Driver is armed with a Mossberg twelve-gauge pump shotgun and a semiautomatic car-bine . . . some kind of newer version of an M16 . . . an M16 A2 we think." He looked around the tight circle of agents, making sure he had everybody's attention. "I don't have to tell any of you what a formidable array of firepower that is . . . especially if it's being wielded by someone of Driver's training and background." He made eye contact again. "We're outgunned here. All things being equal what we probably need is an entry team. Unfortunately, we don't have the luxury of waiting two hours for their arrival. He's got at least two hostages in there."

Rosen pointed. "Timmerman . . ." He pointed again. "Santos . . . I want you and your partners to take up positions opposite the front and back doors of the vehicle." He pointed downhill. "Take a big loop through the woods. Stay out of sight. Come up the far side of the hill and take the closest position you can safely occupy." He wagged a finger. "Hard cover. Remember, with the weapons he's got, he can kill you right through anything rotten or flimsy. Good cover." All four of men nodded solemnly.

He pointed again. "Adams . . . you and your partner get as close as you can to the rear of the vehicle. Buttros . . . you and Speck come along with Westerman and me."

He looked around again. "Everybody got it?" They said they did.

"Be careful," Rosen admonished to their rapidly retreating backs.

He took a deep breath, picked the electronic bullhorn from the ground and started edging downhill. His loafers were never intended for leaf-covered hillsides. He had to use his free hand to grasp bushes and rocks so he wouldn't go skiing down the hill on nothing but his shoes. Westerman, Buttros and Speck were similarly disadvantaged.

It was slow going. One careful step at a time. Halfway across, Rosen stationed Buttros and Speck at the front of the vehicle, while he and Westerman continued on to a place about halfway between the groups.

Westerman used a handheld radio to check with the other teams. She nodded. "Everybody's ready," she pronounced. Rosen pulled out his service piece. A Colt 9mm automatic. Eight in the clip. One in the chamber. Westerman followed suit.

All the curtains were closed, leaving nothing to the eye except occasional patches of ceiling. Just as Rosen was wondering if perhaps the RV wasn't empty, voices suddenly could be heard inside. The vehicle rocked slightly on its springs. A light came on in the ceiling. The hair on Rosen's arms began to tingle.

Rosen brought the bullhorn to his lips and pulled the trigger. *"This is the FBI,"* he said. *"Put your hands on your heads and exit the vehicle."* A pause. *"This is the FBI. Put your hands on your heads and exit the vehicle."* Nothing.

Rosen got on the radio. Ordered the pair of agents assigned to the rear of the vehicle to approach. It took about a minute for the agents to be pressed up against the rear of the vehicle, peering around the sides in anticipation of what was going to happen next. The bullhorn. *"This is the FBI. Put your . . ."*

And the door began to open. "Easy . . ." Rosen said into the radio. "Easy."

He picked up the bullhorn again. *"Put your hands on your heads and exit the vehicle,"* he squawked.

They came out. Two of them. A man and a woman. The hostages. Melanie Harris and Martin Wells. Driver must have released them.

"Get down. Get down on the ground. Keep your hands on your heads and get down on the ground." Slowly they followed orders.

Westerman squinted to see if she could recognize Melanie Harris, but the wind kept swirling the woman's hair around her face, making it impossible.

Rosen spoke softly the radio, then suddenly everyone was in view. Two teams covered the doors. Another two rushed the prisoners, handcuffing them and pulling them to their feet before rushing them off to the safety of the trees.

"No Driver," Westerman said.

"He's not coming out alive," Rosen said.

"What now?"

"Let's make sure he's not going anywhere," he said. He picked up the radio. "Shoot out the tires," he said. The volley began slowly, then picked up speed. Took maybe forty rounds before all four tires had been rendered flat.

The radio beeped. Rosen pushed the RECEIVE button. "Yeah."

Timmons on the other end. "Guy here . . . the one . . . you know the hostage guy."

"Yeah."

"Says his name is Richard S. Kelly and he doesn't like us shootin' up his new RV one bit."

"Not one damn bit," Rosen heard the voice from the background.

47

Wasn't like he'd been a tree hugger to begin with. No . . . U.S. Forest Service Ranger Bob Temple hadn't begun his career in a spasm of idealism, and a decade in the woods had merely proved what he'd always suspected. That money ruled the world and almost nobody gave a shit about resources, natural or otherwise.

On the positive side, his years in the forest had given him a glimpse of the interconnectedness of all things. A sense of how changes in the smallest of things had unforeseen repercussions up and down a system so complicated and diverse as to make human beings nothing more than spectators. As far as he was concerned, notions that humans were eventually going to ruin the planet were ridiculous. Push came to shove, Mother Earth would pass us like a peach pit. He was certain of it. And so it was with the smallest break in his usual routine that Bob Temple set an invisible web of connections into motion . . . connections he could not possibly have predicted.

Two hours earlier, over breakfast, Bob had lingered longer than was his usual habit. He'd been talking politics with Walt Moller. One of his favorite pastimes. Wasn't a soul there but the two of them, and Bob had just plain lost track. By the time he looked at his watch, he was forty minutes behind schedule and had swallowed probably three times as much coffee as was his custom.

And now, as might have been predicted, he needed to take a piss, so he pulled off the highway at Blue Creek, wheeled into the little area behind the Road Department's gravel piles, got out of the truck, unzipped himself and with a heartfelt exclamation of, "Aaaaaah," had begun to relieve himself of the extra coffee.

That's when he saw the tire tracks. Big wide tracks running away from him, back toward the section of old highway concealed by summer bushes and fall weeds.

Temple finished his business and followed along on foot, walking in the wake of whatever had made the tracks. Recent rains had soaked a small depression in the ground. The tread patterns on the tires were visible in the muddy earth. Scattered leaves and the tips of oak branches littered the ground. Bob Temple looked up into the trees above, where the lowest-hanging branches had been snapped off. Whatever had made the tracks was at least nine feet tall. Some kind of RV, he figured.

If someone had merely busted the lock or clipped the cable, he probably would have gotten on with his business for the day. Going where and when they felt like it was pretty much par for the course as far as the locals were concerned. Way they saw it, since they lived here, it belonged to them. This, however, didn't smell of locals. The locals weren't sneaky about it. They just pulled up, attached their bumper winch to whatever was in the way and yarded the whole thing right out of the ground. Then sooner or later, Bob would see the damage, call a crew in to fix it, and the cycle would begin anew. The fact that whoever this was had bothered to hide their intrusion by putting it back together with a piece of coat hanger wire piqued his interest.

So it was with a dual sense of interest and curiosity that Bob Temple dropped the thick, rusty chain on the ground and drove his U.S. Forest Service truck over onto the cracked pavement of the old Angels Mountain Road, as the gold miners used to call it a hundred fifty years before.

Whoever it was hadn't been up there long. For the first half mile, as he crossed a little clearing, the tire tracks were still visible on the bare pavement. Once the road started up, however, the overhanging trees had covered the pavement with a thick blanket of leaves, obscuring any evidence of recent passing.

Temple dropped the automatic transmission into second gear as the grade began to get steeper. The locals called this section "Lookout Road," after the Angels Mountain Fire Lookout Station, a seasonal fire lookout manned only in the months of June through September. Lookout Road was only one of three sections of the old highway periodically maintained by the Forest Service and the only section where a big RV would be able to turn around.

He slowed as he neared the top. The trees began to thin, then disappeared altogether as he entered the clear-cut at the very top of the rise. Built up high, on stilts, the Angel's Mountain Lookout stood sentinel over the entire eastern sweep of the Sierras. All the way out over Mount Whitney and the Mojave Desert beyond. Back around the north side of the tower sat a big brown-and-white motor home with a white satellite dish pointing at the heavens.

Bob Temple gave the truck a little gas and eased it forward. He rolled down the driver's side window as he crept along. High above the tower a single turkey buzzard floated on the airways, using its giant wings to veer this way and that, rising one second falling the next as it rode the chaotic breezes.

He listened for music, a sure sign that whoever these idiots were, they'd come to party and get down. The afternoon air was silent. The turkey buzzard was spiraling upward on the thermals as Bob Temple brought the truck to a stop behind the RV and got out.

As a precaution, he pulled the seat forward and pulled out his gun and holster. When he'd first started on the job, armed rangers would have been unthinkable, but the world was a meaner place these days and park rangers had become just another authority figure in a uniform. He strapped the gun to his waist and walked around to the passenger side of the RV.

The road fell off on all sides. Prior to the fire tower, the top of this ridge had been a scenic pullout on the old highway . . . a place where the tourists could take a break from the nail-biting ride and take a few pictures. For a while, they'd even had a few of those silver binoculars that required a quarter to operate, but the locals kept shooting them to pieces, eventually convincing the service to remove them altogether.

Bob Temple rose on tiptoes and knocked on the passenger-side window. The road sloped away from window, making it difficult for Temple to see inside. He knocked again, then walked around the front of the vehicle.

And there she was sitting behind the wheel. Looked like she had her eyes scrunched closed. He moved slowly, sidestepping his way across the front of the vehicle. As he approached the driver's side window, her eyes popped open.

The terror in her gaze sent his hand traveling toward his revolver. Unfortunately, the move was about five seconds too late. Before his hand reached its mark, a smashing blow to his face sent him reeling sideways; he felt his nose explode, felt teeth fall onto his tongue, felt the rush of blood to his head, then before his roaring senses could regroup, another blow struck him, this one to the side of his head, dropped him to his knees, coughing blood. The third blow nearly broke his neck.

He fell over onto the ground in the fetal position and did not move.

K enny looked over the pair of concrete dividers blocking the Joe Road entrance to old Route 180 and got back in the truck. "Ain't nobody moved those things lately. Not since last winter anyway."

He slammed the door and threw the truck into reverse. "We can skip the one by the Tolbert house and the other one by the café."

Corso was grim. "We've got to be sure."

"They'd have to have a backhoe," Kenny said as they rocketed across a gravel turnout and bounced out onto the highway. "Road Department bulldozed up a quarter mile of pavement and just left the pile in the way. It ain't all that easy to get my ATV in there." He shifted into third and floored it. "Besides . . . they're all grown over. You got to be careful you don't break your damn neck. No way you're getting any kind of big rig into either of them."

They'd decided to start at the bottom on the west side and work their way to the top. First two they'd tried had been open. Kenny thought they were still open from last winter, but they had little choice but to have a look anyway. First one ran maybe a quarter mile into the bush before the entire roadbed disappeared down a steep embankment. From where they sat, they could see more of the road about a hundred feet in front of the truck, but short of wings there was no way to get over there.

The second stretch of old 180 they'd tried had been in a lot better condition. They'd covered the better part of four miles before they found the road blocked by a landslide. Tire tracks in the dirt showed where people had squeezed motorcycles and ATVs around the edge of the slide, but, once again, nothing the size of an RV was progressing beyond that point. It had taken them twenty minutes in reverse to back their way down to the highway.

"What's next?" Corso asked as they roared upward.

"Burnt Meadow," Kenny answered. "That one'll be open for sure."

48

Bob Temple opened his eyes. Blinked. His nose was completely stopped up. His mouth felt as if was full of soup. He hawked once and spit. The metallic taste on his tongue told him it was blood. The tooth sticking through his upper lip told him it was his. Reason he could see the tooth in his lip was that the lip was swollen up the size and color of an eggplant. He tried to look from side to side but couldn't move his head.

"Paralyzed?" he wondered. "Am I paralyzed?"

He reached . . . or tried to. His hands wouldn't move. He moved his eyes down to his hands. They were on the steering wheel. He rolled his eyes around in his head. He was in his truck. His hands . . . his hands . . . his hands were gray and shiny. He was like the lizard man or something. And then it came to him. Duct tape. His hands were duct-taped to the steering wheel. As a matter of fact, nearly every part of him was duct-taped to something, His ankles were duct-taped to each other, then to something under the seat. Same thing with his head. Taped to something behind the seat. And his torso. And his waist. No matter where he sought room to wiggle, he found himself taped in place.

He spit again and tried to remember. The RV. He remembered

the woman and the look of terror on her face. The fear in her eyes. Recalled the sound of a twig breaking and how he'd turned his head just in time to take a blow to the face. After that it was fuzzy. He tried to lean forward. Gave it everything he had with the biggest muscles in his body. His bonds gave a metallic twang, relented slightly, then pulled him right back into place. The noise told him somebody had slit the seats and attached him to the springs inside the padding. His head throbbed. Felt like somebody was pounding nails in his forehead. He sobbed twice but forced himself to stop.

He tried to yell. To call for help, but his ruined mouth could form no syllables, only long, drawn-out O sounds like a wolf or a howling dog.

Bob Temple howled for all he was worth.

R ay Lofton leaned on the compactor handle. The old truck moaned and groaned with the effort. He stopped, peeked inside and still didn't like what he saw. The Lodge at White Lake had severely underestimated the amount of trash they needed hauled. By the time he got all of the crap in the truck he'd be lucky to have room for the rest of the stops on the way back home. If he'd had any idea they had this much trash he'd have brought one of the newer trucks, something he didn't have to baby up the hill. Hell, he'd have been done by now. Sitting on the couch in front of a football game, working on about his third beer. As it was, he might have to unload, then come back for the bottom half of the run. He leaned on the handle until the truck began to shake.

Coupla wedding parties, they said. What a bunch of shit. How could a pair of nuptials generate this much trash? It was unbelievable. And the bottles. He hadn't even started on the bottle bins. Must be hundreds . . . maybe thousands of bottles of every color and shape imaginable. Beer bottle, booze bottles, enough Cristal to float a canoe. Must have been a hell of party. Some kind of celebrities or something. Maybe a movie star . . . or a rock star. Hell, they get married the way other people change their socks.

He wheeled the empty Dumpster over to the army of bottle bins and began, one by one, to empty the smaller containers into the Dumpster. Must have been twenty of them, filled to the brim and heavy as hell. His back ached by the time he finished.

He changed the setting on the hydraulics and lifted the Dumpster from the ground. The glass bin was forward, over the passenger compartment. He feathered the handle carefully, just in case there wasn't enough room left in the bin. Didn't matter though. Despite his best efforts, the glass came out in a rush, crashing down into the bin with a clamorous crash. He held his breath. The way things had been going today, he figured it would spill over and he'd have to spend the next hour picking up broken bottles.

He got lucky. It all fit. Two more stops and he was home free. He could taste that first cool one already.

49

"Up or down? Whatta you think?" Kenny asked.

"What's down?"

"Blue Creek Road takes you all the way down to the bottom of the canyon. It's where the Forest Service does water samples. They got a shack down there. It's where they test the water table for ground pollution, so they keep the road open."

"And up?"

"Up is the Angel's Mountain Lookout. You know . . . keeping an eye out for fires in the summertime. Up they also maintain in the summertime."

"Let's try up," Corso said.

Kenny threw the truck into gear and nosed out onto the highway. "Gotta be careful here," he said, "from the top the curve is blind." He inched another yard forward, then gave it the gas.

On the far side of the road, three giant piles of gravel filled the turnout. "What's with the piles," Corso asked as they darted across the highway.

"Road Department," Kenny explained. "Right here's about halfway up, so they leave it here, spread it on the roads when they need it."

They bounced across the pavement and looped around the back of the gravel piles. A pair of concrete posts marked the opening. "Wide open . . . ," Kenny said, ". . . which it usually ain't. Looks like we ain't the first one's been up here lately neither."

Corso felt the hair on the back of his neck rise. "Let's go," he said.

They rolled across an open meadow and entered the forest. Unlike the previous forest tracks they'd been down, this one had obviously seen a brush cutter from time to time.

They circled the mountain in silence for ten minutes, until Kenny broke the spell.

"Coupla corners now," he said.

The air seemed lighter and less oppressive. Kenny rolled down his side window. Corso followed suit. The air was damp and smelled of loam. The bank was covered with thick green moss. Small yellow flowers poked their heads from between the rocks. On Kenny's side, the mountain sloped away to oblivion. The trees were thinner here and you could see that the mountainside was mostly shards of rock and any illusion of greenery was to be credited to hardy lichens and mosses that had managed to find purchase in the irregular nooks and crannies of the rocks.

The truck skidded to a stop. Kenny pushed in the clutch and stuck the top half of himself out the side window. The rig began to roll backward, around the last corner, to a long straightaway, where Kenny could wedge the rear tire up against the bank.

Kenny turned off the engine.

"What?" Corso asked.

"It's up there," Kenny whispered. "I seen the front of it. Big old brown-and-white thing."

Corso nodded, grabbed the door handle and clamored down to the ground. Kenny's cowboy boots clicked on the pavement as they moved uphill. Corso worked on his breathing, keeping it steady and even as he contemplated the fact that his planning had run out. That he didn't have any idea what he was going to do if and when they found the RV. He reached out and grabbed Kenny by the shirt.

"You got a gun anywhere in that truck?"

Kenny looked at him like he was crazy. "It's outta season, man," he said.

"Let's be real careful here," Corso whispered. "This is a real dangerous dude. He sees us, we're dead."

Corso took the lead now, covering the last fifty yards in a series of carefully placed footsteps. At the corner, he leaned his back against the bank and peeked around the blind bend in the road. Kenny was right. The RV stood in the middle of the clear-cut. The fire station rose above the barren ground like a giant waterbird. A dark green pickup truck was parked in the middle of the road about twenty yards short of the RV.

Kenny's hand pulled his back around the corner. "That's Bob Temple's truck," he whispered. "He's our local Ranger Rick. Looks like he's just sitting there waiting for something."

Corso peeked again. Kenny was right. Somebody was in the driver's seat.

"We better call the cavalry," Corso said, pulling out Marty's cell phone. He flipped it open. The words "No Service" blinked in front of his eyes. He tried dialing Rosen's number anyway . . . nothing.

He handed Rosen's business card and Marty's cell phone to Kenny. "Take the truck," he said. "Get down somewhere to where you can get some phone service. Call that number. Tell him we found it. You can't get him, call nine-one-one."

"You sure?"

"Hurry now."

"Gonna take forever to back down."

"Go."

And then the noise began. Like the bellowing of a moose or

maybe a cow or something. The breeze seemed to swirl the sound around them, like it was coming from all directions at once.

"Hurry up," Corso said.

Kenny started for the truck, when the noise came again. The sound spoke of fear and agony. Kenny stopped. Corso pointed at him. "Go," Corso mouthed. Kenny went.

50

First thing he heard was a hoarse voice. Then the sound of the door banging against the side of the RV. The sounds sent Corso skittering downhill in search of cover among the rocks. He moved on all fours, fighting for traction on the steep incline, working at moving laterally, not down, so as to maintain his view of the road and the vehicles.

He'd just settled into a mossy crevice between a pair of angular boulders when Marty Wells came into view. He was naked except for his shoes, limping along with a TV camera strapped to his chest. Some kind of head wound had painted a trail of blood down the right side of his face. The sight of Marty Wells naked in the forest was testimony to how far mankind had come since their days as hunter-gatherers. The exact evolutionary direction, Corso decided, was purely a matter of interpretation.

Driver and Melanie came out from behind the RV together. She was naked. Not even shoes. Driver had the carbine strapped across his shoulders, military style. His right hand was entwined in Melanie's hair, dragging her along as she squealed like a stubborn puppy. She tried to dig in her heels, but Driver was far too strong.

Thirty yards in front of the pickup truck, he threw her against the bank. She slipped and landed on her behind in the dirt. Driver pointed at her. "You stay right there," he said. "You move I'll take it out on him," he said, inclining his head toward Marty. "I get through with him, I'll find you and kill you. You understand?"

Driver didn't wait for an answer. He used the flat of his hand to prod Marty down the road another thirty feet. "You ready?"

"I need to refocus," Marty said in the voice of a child.

Corso watched as Driver pulled the radio microphone from his pants pocket and used his thumb to switch it on. He waited an impatient thirty seconds.

"Let's go," he said.

Marty fiddled with a couple dials, then looked up. "I don't have a specific frequency," he said.

"Pick a midrange band. Something a lot of stations are going to pick up."

Marty made a couple of adjustments. "Try the mike," he said.

"Testing, testing," Driver said.

Marty nodded that he was ready to go.

Driver walked to the front fender of the truck and lifted the microphone to his lips. "This is Captain Timothy Driver, U.S. Navy." A smile crossed his lips. "Retired," he added. "As ABC affiliate KYOK in Los Angeles had seen fit to ignore my ultimatum regarding airtime on its affiliates, they have left me no choice but to follow through with my threat." Driver reached over and plucked something from the hood. It was a wallet. Driver flipped it open and began to read. "This is Robert Hayes Temple of . . ." Driver read his address and zip code. "Mr. Temple had the great misfortune to interfere in the natural workings of things. This failure to be in rhythm with the order—" He looked up at the camera. "As is always the case, nature is unforgiving of even the slightest mistake."

Driver switched the mike off and walked to the back of the

trunk. Marty kept shooting as Driver lowered the tailgate, groped around for something, then started back his way. He held the microphone in one hand and a gas can in the other.

"Oh God," Melanie sobbed. "Don't you dare. You son of a bitch . . ." She was running at him, consumed by fury, coming full-tilt boogie down the hill, her fingernails thrust before her like talons. Driver set the gas can on the hood, stuck the mike back in his pocket and stiff-armed her in the solar plexus. She went down in a heap, gasping for air in a series of hiccuping sounds, rocking back and forth on the ground like a stroke victim as she fought for breath.

Driver retrieved the gas can. He walked to the driver's side and pulled open the door. Marty began to sob and shake. Bob Temple saw it coming. Without a word Driver began to pour gasoline over Temple and the interior of the truck. Satisfied with his work, he lobbed the can into the passenger seat. A low wailing scream came rolling out of Temple's mouth as Driver reached into his pocket and pulled out a signal flare.

Driver brought the radio mike to his face. "You have thirty minutes to arrange my network airtime or else Melanie Harris and . . ." He looked at Marty.

"Martin Wells," Marty said.

Marty's words were barely audible above the terrified wailing coming from the cab of the truck.

"Should you decide to ignore me again, Martin Wells and Melanie Harris will be the next to suffer for your foolishness." He pointed at Marty. "Show our audience the attractive Ms. Harris." Marty was nearly in tears as he lowered the nose of the camera for fifteen seconds.

Inside the cab of the truck, Temple was throwing himself from side to side. Driver walked over next to him and smiled. Without a word, he snapped the flare in half, watched as the red flame came pouring from the broken ends, then tossed the flare into the truck and kicked the door shut.

The interior of the truck went up in a whoosh of orange flame, blowing out both side windows and violently rocking the vehicle on its springs. By then Marty was crying. Driver grabbed Melanie by the hair and dragged her all the way up to where he stood.

Inside the cab, the flames had melted some of the tape; Temple had one hand free and was waving it like a flag on the Fourth of July.

Corso had to stop himself. It took all of his willpower to stay hidden in the rocks as Temple's death throes bounced around the hillside. And then . . . the truck began to move. Temple's thrashing must have moved something. The emergency brake or the shift lever maybe. Either way, the truck began to roll backward, gaining speed until it slammed into the bank and caromed right, slipping over the edge one tire at a time.

At first the truck rolled down the nearly vertical incline on its wheels. The first boulder sent the truck pinwheeling, ass over teakettle, back over front, down the hill. On the second bounce, the flames in the cab found the truck's gas tank and the whole thing went off like an artillery shell, scattering flaming pieces of truck all over the hillside.

The smoking carcass came to rest about sixty yards downhill, back on its wheels again, facing west. Parts of Bob Temple were still and silent in the driver's seat. The air smelled of burnt plastic.

51

"How did you get this number?" Rosen asked.

He listened, obviously getting more annoyed by the syllable.

"From whom?" he demanded. "Corso? Frank Corso?" He shook his head in disgust. "I see. You don't know his first name." He rolled his eyes. "And your name was?" He listened again. "Kenneth Grabowski. A message from Mr. Corso you say . . . well . . . Angels Mountain . . . no, no, no. If you don't mind, I've had all the foolishness I can stand for one day. We have far more pressing matters, Mr. Grabowski; lives are at stake here. I hope you don't mind." He broke the connection.

Rosen sounded collected. Truth was, he had a stress headache to drop a rhino. The Kelly affair was a disaster. A public relations nightmare. Kelly's lawyer was going to be all over the Bureau like a cheap suit. Things were ugly. Not ugly enough to get him transferred to Albuquerque, but ugly.

Since Ruby Ridge, the Bureau had become extra sensitive about failures of judgment. Getting the wrong RV was at worst laughable. Shooting out the tires was . . . was . . . perhaps not the best idea he ever had. He was going to end up with a letter in his file over this.

Worse yet, he didn't have clue one as to where Timothy Driver was at that moment. He shuddered at the thought.

Rosen was lost in his own inner world when the Bureau-issue Ford Taurus skidded to a stop about a foot in front of his trousers. Rosen was just about to get in somebody's face about their driving when Special Agent Santos bolted out of the car. His arms were full of equipment. "You gotta see this, boss," he said as he dumped his load of gear on the hood of his car with a bang and began pushing buttons. Looked like he had his satellite phone hooked up to his laptop computer. "This showed up on the Internet six or seven minutes ago."

Rosen wandered over. Sunlight made the screen hard to see. Rosen shaded his eyes, but it didn't help. Santos took off his suit jacket and draped it over the screen. "Here," he said. "Look at it now." Rosen bent at the waist and stuck his head under the suit jacket like an old-time photographer.

Rosen watched in disgust as Driver issued another ultimatum. His reaction turned to horror when Driver came out of the back of the truck with a gas can. "Oh God," slipped from his mouth when Driver cracked the flare. The rest of it he watched in silence. In the end, he pulled his head away as if avoiding a blow.

Santos started the streaming video anew. Westerman put her head under the coat. Rosen watched her body stiffen, then grabbed her by the elbow when her knees deserted her. She put both hands on the hood of the car and took deep breaths. She looked like she was about to puke.

A government green pickup skidded to a halt at the rear of the car. Short, overweight guy with a round red face. "We've got a report of smoke up near the Angel's Mountain Lookout," he said.

"Where?" Rosen asked.

"Angel's Mountain."

Rosen pulled his cell phone from his pocket, pushed star

sixty-nine and got the number of the last incoming call. He dialed the number.

"Mr. Grabowski," he said. "Good . . . yes . . . you meet us out at the highway. We'll be there is less than five minutes. Yes," he said. "Yes. We will."

He pocketed his phone and began to jog toward the Lincoln. "Santos, follow me. Call another unit, whoever's closest. Get a couple of aid cars on the way."

Westerman was still ashen as she threw herself behind the wheel.

"That was . . . ," she began.

"Down," Rosen said. "Give it all she's got."

52

orso saw them coming. Saw the big Lincoln Town Car winding its way up the narrow road. Then a gap and a pair of beige Fords trailing along in the wake. Corso scrambled across the hill, to a place where he was able to pull himself up onto the surface of the road.

Two minutes later he signaled the Lincoln to a halt just below the last bend in the road and a couple of hundred feet above the smoking carcass of Bob Temple's Forest Service truck. Rosen got out one side, Westerman the other. They walked to the edge of the road together and stood gazing down at the carnage below. When the Fords arrived, Rosen motioned for the occupants to stay put.

A layer of vile black smoke cut across the rugged contours of the canyon.

"Couple of public access TV channels in L.A. broadcast it live," Rosen said. "It's been up on the Internet for the past twenty minutes or so."

"What a way to go," Corso said. "Live and in color."

"No kidding."

"I'd love to get his remains out of that truck," Rosen said, "but we're going to have to do something about Driver before we can get a crew up here."

"Where's the RV now?" Westerman wanted to know.

Corso pointed uphill. "Just up around that corner. He hasn't moved. He's just sitting up there waiting for his ultimatum to come around."

Rosen looked grim. "Word is the network isn't going to give him his airtime."

The news left Corso agape. "You're shitting me."

"They're worried about the legal implications."

"Ironic huh?" Westerman added with a bitter laugh. "The paparazzi are worried about their image."

Corso crooked a finger. Rosen and Westerman followed him uphill to the final bend in the road. One above the other, they peeked around the corner.

"There it is," Corso said. "Only way out is right back this way. He's got the high ground. No way to cover the doors without coming into his field of fire."

"We're going to have to try," Rosen said.

Corso and Westerman watched as Rosen marched downhill to the waiting agents. After a quick briefing, all four agents helped one another up the steep, moss-covered bank, climbing up onto the top side of the road. Working their way backward, away from the clear-cut at the top of the hill, they quickly disappeared from view.

Rosen tried his phone, only to find out what Corso already knew. Thwarted by a complete lack of service, Rosen tried his radio. Same result. He walked uphill.

"Think he'll negotiate?" Rosen asked Corso.

"Not a chance. That'd mean he wasn't running the show."

"You think he's got a plan for getting out of here?" Westerman asked.

"I don't think he wants to get out of here," Corso said. "He wants to broadcast his message to the world, then go out in a blaze of glory."

The crash of broken glass was followed by three flat reports, a pause, then three more. More broken glass. Closer this time. A peek around the corner confirmed Driver'd kicked out both the side and the back windows of the RV. Mangled screens and pieces of curtains hung down on the outside of the vehicle. The segmented barrel of the carbine appeared in the side window. Three more flat reports split the air.

Down by the cars, the Hispanic agent came spilling over the side of the bank, landing in the road at a skid. His suit was stained with dirt and moss; his service revolver dangled from his right hand as he hurried up the hill.

"Buttros has been hit bad," the agent said.

"Hit where?"

"In the head." He made a smoothing gesture with his left hand. "He was flat on the ground. Guy shot him in the top of the head." The hitch in his voice said he wasn't far from losing it.

Rosen put a hand on the younger man's shoulder. "Listen to me, Santos. I know he's your partner. I know how hard this is, but we've got to keep our wits about ourselves up here. Soon as I can, I'll get us some help. In the meantime, what's the chances of getting Buttros out of where he is without getting anybody else hurt?"

"Already done," Santos said. "We dragged him back out of range. Timmons and Lange are bringing him . . ."

As if on cue, the pair appeared, Buttros slung between them like a sack of feed. Santos hustled down to be of assistance as they eased Buttros over the bank onto the dappled sunlight of the road surface. Santos took his pulse and looked up. His eyes were wide and wet.

"His vital signs are pretty good. We got to get him some help."

Rosen agreed. "You and Lange. Take the car in the back. Hurry."

"You want us to send help?"

"Not just yet," Rosen said.

The trio of FBI field agents carried their fallen comrade to the rearmost car, carefully packed him into the backseat and began to back down the mountain.

Rosen walked down to Timmons. "Go get Martini. Bring him back here. Be careful. We don't want anybody else hurt."

Corso and Westerman watched Timmons scale the bank and disappear. Rosen made his way to the trunk of the town car and pulled out a bullhorn.

Corso and Westerman stepped aside as Rosen approached. He poked the mouth of the bullhorn around the corner. *"This is the FBI . . . ,"* he began.

A single shot rang out. More of a slap than a boom. The megaphone disintegrated, its plastic and metal body sending a shower of shards into the surrounding air. Rosen leaned back against the bank. His lower lip was split in two and dripping blood down onto the front of his suit. A piece of white plastic was lodged in his right cheek, dangerously close to his eye.

He sensed his wound, dropped the rest of the bullhorn and pulled a white linen handkerchief from his jacket pocket. He dabbed at his lower lip with little effect. Westerman stepped forward, took the hankie from his hand and used it to pull the jagged piece of plastic from his cheek. Rosen winced as Westerman applied pressure to the wound for a few seconds before turning her attention to his lip. She covered the split with the lion's share of the hankie and told him, "Squeeze."

Rosen did as he was told. "Harder," she told him, and once again he did as bidden. The flow of blood stopped.

Agents Timmons and Martini slid down into the road. Rosen beckoned them to his side. He tapped Timmons on the chest.

NO MAN'S LAND 289

"Timmons. You take the car. You get down to somewhere you can use the phone. You call us in a SWAT team. Have them helicopter in. We need them yesterday. You understand me?"

Timmons said he did.

"Take Corso with you," was Rosen's last order.

"I'm not going," Corso said flatly.

"I'm not giving you a choice here, Corso."

"I was you . . . I'd take all the help I was offered," Corso said.

Before another word could be spoken, the screaming began. More like a shout, at first, then rising and rising in pitch until it reached operatic octaves. Then silence.

"Go," Rosen said to Timmons.

Timmons was halfway to the car when the upper half of Martin Wells was thrust out the back window of the RV. His hands were fastened behind his back somehow. His face was covered in sweat. His breathing came in short, ragged gasps. "Please . . . please . . . please . . . ," he begged.

Timmons was in the car, backing crazily down the long-deserted highway. The whine of the transmission was lost around the second corner. Only the sounds of the wind and Marty's agonized pleading reached the ears.

"Forty minutes," Rosen said. "They'll have a team in here in forty minutes." His voice held equal parts authority and conviction.

"I don't think Marty's got forty minutes in him," Corso said.

Rosen kept his thumb and forefinger pinching his lip. "I'm open to suggestion," he said with a trace of sarcasm slipping through the muffle.

"We can't just sit here and wait to see what he's going to do to those people. We've got to *do* something."

"Such as?" Rosen inquired.

Corso shrugged. "Maybe we . . ."

Again, Martin Wells's screams rose to a fever pitch. His

thrusts and convulsions rocked the vehicle. At the moment when it seemed Marty surely could endure no more, the pitch of his protestations rose yet another octave.

The sound was more than Corso could bear. He straight-armed Rosen and walked around the corner. "Stop it, godammit," he shouted up the hill.

53

Westerman threw herself forward in an attempt to stop Corso; that was when Rosen let go of his lip long enough to catch her by the collar and pull her back behind the sheltering escarpment. They could hear Corso's boots slapping on the pavement. The woods rang with his curses. They furrowed their brows and waited for a volley of gunfire to cut him down. Miraculously, no shots were fired.

"Stop it, godammit," Corso shouted again as he walked along. "What the fuck is the matter with you ? Is this how you want this thing to end? This is . . . this is disgraceful . . . this is . . . ."

And then the sound of gunfire filled the air. Corso could feel the slugs as they buzzed inches from his head like angry bees. He waited for an impact that didn't happen. He was nearly at the back of the RV by then. He could hear Marty's low moan coming from somewhere in the interior. He could sense Driver's coal black eyes scouring him.

"This isn't how the story ends, man. I have to live so I can tell everybody how it all came down."

And then . . . *bang* . . . the top half of Melanie Harris was thrust out the rear window of the vehicle. Her hair was wild and tangled; her mouth was taped; her breasts hung down from the window frame.

"Puppet show," Driver shouted from somewhere in the interior. And then Melanie went wild. Her muffled screams painted the air and the trees. Her desperate attempts to escape her bonds shook the big vehicle as whatever was happening to the bottom half of her crossed into primal territory, into a place where only the pain mattered and where screaming was the sole option.

Corso ran at full speed and leapt like a basketball player going for a rebound, trying to get his hands entangled in Melanie's hair, but just a moment too late as Driver jerked her back inside, allowing Corso to slam against the metal siding like an insect against a windshield.

Driver laughed. "Audience participation," he said.

Corso got to his feet. The back window was empty, so he dusted himself off and walked up to the passenger-side door. He grabbed the handle. The door swung open in his hand. He stepped inside.

Driver stood in the middle of the coach. The carbine was slung across his bare chest. Behind him, Melanie and Marty sat huddled on the floor.

"You've got balls. I'll say that for you, Corso," Driver sneered.

"A number of unenlightened souls have called it a death wish."

"Were they right?"

"If you've got a death wish, all you've got to do is step out into traffic."

Driver nodded his agreement. "It's about life," he said. "About choosing how you're willing to live it and how you're not. That's what prison teaches you."

"What's that?"

"Your limits."

Corso changed the subject. "Where's Cutter? He on his way to Canada?"

"Cutter's on his way to hell."

"I don't think he'd be surprised."

"He was planning on it."

Corso took a deep breath. "Looks to me like you've staked out your ground here, Driver." Corso inclined his head toward the pile of humanity at the back of the coach. "Why don't you let me take those two and be on my way. After that, you can play this thing out any way you want."

"Why should I do that?"

"Because leaving them here with you is outside *my* limits."

"You could join them."

"I don't think so."

"Me neither."

"What do you say?"

Driver thought it over. "You see my mother on TV last night?"

Corso said he had.

"I was coming for her. We were going to leave the country together."

"That's why you wanted me along, wasn't it? I was the only person on earth who knew where to find her. You wanted me with you so's I couldn't tell anybody else. That way, you two could have disappeared together."

"I always said you were a smart guy."

"And all that Driver's losing his mind stuff . . ." Corso let it hang.

"Got me out of my cell. If I'd needed a regular doctor, they'd just have brought the prison sawbones to my cell. A shrink they had to let me out for."

"We probably got another best seller in how you pulled that one off."

"Don't patronize me, Corso. I'll kill you where you stand."

"I'm serious."

"So am I."

"So what do you say?" Corso tried again. "Let them go. You need a hostage, I'll be your hostage."

Driver shook his head. "The regular citizens there are the only thing keeping me from getting shot to pieces." He smiled. "I'm like you. I haven't got a death wish either."

"I'm not leaving without them."

"Then you're not leaving."

"So be it," Corso said quietly.

Driver took the carbine in his hands and aimed it at Corso. Right between the eyes. Corso stopped breathing. He closed his eyes and waited.

"It didn't have to end this way," Driver said.

Corso wanted to agree but couldn't force the words from his throat.

54

Corso cracked an eye. The carbine was still pointed directly at his face. The tension had partially revived Melanie. Her eyes were focused on Driver and Corso.

Corso took a deep breath and held it. Driver's impassive black eyes told him nothing. He swallowed a couple of times. "If you're going to do something heroic, you better hurry," Corso said. "They've got SWAT teams and helicopters on the way."

Driver lowered the rifle. "You really fucked things up, Corso."

"Me? You're the one got me into this. You put me in a position where I had to show up at Meza Azul. I was minding my own damn business. Then you made me come along on some cross-country crime junket. I didn't want anything to do with it. I told you every step of the way. All I wanted was out. You owe me."

Driver's eyes were hard and flat as rivets. His lips were thin enough to pass for scars. "Owe you what?"

"You owe me a ticket out of here."

"So go."

"I need to take them with me."

Driver threw a glance at the back of the room.

"Those assholes killed my mother," he said without conviction.

Corso waved a hand at him in disgust. "We both know that's bullshit. They may have been there when it happened, but that doesn't make them the reason she had a heart attack. She had a heart attack because she had a bad heart." He waved his arms. "Hell . . . back when I knew her, she'd already had a couple of heart operations. Who are we kidding here? You remember what you said about Kehoe. How he hurt people because it made him feel better about himself." Driver didn't answer, but Corso kept talking anyway. "You want to be that way . . . well I guess that's between you and your conscience." He pointed at the pile of flesh that was Marty and Melanie. "But don't be telling yourself they had anything to do with your mother's death, because that's crap and you and I both know it."

Driver's eyes flickered. He turned away. Corso kept at him.

"They were just doing what they do, feeding the machine. Making somebody the celebrity of the day." Driver turned his eyes back to Corso. "Celebrity has become the opiate of the people. It's the new heroin. Everybody wants to be famous, even if it's only for a day or an hour or one episode of *Evening Edition*. Everybody wants their fifteen minutes of fame. You and I . . . we've already had ours. It's time to move on. Onward and upward. Bigger and better things. It's not their fault the people they work for won't put you on television. All that proves is their employers think a whole hell of a lot more of themselves than they do of the people who work for them."

A long silence ensued. Finally, Driver pushed his way past Corso and walked to the front of the vehicle. "Take 'em," he said. "Take 'em and get the hell out of here."

Corso moved quickly. He lifted the cushion and the lid, dug around in the storage area and came up with a couple of blankets.

He pulled the tape from Melanie's mouth with a single rip. She squealed and gulped air. Marty wasn't moving. Corso found a pulse.

He found the ends and unwound the tape encircling her wrists and ankles. She was shaky getting to her feet but managed it. She pulled the blanket tight around herself and leaned against the wall while Corso wrapped Marty up in a blanket and lifted him from the floor as if he were a child. "Go," Corso said to Melanie.

Melanie walked unsteadily up the aisle, never letting her eyes come to rest on Driver as she stepped down out of the vehicle. Corso had to turn sideways to squeeze Marty through the door. He turned back and spoke to Driver. "Good luck," he offered.

Driver closed the door. Melanie slipped and fell.

"Get up," Corso said. "I can't carry both of you."

She struggled to her feet and began to shuffle forward.

Corso turned back. "Just for the record . . . in case anybody asks me . . . what was it you wanted to say?"

"What?" Driver appeared dumbfounded.

"You wanted all this airtime from ABC. What were you going to say?"

Driver gave a halfhearted shrug. "I don't know," he said. "I figured I'd make it up as I went along. Maybe . . ." He stopped and seemed to laugh at himself for a moment. "I just wanted to go out with a bang was all. Just wanted people to remember I was here on this planet with the rest of them."

"They'll remember," Corso said.

The RV started. The rumble of its engine filled their ears as they moved downhill. Corso heard the RV drop into gear and begin to move. He picked up his pace. Ahead of them, down at the corner, Westerman took a peek. Then Rosen and Marino.

Westerman hustled out and threw an arm around Melanie. Martini offered his arms to Marty, but Corso shook him off.

"He's coming," Corso said as he bent low and set Marty on the edge of the road. He stood for a moment and shook out his trembling arms.

Melanie stood in Westerman's encircling arms. Corso called her name. Melanie looked at him. "Come on," he said. "We need to get out of the way."

She moved like she was in a trance, crossing the two-lane highway to Corso's side. She wanted to say something . . . to express her thanks . . . something kind, something loving . . . maybe even something more than that, but her lips couldn't form words. He body felt like a tree in a windstorm, waving back and forth, at the mercy of forces beyond her control.

Corso lifted her from her feet and placed her among the rocks on the low side of the road. He slipped over the edge, rolled Marty into his arms, and began to pick his way down the hillside. "Come on," he said over his shoulder to Melanie.

She sidestepped along, unwilling to remove either hand from the blanket, following Corso downward to the same crevice he'd occupied earlier. He set Marty carefully on the thick moss, then hurried to her side.

The sound of an engine pulled his head around. He picked her up, covered the ground quickly and set her down next to Marty. "We'll be okay here," he told her.

"Is he coming?" Her eyes overflowed with terror.

"Not here," Corso said, smoothing her tangled hair away from her face. The gesture seemed to send her back to the last happy moment she could remember. She brought a hand to Corso's cheek.

"The sex was great," she said with a loopy smile.

Corso looked around to see if anyone else had heard. Mercifully, Marty was out of it and the feds were too busy figuring out what to do next to pay any attention to civilians. "We'll talk about it," he said. "You know, when things aren't so . . . you know . . . aren't so . . ."

The roar of an engine snapped his head around. The big RV came barreling around the corner, scattering the FBI like so many leaves.

55

They got off one shot each. One slug went wide right. Would have hit a passenger right in the face if there'd been one. One lodged somewhere in the body of the vehicle. Driver felt the impact of metal on metal. The third bullet plowed through the windshield and into the tabletop Driver was holding between his legs as he drove. Half again as long as it was wide, the tabletop covered Driver from the chin down, except for his hands and arms, which he needed to steer. The tapered end was down by his feet, allowing him to work the pedals. The piece of laminated three-quarter-inch particle board stopped the slug cold.

Rosen and Westerman had each gotten off one round, then thrown themselves over the edge to get out of the way. Martini had proved less nimble and had found himself pinned against the bank as the RV came sliding around the bend.

Corso got to his feet. He scrambled up the hillside. By the time he got to road level, Martini was down in the ditch, rolling around on his shoulder blades, clutching his head and moaning. Rosen was trying to climb the grade in loafers. Westerman was sitting with her back against a boulder, teeth bared, eyes screwed shut, cradling her right shin with both hands. Fifty yards down-hill, the RV was nose to nose with the Lincoln.

Driver fed the engine more gas and, between the power of the big RV and the effects of gravity, the Lincoln began to move. More gas meant more speed. The Town Car was sliding sideways at a pretty good clip when it left the roadway and became air-borne, turning a lazy somersault in the air and landing on its roof, where it lay tinkling and steaming in the cool afternoon breeze.

Driver had negotiated the turn and was speeding along the next straightaway when the beige government-issue Ford Taurus came into view. The car was packed to the rafters with FBI agents. Driver leaned on the horn and fed the big rig more gas.

The agent behind the wheel of the Taurus decided to make a run for it, in reverse. Driver applied just enough pressure to keep them weaving ahead of him, but not so as to make them feel any more threatened than necessary. He knew from command experi-ence what came next. The blind curve was just ahead. Driver slowed, allowing them to increase the distance between the vehi-cles. The Taurus veered wide and disappeared from view.

Driver put the gas pedal to the floor. Swung the RV as wide as the road would allow, crimped the wheel hard to the left and put the big rig into a power slide around the bend. Just as he'd figured, they'd tired of running and had decided to fight. Young men were like that. Always spoiling for a fight.

Driver caught them half-in, half-out of the car. He put the middle of the rig on the double yellow line and ducked his head. In the five seconds before impact, the windshield exploded. Shouts and screams ricocheted among the trees. Half a dozen rounds plowed into the tabletop. The staccato rap of automatic weapons rose above the roar of the engine, then *bam*, the RV hit the Taurus like a runaway freight, driving the smaller vehicle up onto its side and propelling it over the edge, pinwheeling down into the steep gully below.

Inside the RV, the air bag had deployed, completely obscuring Driver's view of the road. Bullets slammed into the metal siding as he threw the tabletop aside, grabbed the air bag in both hands and jerked it completely out of the steering wheel.

By the time he threw it aside, the RV had smacked into the inside bank, plowing a deep furrow in the brown dirt and very nearly coming to a halt. Driver steered right and floored it again, forcing himself back onto the highway.

Steering had become the problem. The right front suspension was seriously out of whack. Driving in a straight line required keeping the steering wheel turned nearly all the way to the left. He was dragging something. The radiator had begun to leak steam.

Worse yet, Driver had a bullet in his side. He could feel blood leaking down over his belt line onto the side of his pants. He groaned from the effort of steering. His vision strobed a couple of times, going white, then black, then back to normal again.

He drove the last couple of miles at a placid pace. Wasn't like anybody was chasing him down the hill. He stopped at the crest of the final grade. Two hundred yards ahead a pair of FBI Fords were nosed up to one another blocking the mouth of the road. He cleared the glass from his shoes, took several deep breaths, then gave it all he had. The fan belt screamed as he started down the hill toward the roadblock.

The gunfire started almost immediately, so he leaned over to the right, getting the upper part of his torso all the way over to the passenger seat. Bullets slammed into everything. The interior of the RV was disintegrating around him, blown to dust and slivers by a torrent of gunfire.

The RV rammed through the roadblock, brushing the cars aside like a cow shoos flies. He sat up just in time to steer around the pile of gravel, then quick to the left, sending him out onto the highway, where he skidded to a tire-shredding halt.

Amazed to be alive, Driver smiled as he popped his seat belt. He groaned as he leaned over and picked the carbine from among the debris covering the floor. He pulled the door handle upward and began to step out onto the ground when he thought he heard somebody singing. He looked up.

56

The boys called her Wanda. Wanda Lackanooky. The spring-loaded hula doll superglued to the dashboard was dancing up a storm. Ray Lofton had his little radio wedged between Wanda and the windshield. Jimmy Buffett was *"wastin' away again in Margaritaville"* and Ray Lofton was about to join him.

He had the old truck going flat out in high gear, running downhill like the Atchison, Topeka and Santa Fe. *"But there's booze in the blender. And soon it will render that frozen concoction that helps me hang on."* Packed full, stuffed with more refuse than she'd probably ever had crammed in her innards before, she was top-heavy and unresponsive. "A lot like my first wife," he thought to himself with a big smile.

Lest anything spoil his plans for the afternoon, Ray opted for caution and thus began feathering the brakes well before he went into the steep turn at Blue Creek. He moved her as far out into the top of the turn as he dared, then leaned into it. *"Searching for my lost shaker of salt."* He howled the lyrics and turned the wheel.

Ray was still warbling at the top of his lungs when his worst nightmare was realized. Midway around the turn, sitting sideways across both lanes, was a huge brown-and-white motor home.

"*. . . Nibblin' on sponge cake . . .*" The lyrics died in his throat. He had nowhere to go. In the brief seconds prior to impact he managed to get both feet on the brakes, but the effect was minimal. The rig began to slide sideways.

He hit the motor home nearly dead on, just about in the middle of the driver's door. The impact tore the cab section completely off the rig, sending it skidding along the pavement in front of the runaway garbage truck in a hail of sparks and dust.

Ray knew what was coming. He saw the guy with the gun, half-in, half-out of the door. Felt his rig start to go. Felt the tons of bottles in the overhead beginning to pull her over. He jacked the wheel hard the other way but to no avail. Gravity and centrifugal force had taken over. With all the grace of a wallowing pig, his rig rolled over onto its side.

Ray lost his grip on the steering wheel and fell hard to the low side of the cab. Below his right shoulder, Ray could feel the pavement tearing the door to pieces. And then he heard the bottles go. Crashing and clanging, making a sound like a thousand drunken bell ringers as the tons of glass spilled from the truck and shattered on the pavement.

And then suddenly the truck stopped skidding and all was silent.

Only the radio played on. "*Some people claim that there's a woman to blame . . . and I know . . . it's my own damn fault.*"

57

The last ambulance down the mountain carried the remains of Bob Temple, or at least those parts they'd been able to find before darkness settled in. Corso overheard the Forest Service supervisor arranging a ten-man search party for seven the next morning, in hopes of finding the rest of their fallen comrade's remains.

Before that, the professionals had satisfied themselves with carting off the living. He'd heard an EMT say they'd called in every ambulance and aid car within a hundred-mile radius and had still come up two short. Westerman had broken her lower leg when she'd leapt from the roadway. Martini had taken the RV's side mirror flush in the face, breaking his jaw and plowing a bloody divot across his forehead. They'd shared an ambulance down the mountain, as had a couple of minimally injured FBI agents who'd gone over the side in the car.

Melanie and Marty had gone separately. Both of them down to the airport at Caldwell, where an air ambulance was waiting to whisk them back to Los Angeles.

When the pair of giant tow trucks had successfully lifted Ray's rig back onto its tires, what was left of Driver could have been most anything . . . a deer . . . or a dog . . . anything made of meat. Driver and the flattened remains of the cab went down the hill on the back of a flatbed truck, bound for the state crime lab at Glendora, where highly trained personnel could poke and prod him to their heart's content.

Rosen had refused to leave until every one of his agents was accounted for and had received appropriate medical treatment. Two shots of Novocaine and eighteen stitches had put his lip back together.

Corso sat on the running board of Kenny's truck, which, interestingly enough, had been the only vehicle still in running condition when the smoke had cleared.

"I don't see what you so damn glum about Ray Ray. It was like Rambo, man," Kenny said. "This one badass dude come in here and just fucked everybody up. And you . . ." He shook his friend's shoulder with his big hand. ". . . you single-handedly put an end to his reign of terror."

Ray Lofton looked dubious. "I seen 'em, Kenny. He had some kinda rifle in one hand. He had one foot out the door." He shook his head. "I ain't never . . . you know . . . hurt anybody before . . . you know what I mean. I never figured . . ." Ray began to weep. Kenny took him in his arms.

Rosen strode over to Corso. "I've got a car," he said. "You headed for L.A.?" Corso thought it over. If he hadn't been so tired, he'd have laughed. A week of madness. A trail of dead bodies from Arizona to California, leaving untold lives changed forever. National news coverage. Murder, mayhem, kidnapping, you name it . . . and somehow it all boiled down to same old question. Whether what everybody said was true. Whether victories were only worth savoring, defeats only worth weathering, if you had somebody to share it with. Whether, like the old song said: *in the end the love you get is equal to the love you give.*

Or whether, as he liked to think, some strand of nobility

could only be found in solitude. As if silence were required for serious thought and the only true joys were self-generated. The
older he got, the more of a statistical anomaly he became. To
him . . . the best moments in life were silent, like sitting alone in
the cool grass.

"So?" Rosen said.

"Seattle," he said after a minute's hesitation. "I've got a boat
to look after."

58

"It was awful," Heidi said. "That Harry Gibbs shot my papa right there in our front room. Just walked up to him and shot him in the head." Tears began to leak from her big blue eyes. "He drug me off and raped me over and over. Kept at me day and night, like some kinda animal." She stopped to collect herself. "Kept me locked up. Kept me tied to him all the time. I didn't have nothin to do with any of them killings. That was all Harry. I'da tried to stop him, he'da killed me for sure." She pointed at the back of the room, where a phalanx of uniformed police officers stood. "I can't imagine why the police don't believe me. Why they think I must have . . ."

Her recitation was interrupted when the door directly behind her chair opened and a large middle-aged blond woman entered the room. She threw her briefcase onto the table, then leaned over and whispered in Heidi's ear. Heidi nodded.

The woman looked the assembled media over with an expression of thinly disguised disgust. "My name is Lisa McClendon," she said. "I have been retained by the Women's Domestic Violence Commission to act as Ms. Spearbeck's attorney until her permanent representation has an opportunity to arrive. Ms.

Spearbeck will neither be answering any further questions nor
holding future press conferences until such time as Mr. Cochrane
arrives from Los Angeles."

   "He was sooo nice on the phone," Heidi cooed.

   "That's all," McClendon said.

   Heidi waved good-bye.